The Blood Pact

The Notturno Affair, Volume 1

R. Stellan

Published by R. Stellan, 2024.

This is a work of fiction. Similarities to real people, places, or events are entirely coincidental.

THE BLOOD PACT

First edition. November 20, 2024.

Copyright © 2024 R. Stellan.

ISBN: 979-8230284680

Written by R. Stellan.

Table of Contents

The Choice 1
New Beginnings 5
Unseen Shadows 31
Meeting Ruby 53
Complications (Ruby) 75
Unwanted Attention 105
Confronting the Past 121
Shadows of Loyalty 137
A Test of Trust 153
Breaking Point 165
Choices Made 187
Paths Diverged 207
A Blood Pact 223
Echoes of the Past 237
Unforeseen Alliances 247
Dangerous Games 257
Next to come! 263

Dedication

To those who dare to break free from the chains of their past, who seek light even in the darkest of shadows, and who fight for a life of their own making.

This is for the dreamers, the survivors, and the rebels at heart. May you always find the strength to write your own story.

And to my loved ones, for your unwavering belief in me—this journey wouldn't have been possible without you.

"In the shadows of loyalty lies the fine line between love and betrayal. To forge a pact in blood is to bind your soul, for better or worse."

The Choice

The heavy oak door creaked shut behind Ryan as he stepped into the dimly lit study. The scent of expensive cigar smoke lingered in the air, mixing with the musty, old leather of the chairs and the faint trace of aged whiskey. The room felt suffocating, heavy with the weight of years spent in the shadows. Every piece of furniture, every ornate painting, every polished surface exuded power—Dom Giovanetti's power.

Ryan straightened his back as he approached his father's massive desk, his heart pounding beneath the weight of the moment. Domenico "Dom" Giovanetti sat behind the desk, his eyes narrowing over the rim of his glass. The older man's face was a mask of calm, but his eyes betrayed the storm brewing beneath, the same storm that had roiled within Ryan since his mother's death.

"You think you can just leave, boy?" Dom's voice cut through the silence, low and dangerous. His hands, calloused from years of dealing in power, set his glass down with a heavy thud. "You think that's something you can just do?"

Ryan clenched his fists, feeling the ghost of his mother's words echo in his mind— "Be brave, my boy." He stood his ground. "I'm leaving, Father. I'm done with this life. With this family."

Dom's expression darkened, his brows furrowing. "And what will you do, huh? You think you can walk away from your blood? From everything I've built. The power, the respect... the legacy?"

A memory flashed in Ryan's mind—his mother, looking weary and worn, urging him to pursue education instead of violence. He swallowed hard, steeling himself. "I don't want your legacy, Dom. I want my own. I'm not going to be the next don, and I'm not going to live in your shadow. I'm going to school, to study criminal justice. I want to help people, not hurt them."

For a moment, the room was silent, save for the low crackle of the fire burning in the hearth. Dom didn't move, didn't speak. Ryan felt his father's glare like an invisible weight, threatening to crush his resolve, but he didn't break. Not anymore. He remembered the bruises on his friends and the nights spent listening to the chaos outside, and he knew he had to fight for himself.

Finally, Dom stood, his chair scraping loudly against the polished floor. He walked around his desk slowly, his movements calculated, almost predatory. "You think I haven't seen this coming? You think you can just turn your back on everything you've been raised to do? To be?"

Ryan's throat tightened but he maintained his composure. "I'm not you. I don't—" He hesitated, breath hitching as memories threatened to surge. Taking a steadying breath, he pressed on, "I want to make something of myself. I'm done with the lies, the violence... the bloodshed." Dom's lips curled into a dark smile, but there was no warmth in it."

You'll never escape it, Roy. No matter where you go, no matter what you do. You were born into this life. You were chosen to take over when the time came. You can run, but you'll always be a Giovanetti."

Ryan's hands trembled slightly, but his voice was steadier. "Not anymore. I'm cutting ties, Dom. This is the last time we'll speak of it."

THE BLOOD PACT

For a moment, Dom didn't respond. The fire crackled in the hearth, the tension palpable, an oppressive silence hanging between them. Then, without warning, Dom slammed his palm on the desk with such force that the glassware rattled. "You think you can leave this family?" he hissed, his voice sharp as a knife. "You think you can just walk away from me? You are all I have left after your mother died!"

Ryan's heart ached at the mention of his mother, but he clenched his jaw and clenched his fists until his knuckles turned white. "I already have."

Dom's gaze narrowed, cold and calculating. "You'll regret this, Roy. No one leaves the Notturno, not truly. The world isn't done with you. I'll make sure of it."

Ryan stepped back, every beat of his heart echoing his determination. He had made his choice, and with it came a fierce clarity. "I'm not you, Dom. I'm leaving."

Dom didn't move. He didn't need to. The air was thick with unspoken threats, promises of a dark future. "We'll see about that," he muttered, his voice so quiet that it sent a chill down Ryan's spine.

R. STELLAN

New Beginnings

I've never felt this free in my entire life.

As the plane touched down at Horizon View Airport, I exhaled deeply, feeling the weight of the past slip away with each heartbeat. The wheels met the tarmac, and the thrill of a new city filled me. A new life—and the chance to be someone else. Someone who wasn't tethered to the darkness that had always lurked in my shadows. Someone who wasn't Roy Giovannetti.

No more family business. No more mafia. Just me. Just Ryan Rossi.

I adjusted the strap on my duffel bag, my eyes darting across the bustling airport terminal. The air smelled different here, fresh and alive, infused with the promise of new beginnings. I could almost taste it—freedom. For once, I didn't have to look over my shoulder. For once, I didn't have to live in the shadow of my last name.

"Ryan Rossi," I whispered to myself, testing the sound of it.

I liked it. It felt clean, unburdened. Giovannetti felt like a stone around my neck, but Rossi felt lighter, like the first breath after emerging from deep water. I had envisioned this moment for years, planning and plotting my escape. There was no way back to the family business. I had made my choice. I took a cab ride to the university, my heart racing with a blend of anticipation and anxiety as we navigated the busy streets. By the time I stepped out, my resolve was solidified.

"Hey, Ryan! You made it!"

I turned toward the voice, and there he was—Dylan Johnson, my new roommate.

"Yeah, I'm here." My voice steadied, although I could hear the faint thrill of excitement creeping in.

Dylan slapped me on the back, his gesture friendly but assertive. "Good to hear, man! Welcome to the chaos." He laughed, the sentiment light, but those sharp, watchful eyes of his made me pause.

"Thanks," I replied, unsure what to add to the conversation with someone I barely knew. "You been here long?"

"Long enough to know the ropes. Follow me; I'll show you, our place."

Dylan led the way through the bustling crowd of students rushing to catch their futures. I trailed behind, my mind occupied with fears of being discovered, the past trailing me like a sinister shadow.

Dylan's room was on the second floor—a simple space filled with essentials that could easily belong to any guy navigating college life. It was comforting in its ordinariness, a stark contrast to the chaos I'd left behind. We reached our room, and Dylan flung open the door. "Here it is. Make yourself at home." Inside, I dropped my bag beside the single bed, taking a moment to absorb it all. Basic but functional—it had everything I needed. No frills, no excess, just enough for a fresh start.

"So, what's the plan, Rossi? You here to have fun or get some work done?"

I laughed, shrugging as I unzipped my bag. "A little bit of both, I guess."

"Well, don't worry. You'll learn fast. This place knows how to have fun," he said, his grin widening.

THE BLOOD PACT

But again, that look in his eyes—calculating, dissecting—still sent a strange chill down my spine. Maybe it was just his personality, but the intensity of it didn't sit right.

"Cool, I'll keep that in mind," I responded, trying to keep things light despite the heaviness I felt.

Dylan tossed me a key. "You'll need this for the dorm study room. Just in case you want some quiet time away from the madness." He paused, his gaze assessing. "We all need a little peace and quiet, right?"

"Yeah," I said, accepting the key but still unsure. A quiet space would be good. After everything I'd left behind, I needed it more than I realized. "Thanks."

After Dylan left, I stood in the middle of the room, taking it all in. No one to answer to here. No father's expectations. No Famiglia Notturno. Just me. Ryan Rossi. It was exactly what I wanted—freedom without looking over my shoulder. The first night in my new room passed quietly. The dorms were alive with laughter and voices, sounds drifting through the walls like a distant echo compared to the noise of my former life. No matter how much noise surrounded me, I couldn't hear my father's voice pressuring me into the life he'd chosen. I was grateful for that stark contrast, though it was tinged with nostalgia.

Before I fell asleep, my phone buzzed with an unexpected message.

"Protection."

I stared at the screen, my brow furrowing. I didn't recognize the number. Just some random text. I shrugged it off, setting the phone down on the nightstand. The past is the past, I told myself. Here, I'm Ryan Rossi. That's all that matters now. But the next morning greeted me with the sharp sting of reality. I rolled out of bed, and the familiar routine unfolded: shower, dress, grab a quick breakfast. As I passed through the bustling dorm hallways and down the stairs, the weight of my new life began to settle in like a heavy cloak. It wouldn't be as easy as I'd envisioned. Horizon View University was a sprawling maze of possibility, full of students rushing past with their own lives and histories. I walked through the campus, feeling like an outsider who didn't quite belong. No looming threats here, no hidden eyes watching, but even in this vibrant space, an undeniable sense of unease gnawed at me, a reminder that the shadows I thought I'd escaped had a way of lingering.

I kept whispering to myself that it was just nerves, that it was normal to feel out of place. Yet, an unsettling feeling remained, a reminder of the life I was striving so hard to erase.

The first class was Criminal Law 101. I read the plate next to the door:

Classroom Door Plate:
Dr. Landon Finch, Ph.D.
Professor of Criminal Justice
Specializing in Organized Crime and Criminal Psychology

I settled into my seat as a familiar tension ebbed and flowed within me. Students around me were eager—potential lawyers, some likely from privileged backgrounds insulated from the life I had known. But for me, the class was a stark reminder of my past. I wasn't here to embrace the law; I was here to escape everything I knew about it.

The professor strode in, tall and sharp-eyed, with salt-and-pepper hair that gave him an air of authority.

His presence commanded attention the moment he entered; the room fell silent like a drawn bowstring. I could sense that he was the kind of man who demanded respect, not just with words but with presence.

THE BLOOD PACT

"Welcome to Criminal Law 101," he said, his voice carrying across the hall. "This isn't a class about what you think you know. It's about understanding the system—the flaws, the strengths, the hidden truths. Believe me, there are truths in this field most people would prefer to keep buried."

I leaned back, watching him carefully. There was something unsettling about the way he spoke, as though he could see through the polished veneer, I had worked so hard to maintain.

"So, who here plans to become a criminal lawyer?" he asked, scanning the room. A few hands went up, but they were few and far between. "And who's here because they've seen it firsthand, from the other side?"

Before I could think, my hand shot up.

Dr. Finch's eyes locked onto mine, a moment of silence stretching between us, thick with unspoken understanding. I shifted uncomfortably but didn't look away. There was a subtle power shift; I could almost feel the air around us crackle.

"Ah, Mr. Rossi," he said, his voice cool yet tinged with curiosity. "What makes you so eager to dive into the criminal world?"

My throat tightened. "I—uh, I want to understand it better. You know, the way it works. The people involved."

He raised an eyebrow, his scrutiny piercing. "And why is that Mr. Rossi?"

A thousand thoughts swirled in my mind. I wanted to explain—to open about my upbringing, about the family steeped in crime, the blurred lines between law and illegality that haunted my childhood. But the fear of exposure clamped down hard.

"I think it's important to know both sides of the coin," I answered, striving for nonchalance, hiding the storm within me. "To understand what drives people, what pushes them to break the law."

Dr. Finch nodded, though I could see he wasn't fully convinced. "Fair enough. We'll explore that in due time."

The rest of the class washed over me in a blur of information and anxiety. Thoughts of my past whispered incessantly: What if he knows? What if he's already figured me out?

The day wore on. Classes, new faces, and a myriad of questions I still couldn't answer as I adjusted to the unfamiliar rhythm of this life that wasn't really mine. With each step I took across campus, trying to blend in, the harder it grew to escape the ghosts of my former life.

As I headed back to the dorm later that afternoon, a new message pinged on my phone:

"You can't run forever, Ryan."

My heart dropped as I read it, fingers trembling slightly.

I quickly glanced around. The pathway was empty; no one was there. Yet the words felt real and chilling, hanging in the air like an ominous cloud. The message had come from yet another unfamiliar number, but those words... they sliced too close to the bone. My father's reach was longer than I'd imagined. Even here, in this new city, this life I had fought for, I couldn't escape him.

I forced myself to breathe, fighting off the creeping panic. It was just a prank. Just someone messing with me. But deep down, a voice whispered that I knew better. The shadows I thought I had outrun had an uncanny way of following me, and no matter how far I ran, they'd always be there.

I had to be smarter. I had to keep my head down, focus on the future, and not let the past catch me.

But that night, as I lay in bed staring at the ceiling, the echoes of the message pulsed in my mind: You can't run forever.

THE BLOOD PACT

And for the first time since my arrival, the weight of doubt settled over me like a heavy blanket, blurring the line between hope and despair. The night stretched on, and I found it difficult to shake off the weight of that text. "You can't run forever." It echoed in my mind like a reminder that my past wasn't going to let go so easily. Just as I thought I could shed my old life, the shadows twisted and beckoned, making me question if freedom was truly within my grasp.

The next morning, I woke up with a dull ache in my chest that refused to subside. I slipped out of bed, taking a deep breath to calm my nerves. The light filtering through the window felt false, a bright façade hiding the uncertainties lurking beneath the surface.

"Hey, Ryan! You good?" Dylan called from the bathroom, his voice echoing as he brushed his teeth.

"Yeah, just... adjusting," I replied, forcing a smile. I didn't want to burden him with the weight I carried, nor did I want to explain that my adjustment was complicated by the haunting presence of my past.

As I got ready, I caught a glimpse of myself in the mirror. My dark hair was a mess, and the remnants of sleep still clung to my features. I needed to get my act together. College was supposed to be my starting line, not a reminder of everything I wanted to escape.

Breakfast was a whirlwind of noise and chatter in the dining hall. Students crowded around tables, laughing and sharing stories, but I felt like an imposter in this world of carefree youth. Dylan was in his element, bouncing between tables of friends, teasing and joking with easy confidence. I envied him, the way he moved through life unburdened.

"Come on, Rossi! Sit with us!" Dylan waved me over to a table where a group of his friends congregated.

I hesitated but finally made my way over, forcing a smile as I plopped down.

"This is Ryan, my new roommate," Dylan introduced, beaming.

"He's got some interesting stories. Isn't that, right?"

I shrugged, avoiding their curious gazes. "Just trying to survive my first week."

"Surviving is overrated! You've got to make the most of it," a girl with curly brown hair said, nudging my shoulder. "I'm Sarah, and believe me, this place can be a blast if you let it!"

"I'll keep that in mind," I said, though the thought of letting loose felt distant, like a lifeline thrown into choppy waters.

Before long, Dylan's friends began talking about the upcoming football season, their enthusiasm infectious. I watched him as he animatedly discussed strategies and workouts, the passion he had for the sport evident. It was a world I knew nothing about, yet I felt drawn to his energy—a reminder that life could still be vibrant despite the storms brewing within me.

"Ryan, you should come to one of our games!" Sarah said, her green eyes sparkling with excitement. "It'll be fun, and you'll get to see Dylan in action."

"Yeah, I'll think about it," I said, though the thought was intimidating.

Attending an event like that felt like stepping into a spotlight I wasn't ready for.

Classes resumed, and with each lecture, I felt myself slowly acclimating to the rhythm of university life. Yet, as I sat through discussions about criminal law and justice, the shadows of my past lingered just beneath the surface. Dr. Finch's lectures provoked thoughts that stirred my mind like a tempest. I found myself engaged—both intrigued and nervous by the topics he brought up regarding organized crime. He had a way of weaving real-world implications into the curriculum, drawing us into discussions that felt both distant and hauntingly familiar.

THE BLOOD PACT

"Today, we're going to delve into the psychology behind criminal behaviour," Dr. Finch announced, leaning against his desk with authority. He scanned the room with those sharp blue eyes, his gaze lingering on me for a moment. "Understanding motivation is crucial. Not every criminal is a monster; sometimes, the line between right and wrong is blurred."

My heart raced at his words, each one echoing my own inner conflict. I couldn't help but wonder what he saw when he looked at me. Did he sense that I carried shadows of my own?

"Let's discuss organized crime. Who can give me an example of a well-known figure and their motives?" he asked, and several hands shot up around the room.

Dylan's hand was one of the first. "Al Capone! He used his power to control the illegal liquor trade during Prohibition, right?"

"Exactly. Capone's rise to power was fuelled by opportunity and a desire for control. But what about the human cost? What does that tell us about the nature of crime?" He turned his gaze to the class, waiting for an answer.

I felt a surge of determination. "It shows that circumstances often drive people to make choices they wouldn't normally consider. Sometimes, survival takes precedence over morality."

Dr. Finch's eyes locked onto mine, a flicker of interest sparking in his gaze. "Well said, Mr. Rossi. The balance of survival versus morality is a theme we'll explore further. Crime isn't just about the act itself; it's about understanding the underlying motivations."

I could feel the weight of his scrutiny. The words hovered between us like a thin thread, the tension palpable. It was as though he was peeling back layers, trying to see what lay beneath the surface of my carefully maintained façade.

As the class continued, I stayed focused, pushing aside the anxious knot in my stomach. But when the bell rang, releasing us from the confines of the classroom, I felt the weight of Dr. Finch's gaze upon me once more. I wasn't sure whether it was encouragement or suspicion, but I had to navigate this new life with care.

After class, I made my way to the campus quad, the vibrant greenery brightened by the afternoon sun. Students sprawled across the lawns, engaged in laughter and conversation. I half-heartedly scrolled through my phone, still haunted by the anonymous text.

"Hey, Rossi!" Dylan's voice broke through my thoughts, and I turned to see him jogging toward me. "You up for some football practice today? We need all the support we can get!"

I hesitated, glancing at the throngs of energetic students around me. "I don't really know much about football."

"Trust me, you'll catch on fast! It's mostly just about cheering loudly and making a fool of yourself. Besides, it'll be fun!" His enthusiasm was hard to resist, and part of me yearned to break free from the confines of anxiety and isolation.

"Okay, I'll come," I said, forcing a smile.

"That's the spirit! You'll meet the whole team, and I promise you, we know how to have a good time."

As we made our way to the football field, I tried to shake off my lingering doubts. Maybe I could blend in, be just another face in the crowd. But even as I walked beside Dylan, the thrill of stepping into that arena filled with energy and excitement flickered like a distant flame.

As I approached the field, a sense of apprehension washed over me. The boisterous sounds of laughter and shouts enveloped me, and my heart raced. I was stepping into a new world, one that was supposed to be filled with joy and camaraderie, yet the ghosts of my past followed, shrouding it all in uncertainty.

THE BLOOD PACT

Maybe, just maybe, I could find a way to let go, if only for a little while. I took a deep breath and stepped into the chaos of the football field, ready to embrace whatever moments lay ahead.

But a sense of dread gnawed at the back of my mind—an unsettling reminder of the message in my inbox. No matter how hard I tried to break free, the past had a way of creeping back in, lurking at the periphery, waiting for the moment to reveal itself.

As we neared the football field, the sound of whistles and shouts grew louder, blending with the enthusiasm of players and spectators alike. A group of students were gathered on the sidelines, some tossing a football back and forth while others cheered loudly for their friends on the field. The energy was infectious, a different world compared to the shadows that clung to me.

"Come on, let's get in there," Dylan said, his eyes sparkling with enthusiasm as he pulled me toward the sidelines. "You'll love it!"

I tried to suppress my anxiety, forcing a grin. "Right. Just stand there and cheer, right?"

"Pretty much! But don't worry, you'll get a chance to show off your arm later." He grinned, tossing an arm around my shoulder, drawing me into the fray.

As we reached the sidelines, the smell of grass and sweat filled the air, mingling with the sunlight that cast everything in a golden hue. Dylan introduced me to other players and friends, their laughter and camaraderie swallowing me up in a comforting wave. Still, a part of me felt like a stranger at a party where I didn't know anyone—a reminder of how far I came from being the person I once was.

"Hey, everyone! This is my roommate, Ryan!" Dylan announced, drawing attention to me. "He's new and needs to learn how we celebrate a win!"

"Welcome to the jungle, Ryan!" shouted a player with a broad grin, yellow mouthguard glinting in the sun. "Get ready to cheer like you mean it!"

I chuckled, trying to go along with the light-hearted vibe but aware that my heart was pounding in my chest.

As practice started, I watched the intensity of the drills, players moving in sync, executing plays like a well-oiled machine. The field buzzed with energy, and I couldn't help but feel a twinge of admiration. I was drawn into the rhythm of it all, the shouts of encouragement and challenge setting a tempo I felt I could almost follow.

"Alright, time for some scrimmaging!" the coach hollered, clapping his hands to gather attention. "We're working on our defence tonight! Let's show some spirit! And I expect our newest fan—Ryan—to lead the charge over here!"

Dylan shot me a conspiratorial grin and pointed me toward the makeshift bleachers where other students had gathered. "Go on! Get your cheer on!"

With an exaggerated sigh, I climbed up onto the bleachers, hearing the laughter and excitement drift behind me. "I'm not really a cheerleader, you know that, right?" I called back.

"Just give it a shot!" Dylan shot back, already layering himself in pads to rejoin the cramped circle on the field. "You might surprise yourself!"

So, I stood there, watching as the players lined up, the atmosphere buzzing with anticipation. As the play began, I found myself lost in the moment, shouting and cheering, trying to mimic the enthusiasm around me. It felt liberating—maybe I could play a part in this new chapter, even if just as a bystander for now.

Yet, even in this brand-new place, memories of my old life flickered at the edges. I squashed the nagging thought that I was somehow betraying my past by trying to live freely; I could navigate through this. I had to.

THE BLOOD PACT

As practice wound down and the players gathered on the sidelines, Dylan trotted over, sweaty and hyper, his green eyes shining with energy. "Alright, Ryan! Time to show us what you've got. Let's see if you can throw a spiral!"

With a hesitant laugh, I took the football he tossed my way and took a few steps back. The weight of the ball felt foreign in my hand, and I wondered if I was about to embarrass myself in front of my new friends. But I couldn't let Dylan down—not this early.

"Come on, man! You've got this!" someone shouted from the sidelines, and I felt the pressure mount slightly, a mix of encouragement and challenge.

Here was the moment. No one knew about my past; I was just Ryan. I threw a deep breath into my lungs and focused on the target. I wound up my arm and let it fly, releasing the ball with more force than I anticipated. To my surprise, it soared straight and true, landing squarely into the hands of a receiver, who barely managed to keep his feet as he caught it.

"Nice throw!" Dylan cheered, clapping his hands. I felt a rush of adrenaline, layered with the happiness of having done something right in this new setting.

"Looks like we have a new QB in training!" another player called, laughing as they all mimicked a quarterback stance.

I smiled, feeling a sense of belonging shimmer just beneath the surface. Maybe I really could carve a niche for myself here. I spent the rest of practice joining in on the playful banter, enjoying the camaraderie that was slowly forming.

As the afternoon settled and twilight crept in, I felt lighter, my earlier anxieties dissipating—until my phone buzzed again, slicing through the moment like a knife.

The message was from the same unknown number.

"Don't think you can just run away from your family. We know where you are."

My stomach dropped as dread settled in. I quickly moved away from the group, my smile fading, heart racing as I clutch the phone tighter. I needed to stay calm, to not let panic take control. But how could I pretend everything was fine when my past was clawing its way back in?

I looked around, searching for any unfamiliar faces among the crowd. Was someone watching me?

"Ryan! You good?" Dylan called, breaking into my thoughts.

I plastered a smile on my face, trying to bury the fear. "Yeah, just taking it all in!"

As I returned to the group, I felt the weight of the message in my pocket—a reminder that even in this newfound excitement, my past was just a text away.

The evening rolled on, and just when I thought I could breathe a little easier, Dr. Finch's words echoed back in my mind: Understanding the motivations behind crime and knowing how thin the line could be.

How thin indeed.

With a head full of thoughts, laughter, and unease, I participated in the celebrations around me yet felt distanced from it all. The freedom I craved felt like a mirage in the desert of my reality.

As night fell and we wrapped up practice, the glow of streetlights framed the scene in a warm halo. I lingered on the sidelines, watching as Dylan and his teammates celebrated the day's practice. I wanted to feel relief, but as I stood there, I realized a part of me was still haunted by questions.

Would I ever truly escape my past? And if not, how close was I to its dangerous edge?

With a heavy heart, I took a deep breath and faced the darkness creeping in. Maybe tomorrow would bring some clarity, or maybe I would find a way to fight against the chaos that had followed me here.

THE BLOOD PACT

And for now, I just needed to put one foot in front of the other—Ryan Rossi, finding my way in a world that begged me to belong.

As the sun dipped below the horizon, painting the sky with hues of orange and purple, I found myself leaning against the bleachers, watching the post-practice banter unfold. The laughter was contagious, and for a fleeting moment, I let myself believe that I could truly belong here. But the weight of that text gnawed at me like a persistent itch I couldn't scratch.

"Hey, Ryan!" A voice called, shattering my introspection. It was Sarah, her hair bouncing as she approached with an enthusiastic smile. "You really did great out there! I didn't know you had it in you!"

"Thanks!" I replied, attempting to mirror her cheerfulness. "Just trying to keep up with you all."

"Don't sell yourself short! You've got potential." She leaned against the bleacher beside me, her presence warm and inviting. "Are you going to come to the actual game on Saturday? It'll be a blast!"

My mind raced with possibilities. Part of me felt drawn to the idea of being part of this community—my newfound friends, the excitement of what lay ahead. But another part hesitated, held back by the creeping fear that had settled in since I received that ominous message.

"I... I'll try," I said, hoping it sounded more enthusiastic than I felt. "It depends on how things go."

"Just promise me you'll at least consider it. You can't do college without a game day experience!" She grinned, and I couldn't help but return her smile, even if it felt a bit forced.

"Deal," I said, trying to maintain a light-hearted tone to mask my inner turmoil.

As the festivities continued, the weight of my phone in my pocket felt like a lead weight. I excused myself under the pretence of needing to call home. In truth, I just needed a moment alone to process everything swirling in my mind.

The campus, drenched in warm light, felt breathtakingly vibrant, yet I was a storm cloud within it. I walked toward a nearby garden, hoping to shield myself from the noise and distraction for just a moment.

Finding a secluded bench, I pulled my phone from my pocket, hesitating before unlocking the screen. I stared at the message again. "Don't think you can just run away from your family. We know where you are."

My pulse quickened, each syllable igniting a fresh wave of anxiety. I had thought I was escaping, free from the shadows of my past. But now, the reality hit hard: no matter how far I ran, they would always find a way back into my life.

What did they want from me? Would they come here? I couldn't let that happen. I would have to end this once and for all; I needed a plan.

I couldn't keep the fear bottled inside. I had to talk to someone, maybe even share my past with Dylan—someone I was beginning to trust. But as I sat there, I wondered if that was even an option. Could I really burden someone with the weight of my history? Would he understand?

A rustle in the bushes brought me back to reality, and I glanced up, instinctively tensing. There was a figure emerging from the shadows, and for a split second, my heart raced with fear. But then I recognized him: it was Dylan.

"Hey! There you are!" he called, his voice cheerful despite the dusky surroundings. "We were looking for you. Are you alright? You've been gone a while."

THE BLOOD PACT

I plastered on a smile, willing myself to appear nonchalant. "Yeah, just needed to catch my breath. It's a lot to take in, you know?"

He nodded, his face suddenly serious. "I get that. Moving away from home and starting fresh is a big deal. If you ever need to talk—about anything—I'm here for you."

His sincerity overwhelmed me, and for a moment, I considered confiding in him. But the thought of unloading my troubles, the gravity of my situation, felt impossible. I just couldn't.

"Thanks, Dylan. That means a lot," I managed, grateful he was looking out for me.

"Come on, let's head back. The guys are planning some food, and it would be a shame to miss out on that."

As we walked back toward the gathering crowd, I felt a sense of longing for normality. But the weight of my past pressed relentlessly against me, reminding me that I couldn't stay hidden in the shadows forever. With each step, I grappled with the notion that my new life was at stake, teetering on a precipice.

Back at the group, laughter echoed as food was served, the sights and sounds of camaraderie enveloping me like a warm blanket. But I remained teetering on the edge, uncertainty lurking in every smile, every joke shared.

"Hey, Ryan! You're just in time for the taco bar!" Sarah announced, drawing my attention back. "What's your favourite topping?"

"Uh, I think I'm a classic salsa kind of guy," I replied, forcing a smile.

"Tacos and football—a winning combination for sure!" she laughed, and for a moment, I was swept away in the ease of their interactions.

But in the back of my mind, the text loomed, its implications circling like hawks waiting for the right moment to swoop down.

As I took a taco and joined the banter, I felt a sense of distance growing within me. I watched Dylan and his friends laugh and challenge one another over their meals. It was comforting yet painful, a reminder of what I yearned for and what felt just out of reach.

"Hey, Ryan! You're unusually quiet tonight," Dylan nudged me with a grin. "Are you sure you're not hiding some secret salsa recipe?"

"Just taking it all in, man," I said, forcing lightness into my voice while understanding that the secret I hid was far from simple.

The group continued to banter around me, but my mind drifted. Would I be able to enjoy moments like these, or was I destined to relive the darkness? I had to find a way to sever the ties that bound me to my past, maybe even confront it, but how?

As the evening wind blew gently, I made a silent promise to myself. I couldn't live in fear. I wanted the freedom to explore this new life on my terms. But to do that, I had to confront my demons—wherever they might lead.

And as they cheered for another round of touchdowns yet to come, I steeled myself, ready to push back against the shackles of my past. I was Ryan Rossi, newly diving into the depths of college life, and I would not be defined by the shadows that sought to catch up with me. The night wore on, and the atmosphere buzzed with excitement as Dylan and his teammates swapped stories, pushing each other for laughs. I took a sip of my soda, faking a smile and engaging with the banter, yet my mind continuously drifted back to that ominous message.

"Hey, Ryan! Salsa or guac?" Dylan shouted over the noise, holding up two bowls. His eyes were wide with mock seriousness. "This could be a make-or-break moment for you!"

"Definitely guac!" I replied, not wanting to engage in a hypothetical debate while already battling thoughts of my own hybrid turmoil.

THE BLOOD PACT

The laughter around me swelled, and I felt a flicker of warmth from their acceptance mixed with a hollowness that nagged at me.

As the food dwindled and stories escalated in intensity, I found myself sitting next to Sarah. She leaned in conspiratorially, her eyes sparkling with mischief. "So, are you officially a part of the team now? Because I've heard taco-eating is the secret initiation rite!"

"Is that so? Maybe I should've packed more toppings," I joked, trying to keep the mood light.

But the laughter from my friends felt like a double-edged sword, amplifying my feeling of disconnection beneath the surface.

"Just wait until you get to the home game. The atmosphere is unlike anything you've experienced," she replied, her enthusiasm rejuvenating a sense of hope within me.

"Yeah, I'm looking forward to it," I stated, though my heart was battling with doubts about my past clouds hovering over my head.

Dylan broke in, "Speaking of the home game, we'd better come up with some epic cheers.

I'm thinking a few surprises could get the crowd hyped, don't you think, Ryan?"

"Absolutely," I responded, instinctively wanting to be included and yet feeling like a shadow on the sidelines of my own life. I watched Dylan step forward to grab his phone — undoubtedly to rally the team for another spirited discussion about game day.

The moment felt heavy, as if each laugh echoed a reminder I was still tethered to the possibilities of my past, lurking in the corners of my mind.

"Hey," Sarah said, nudging my shoulder lightly. "What's really going on? You seem... far away"

The genuine concern in her voice broke through my inner turmoil. It was tempting to spill everything — the fear, the past, the weight of the unknown. But the truth was a monster I wasn't sure I could face, let alone share with someone as vibrant as her.

"I guess I'm just trying to find my footing in all of this," I admitted, swallowing the lingering bitterness in my throat. "New places, new faces. It's a lot."

"I get it," she replied, nodding with an understanding that made me feel slightly less alone. "It's okay to take your time. Just know that no one expects you to have everything figured out right away. We're all just figuring it out together."

Her words resonated with me, a gentle reminder that I wasn't alone despite feeling the isolation of my struggles. But as the conversation shifted back to football, I felt my heart harden. Here I was, just hanging on by a thread, trying to be a part of their world, but shadows still clouded my memory and my future.

"Ryan?" Dylan called out, snapping me back to the moment. "You in or out? We're planning a practice scrimmage for tomorrow afternoon. You should totally join us."

"Yeah, I'll be there," I said, surprised by the certainty in my voice. It felt powerful to say it; maybe I needed that edge to reignite my determination to break free from the fear.

As we wrapped up the night, I glanced around at the group. Dylan was animatedly talking with another player, Sarah was laughing with a couple of girls, and a certain warmth enveloped me — a feeling I nearly thought I had lost forever.

But just then, my phone buzzed in my pocket again. I could feel my breath hitch as I fished it out, the dread flooding back. It was another message from the unknown number.

"Don't think you can hide from us. You're still one of us. We'll be watching."

THE BLOOD PACT

My heart dropped; the walls around me drew tighter. Anxiety surged, and I fought to remain still while the laughter of my new friends echoed around me. As I slipped the phone back into my pocket, I felt the hot whiplash of fear against the joyful atmosphere.

"Hey, you good?" Dylan's voice cut through the fog, his brow furrowing with concern. "You look like you just saw a ghost."

"Yeah, just... tired, I guess," I replied, plastering on a smile that felt strained. "Long day."

"Alright, man. Remember, if you ever need an escape or just want to chill, you're welcome at our place anytime," he said earnestly, clapping a hand on my shoulder.

I took a moment to soak in the offered camaraderie, grounding myself in the reality that maybe I wasn't as alone as I feared.

As we stood up and began to gather our things, I felt the last tendrils of the night begin to settle over us. I met Sarah's gaze, who shot me a warm smile that lingered with promise—a flicker of what a brighter future could hold, while the shadows of my past loomed behind, hungry for my attention.

I stepped out into the cool night air, sharing a few final laughs with the crew as we parted ways. But behind the jovial smiles and relaxed chatter, I held tightly to the burgeoning determination that I needed to face whatever came my way.

The promise of tomorrow echoed in my mind as I walked back to my dorm, fingers brushing against the hard outline of my phone. My reality was a complex web of excitement and apprehension. But if I wanted to reclaim my life, I needed to confront these threats head-on.

Tomorrow would be a new day, and I would decide how to turn the tides in my Favor. I was Ryan Rossi — a fighter. And I would not be defined by the shadows that followed. I would break free. As I walked back to my dorm, the night air filled with a crisp coolness that felt refreshing against my skin, though it couldn't quite dispel the heaviness still weighing on my chest. The comforting sounds of the campus winding down—the distant laughter of students, the soft rustle of leaves—were juxtaposed with the chaos that churned within me. Loneliness often felt like a dark pool, and the shadows were closing in, but perhaps I was beginning to learn how to swim in those depths.

Unlocking the door to my room, I stepped inside and immediately flicked on the light. The familiar sanctuary greeted me, lined with boxes and unmade bedsheets, remnants of my hasty move. I kicked off my shoes, feeling the familiar comfort of the floor beneath my feet, but I couldn't shake the nagging thought about the text.

I dropped my backpack on the bed and sank down beside it, pulling my phone out again. My hands trembled slightly as I navigated to the messaging app. The name still read as "Unknown," a title that seemed to mock me with its anonymity.

Taking a deep breath, I typed back, my heart racing at the thought of engaging with whoever was on the other end.

"What do you want from me?"

I hit send before I could lose my nerve. For a moment, I just stared at the screen, my pulse pounding in my ears. As the seconds passed, every tick felt like a countdown, a reminder of the evasive peace I was searching for. Why was I even taking this chance? I could just block the number, ignore the messages, and try to move on. But something compelled me to confront it head-on. Part of me wanted answers and to wrest control back from the shadows.

Moments later, my phone buzzed with a response, breaking the tension in my chest like a pop of firecrackers.

"You may think you're safe, but you can't outrun us."

THE BLOOD PACT

Every word sent chills down my spine, a stark reminder of my fears. I cursed under my breath, tossing the phone onto the bed in frustration. Anger replaced my fear for a moment, my heart racing not just with anxiety but with a reckless urge to regain control. This was my life now, and I couldn't allow my past to drag me down.

I paced around the small room, the cluttered space reflecting my chaotic thoughts. The people I had met tonight were the first real connections I had forged away from home—the first hints of a new start. I couldn't let the darkness swallow that burgeoning hope.

With newfound determination, I grabbed my notebook from the desk, flicking to a blank page. Writing always cleared my mind, a way to channel my turmoil into something tangible.

I scrawled down my thoughts, pouring out my frustrations and fears, the text messages, and my hatred for feeling trapped. Writing about it felt oddly liberating, like I was releasing the shadows from the depths of my mind onto the page.

But just as I began to feel clarity, my phone buzzed again, interrupting my flow. I picked it up, and a knot tightened in my stomach.

"We'll find you, Ryan. You can count on it."

I slammed the phone down, breathing heavily, angry tears prickling at the corners of my eyes. I was tired—tired of running, tired of looking over my shoulder. I couldn't hide. The threat wasn't just a message; it was a reminder of the reality I had been fleeing.

Suddenly, the door swung open, and Dylan stepped inside, his expression shifting from one of enthusiasm to concern as he caught a glimpse of my distress. "Hey, man! I thought I'd check if you wanted to—wow, everything okay?"

I hesitated, heart racing at the thought of exposing my turmoil. "Yeah, just... dealing with some stuff," I said, attempting to regain a semblance of calm.

Dylan stepped closer, a frown etched on his face. "You don't look fine. Do you want to talk about it?"

The genuine concern in his eyes made my heart swell and ache at the same time. I wanted to trust him, to let him in. But how could I explain something that even I struggled to comprehend? "It's just..." I faltered, my mind racing, but I forced myself to maintain eye contact. "I'm still processing everything. Moving here, starting fresh. It's been a lot."

"I get that," he replied, leaning against the wall. "Change is tough. But you don't have to carry that weight alone, you know? We're here for you. Besides, if you have anything on your mind, you can trust me. I swear I won't tell anyone."

The sincerity in his voice tugged at me, and I recognized the promise laced within. It would be so easy to unburden myself, to let him hold part of my fears. "It's just... I'm dealing with some personal stuff," I managed, keeping my tone even. "Nothing dangerous, just... you know, history I'm trying to shake off."

His brow furrowed, and I could tell he wanted to pry deeper, but instead, he nodded. "I know what that feels like. Honestly, I've had my share of baggage too," he admitted, his voice softening. "Maybe one day we could swap stories over pizza and bad horror movies?"

I chuckled lightly, grateful for his attempt at levity, even if I could sense the heaviness beneath it. "Yeah, for sure. I'd like that."

"Good. Just remember, you're not alone in this." He stepped towards the door but paused before leaving. "And if those messages keep bothering you, just let me know. I can help you figure it out."

"Thanks, Dylan," I said, my voice earnest.

I could see the concern still lingering in his eyes, but I also felt a small flicker of comfort in knowing that someone cared—someone was willing to stand by me as I navigated this uncertainty.

THE BLOOD PACT

Once he left, the room fell into solitude once again. I exhaled deeply, wrestling with the weight of my decision. I could stay in this cluttered space of fear and doubt, or I could fight against it. My new friends were offering a lifeline, and I could never have imagined that I'd find a hint of home here.

I picked up my notebook and wrote a new line: "I will confront my fears, not run from them." A small but powerful mantra, as my resolve started to solidify. The shadows of my past could try to overwhelm me, but they wouldn't win. I envisioned myself taking control of my narrative instead of letting it dictate me.

Tonight, I would find a way to share pieces of who I was and build a bridge to who I wanted to be. Tomorrow would bring a new day, and with it, new opportunities to forge my path. The battle wasn't over, but I wouldn't face it alone anymore.

The phone lay silent beside me, the oppressive weight of uncertainty still looming, but now I felt a surge of determination rising within. I was Ryan Rossi, on the brink of redefining my life. I would seek out the light amid the shadows, no matter how daunting they appeared.

R. STELLAN

Unseen Shadows

As I settled into my bed, the faint murmur of laughter and chatter from the campus drifted in through my window, an echo of the life I was trying to build. Yet, the weight of the unknown pressed heavily on my chest. I had stepped into a new life as Ryan Rossi; a fresh start filled with possibilities. But doubts clawed at the edges of that hope, refusing to let go.

Dylan's words rang in my mind— "You're not alone in this." The warmth of his assurance felt comforting, yet there was a flicker of concern that lingered in the back of my thoughts. In my world, genuine concern often came with hidden motives, and I couldn't shake the feeling that Dylan was somehow observing me far more closely than most friends would. Yet, the logical part of me acknowledged that I was simply overthinking it. After all, he had offered me friendship at a time when I felt untethered.

In the following days, I immersed myself in classes and tried to engage with colleagues, forcing smiles while my mind wrestled with unsettling messages and covert threats. Each conversation felt rehearsed, as if I were playing a part in a drama where I was constantly on edge, teetering between my past and an uncertain future.

During one of my late-night strolls across the campus, the cool autumn air brushed against my skin, refreshing yet chilling. I found comfort in the rhythmic crunch of leaves beneath my feet, their crackling sound a reminder that change was constant, even if it frightened me. As I passed groups of laughing students, carefree and oblivious to my turmoil, I felt a pang of envy. I longed for that kind of peace.

Tonight, I stopped at the bench beneath the oak tree where I had encountered the stranger—the man who had cast a long shadow over my newfound life. His words haunted me like a spectre: "You're being watched."

Pulling out my phone, my heartbeat quickened at a new notification. My stomach dropped as the familiar message blinked on the screen.

"You're not as invisible as you think."

It was a different message but echoed the same threat. My skin prickled. I glanced around, the campus bathed in moonlight, but it felt like the darkness was closing in on me. The tranquil silence only heightened my anxiety; it was too quiet, too serene. It felt like the calm before a storm.

My thoughts spiralled, caught between the life I was trying to live and the past from which I was desperate to escape. Suddenly, I became aware of footsteps behind me. I held my breath, my body tensing as I tried to remain composed. I refused to give anyone the satisfaction of knowing I felt like prey.

The footsteps approached and stopped, just inches away.

"You seem deep in thought, Rossi."

The voice was low, smooth, and unmistakably familiar. I turned slowly, my hand slipping cautiously into my jacket pocket, ready to grasp my phone if I needed it. It wasn't Dylan standing there. It was the tall guy with the calculating eyes—the one who had invoked a chill down my spine the last time we met.

THE BLOOD PACT

"Do I know you?" My voice felt steadier than my pulse racing in my chest.

He smiled, but it didn't reach his eyes. It was more of a smirk, as though he found amusement in my confusion. "No, but I know you. I know exactly who you are, where you've come from, and where you're going." Panic surged through me, making it hard to breathe. "What do you want?" I managed to ask, my voice sharper than I intended.

He raised his hands in a placating gesture, a mockery of surrender.

"Easy, Rossi. No need to get hostile. I'm just here to give you a little heads-up."

"A heads-up?" I repeated, stepping back instinctively, reclaiming a breath of distance.

"You're not as invisible as you think," he said, his tone dripping with condescension. "You may have left your family, but your family hasn't left you. You're a part of something much bigger than yourself now. And you're being watched—every move you make."

I swallowed hard, the knot in my stomach tightening. "I don't know what you're talking about," I said, though my voice wavered. He nodded slowly, almost with sympathy, as if waiting for me to come around—a cue that terrified me.

"You will. Soon enough," he said, his voice low, almost conspiratorial. "Remember this, Ryan. The name you're trying to outrun—it's still with you. Whether you like it or not."

And just like that, he turned and faded into the shadows, leaving me trembling beneath the oak tree. For a moment, I stood there, frozen, amidst the echoes of laughter from the nearby students, grappling with the weight of his words. I was not free—not yet. I needed answers. As I returned to the dorm, my thoughts churned with uncertainty. When I opened the door, Dylan was gone, leaving the room cloaked in silence and the dim glow of the desk lamp. I paced, rubbing the back of my neck as I tried to process the strange encounter. What did that guy know? How was he connected to my past? Suddenly, a knock at the door jolted me. I wasn't expecting anyone at this hour. My heart raced as I hesitated before opening it. Dylan stood there, looking casual but with an undertone of concern in his demeanour.

"Yo, Rossi! You in there?" he called, a friendly smile masking whatever was brewing beneath the surface.

I forced a smile, even though my heart was still pounding in my chest. "Yeah, I'm here. Just... taking a break."

"Cool, just wanted to check on you. You've been kind of quiet lately," he said, leaning against the doorframe.

I shrugged, instinctively moving aside for him to enter. "Getting used to things, I guess. This place is... different." Dylan walked in, shifting his gaze around the room before settling his gaze back on me, studying me with an intensity that made me uncomfortable. "I get that. But you've got a fresh start, man. New city, new life... all that. Just go for it."

"Yeah, a fresh start," I muttered, half-heartedly.

The silence stretched, feeling heavy with unspoken thoughts. Dylan scrutinized me, as though he could read the flickering emotions swirling behind my composure.

"Well, if you need anything or just want to talk, I'm here," he offered, his voice shifting to an earnest tone.

"Thanks, I will," I replied quickly, desperate to dispel any hint of my troubles.

Dylan smiled again but lingered, as if waiting for something more from me. Finally, he shrugged, breaking the tension. "Alright, man. Just remember, you don't have to carry it all alone."

"Goodnight, Dylan," I said, my voice softening.

THE BLOOD PACT

 He hesitated a moment longer before stepping back out into the hall. I closed the door behind him, instantly feeling the once-familiar silence swallow me whole.

 I sat on my bed, overwhelmed by the whirlwind of thoughts. The room felt too quiet now, too still, amplifying the distant echo of the stranger's warning. I picked up my phone but saw no new messages—only the void reminder of my growing paranoia. The lurking sensation of being watched loomed over me, a shadow extending far beyond my choices. I had left a life fraught with danger, yet the threads of my past clung to me, tightening with every breath I took.

 With a heavy sigh, I set my phone down and stared into the darkness where the threat lingered, feeling the weight of uncertainty settle in my bones. I knew I had to remain vigilant; the peace I had found was only a fragile veneer, one that could shatter at any moment. When the shadows inevitably returned, I promised myself I would be ready. The hours trickled by slowly, each tick of the clock a reminder of my restless mind. Sleep felt impossible, elusive as a wisp of smoke. I sat on my bed, staring blankly at the ceiling. Would I ever truly escape? The question looped inside my head like an unanswered prayer.

 Dylan's earlier words echoed in the silence: "You don't have to carry it all alone." Part of me wished I could confide in him, share the burden of my past. But the thoughts of my old life, the danger that lurked, forbade me from trusting anyone. My secrets felt like a weight I shouldered alone, an invisible cloak that both sheltered and stifled me. Eventually, I rolled over to grab my phone, letting the soft glow of the screen provide brief comfort. I opened my messages again, hoping for some sign of normalcy to distract me from the chaos swirling around me. A text from an old friend popped up, a picture of a crowded bar with laugh lines of joy radiating through the screen—a stark contrast to my current reality. I quickly swiped it away, the image a harsh reminder of what I'd given up. With a heavy sigh, I finally turned off the light, letting the darkness envelop me. In the quiet, my mind wandered. Maybe it was time to confront my past rather than run from it. First things first: I needed to figure out who'd sent me those messages. They weren't just warnings; they were a threat, a tether to the life I had left behind. If there was one thing I had learned, it was that pretending everything would just go away would not keep me safe. Sleep came reluctantly, punctuated by restless dreams filled with shadowy figures and whispered warnings.

I awoke the next morning to the sound of my phone buzzing on the bedside table. My heart raced as I grabbed it, half-expecting another cryptic message. Instead, it was a notification from a campus event:

"Welcome Back Fair! Join us at the Student Union for games, food, and friends!"

I sighed, glancing at the time—it was already noon. A part of me craved the distraction of the fair, while another still wanted to hide away in my dorm room, cocooned in the safety of solitude. After a few moments of internal debate, I decided a change of scenery might do me good. I needed to get out, if only to clear my head and regain some semblance of normalcy. After a quick shower and a change of clothes, I headed out, the crisp air hitting me like a gentle slap. The campus buzzed with energy as students mingled, laughter and shouts bouncing off the brick buildings. It felt surreal, a world apart from the shadows that haunted me.

As I entered the Student Union, vibrant streamers hung from the ceiling, and tables were adorned with colourful flyers and products from various student organizations. Decisions lay ahead: join a club, find a hobby, make friends. I could almost feel the pressure to blend in, to be the person I wanted to be rather than the ghost trailing in the background. I navigated through the crowd, grabbing a slice of pizza from the food table. It was then that I spotted Dylan, chatting

THE BLOOD PACT

animatedly with a few other students, his infectious smile brightening the room. A small voice in my head urged me to go over, to seize the opportunity for camaraderie. I took a deep breath and walked toward him. As I approached, he turned and waved, his demeanour welcoming. "Hey, Rossi! You made it!"

"Yeah, I figured it was time to get out of my head," I replied, trying to match his enthusiasm.

"Smart move," he said, clapping me on the back. "Come meet some friends! We were just talking about joining the hiking club."

"Sounds great," I said, even as a different part of me bristled at the thought of exploring the wilderness, far from the safety of my new routine.

Dylan introduced me to a group of energetic students, each eager to share what the hiking club had to offer. As they spoke, I found myself relaxing, laughing at silly stories and feeling the faint warmth of belonging. Yet, amid the conversations, a nagging feeling lurked at the back of my mind—a persistent reminder to remain vigilant. After a while, Dylan pulled me aside, an expectant look on his face. "You're doing good, man. This is the most I've seen you smile since you got here." I offered a half-smile, the gesture light, but my mind was still reeling. "Thanks. But it's hard to shake the feeling that something's not right." Dylan studied me for a moment, his eyebrows furrowing with concern. "What do you mean? You think someone's bothering you?"

"It's more complicated than that," I replied cautiously, weighing my words. "I just... I feel like I'm being watched, like there are things I can't escape."

His expression softened, and he nodded slowly as if he could understand that sentiment. "I get that. Can I be honest with you? Everyone feels a little out of place at first, especially in a new environment. Just give it time."

"Yeah, I guess," I admitted, though the knot in my stomach flickered with unease.

With our conversation, the fair continued around us, laughter and chatter mixing with the enticing aromas of popcorn and cotton candy. Despite the warmth of connection, I couldn't fully let my guard down. The fair ended, students dispersing into groups as the sun dipped below the horizon, casting long shadows across the campus. I took one last glance at the flickering lights and vibrant decorations, a fleeting sense of hope blooming in my chest—maybe my new life wouldn't be so bad after all. But as I turned to leave, my phone buzzed yet again. Heart racing, I pulled it out, praying for something different. Another message from the unknown number greeted me, tauntingly familiar.

"You think you can outrun your past? Think again."

My pulse thundered in my ears as dread washed over me. They were still watching. I abruptly felt the walls of my new world rushing in around me, suffocating and confining. I quickly tucked my phone away, forcing myself to breathe. I had to regain control. The fair, the laughter—it all felt distant now, a ruse that couldn't camouflage the chilling truth. I wasn't safe. I had to confront my past before it brought its darkness crashing into this fragile life I was trying to build. As I slipped into my dorm room, the shadows deepened and danced at the edges of my consciousness. I needed a plan. Answers. I couldn't wait any longer. If I wanted to escape the unseen threat hovering over me, I had to act. And I needed to start now.

The following morning felt uneasily familiar, as I woke to sunlight streaming through my window, illuminating the room with a bright glow that contrasted sharply with the darkness in my mind. The messages still weighed heavily, their implications echoing relentlessly. It was time to confront the reality that my past was intruding on my present far more than I had anticipated. After a quick shower, I decided to head to the campus library—a sacred fortress of knowledge and relative quiet. It was there I could research anything and everything I needed to know about my old life, my family, and the potential dangers lurking on the periphery of my new normal. Deep down, I knew that understanding my past might bring me one step closer to reclaiming my life. The library was bustling. Students sprawled over tables with textbooks open, some lost in conversations, others immersed in their own worlds. I found a secluded corner in the back, where the lighting was dim and the atmosphere conducive to concentration. As I settled into a plush armchair, I powered on my laptop, each click of the keys feeling deliberate.

I began with a search for any recent news related to my past—anything that could provide insight into what lingering shadows might be creeping into my life. I steeled myself for the worst as the pages loaded. My heart raced as I scrolled through article after article, my pulse quickening with each mention of a familiar name. But no matter where I looked, the stories ended with vague references—a string of events that felt systematically brushed aside, as if the world wanted to forget. Then, buried deep within a string of links, I found something. A recent article regarding a crime syndicate closely tied to my old life, its tentacles reaching out far beyond what I had imagined. The chilling details made my fingers tremble as I read about their connections, their influence spreading insidiously into everyday lives. Suddenly, a voice broke my concentration. "Hey! Is that you, Ryan?"

I looked up to find Dylan standing nearby, a stack of books in his arms and a grin lighting up his face. "Mind if I join you?"

I gestured toward the empty chair across from me. "Sure, what are you up to?"

"Just picking up some reading material for my history class," he said, plopping down and stacking the books on the table. "You are diving into weighty topics too?"

"Just some research," I replied, setting my laptop aside and trying to hide my growing apprehension. "Nothing too serious."

He arched an eyebrow, clearly unconvinced but choosing not to press. Instead, he launched into a discussion about the most interesting historical figures he had come across recently. I nodded along, grateful for his attempt to lighten the mood, but my mind drifted back to the articles I had just read. The looming danger felt both near and distant simultaneously, yet the fear swirled within me like a storm. As the conversation continued, I stole covert glances at my laptop, half-listening, half-plotting my next move. I knew I needed to find out who had sent me those threatening messages, and Dylan's presence, while comforting, impeded my ability to think clearly. He was such a stark contrast to the tension unravelling in my mind. Maybe it was time to let him in, at least a little.

"Dylan," I interrupted, my voice steadying as I made my decision. "What do you know about criminal organizations in the area? Or—let's say... organized crime?"

His expression shifted; surprise caught in his features. "That's a heavy topic. There's been some chatter around campus, but no one's ever really mentioned it seriously. Why do you ask?" I hesitated. "Just... some stuff from my past has been creeping up on me. I need to know what to look out for."

He frowned, concern flickering across his face. "Well, I don't know much, but I know the local police have been working hard on a few cases involving drug trafficking and extortion. The city's trying to clean things up after a string of incidents. It's a lot to keep track of."

"Is it really that bad?" I pressed, my pulse quickening at the disquieting implications.

THE BLOOD PACT

"Depends on who you ask," he admitted, leaning back in his chair. "But some say it's still rampant in certain neighbourhoods. Most people avoid it. Just stay away from any shady deals or—well, you know the type."

I looked down at my hands, recalling the stranger's words—how he had made it sound like I was irrevocably tied to something dark. "What if you can't avoid it?" I mumbled, more to myself than to Dylan.

"Well, that's the scary part, isn't it?" he replied, his tone shifting to one of seriousness. "But you have the power to change your path, Ryan. You can determine your future and distance yourself from whatever that was."

I met his gaze, searching for the sincerity behind his words. For a moment, I felt a flicker of hope, but it was swiftly extinguished by the familiar weight of paranoia. "I want to believe that" I said softly. Just then, a notification pinged from my laptop, and I reached for it almost instinctively, my heart racing in anticipation. A new message had appeared, and the blood drained from my face when I saw the sender. My stomach churned as I read it:

"Don't think you can hide forever. The past will always catch up."

Dylan's attention shifted to the screen, and he leaned closer, curiosity etched on his face. "What's that?"

"It's—" I quickly closed the laptop, my heart pounding in my chest. "It's nothing, just spam."

He narrowed his eyes, unconvinced. "Spam, huh? Right. You know you can tell me anything, right?"

"I appreciate that, Dylan. But I need to handle this on my own," I replied, the tension thickening in the air.

Dylan studied me for a long moment, the concern etched on his features deepening. "Okay, but just remember, the offer stands. If you ever want to talk, I'm here," he said, his voice surprisingly gentle. "I know you're going through something." Once again, the warmth of his friendship stirred a conflict within me. Could I trust him, or would opening only serve to complicate matters further?

"I think I just need to take some time to think," I finally said, my tone apologetic.

"Sure, man. I get it. Just, you know, take care of yourself." He pushed back from the table, gathering his stack of books. "I'll catch you around, yeah?"

"Yeah, definitely."

After Dylan departed, I focused on regaining my composure, but the words from the message reverberated through my mind, each syllable sharpening my resolve. I wasn't about to let fear dictate my actions. Once I was alone, I pulled out the laptop again, searching for the syndicate's name that had emerged in my previous research. It was now or never. I needed answers, and I was done waiting for them to come to me.

The screen flickered as I opened multiple tabs, pouring over links filled with information about connections, players, and key events related to organized crime in the area. The more I read, the more I began to piece together a world I thought I had left behind. Then, I stumbled onto an online forum where people discussed their experiences with various syndicates—stories woven with desperation, fear, and survival. It became a tapestry of voices warning of dangers I had only begun to comprehend. One post caught my eye in particular—the author had been in a similar situation, detailing interactions that mirrored my own wild encounters with shadowy figures.

THE BLOOD PACT

I held my breath as I eagerly read through it, my eyes widening when I reached the conclusion. The user described someone who had narrowly escaped and found a way to dismantle their hold—someone who had encountered the same menacing presence in the shadows.

"They never forget," the post read ominously. "They will always be lurking, watching. Protect yourself at all costs."

Adrenaline surged through me. This was not just some isolated warning; it felt personal, and I needed to connect the dots. Could that stranger I had encountered be tied to this all? I realized it was possible I hadn't just fled my past; I had inadvertently stumbled back into its path. What if they were right? What if my new life was a facade built on a foundation of secrets only waiting to crumble? I knew I had to dig deeper. As dusk settled outside, casting shadows that curled around my room, I felt a surge of determination. This was my life, and I wouldn't let it be governed by fear. With a newly sparked sense of agency, I began drafting a plan. First, I needed to gather information about the people associated with the syndicate, establish a network, and build connections—all while keeping my identity hidden.

The door to the library was open, and the outside world felt just a bit brighter. I had taken a step into the light, yet the dark shapes echoed in the recesses of my mind. Tomorrow would be another day of research. Another day of preparing myself. This time, I would be ready. The hours of the night slipped away as I dove deeper into research, losing myself in a labyrinth of information. My laptop screen illuminated my face as I sifted through articles, forum posts, and news archives, piecing together a puzzle that stubbornly refused to form a clear picture. The name of the syndicate had recurring mentions—**The Black Serpent**. As I read, I noted their history, their methods, and their notorious figures. They thrived in the shadows and had a choking grip on the underbelly of the city. This was more than just a gang; it was an organization built on fear, and now it seemed to have its sights set on me.

I skimmed through various reports. Members of The Black Serpent didn't simply let their enemies walk free. They were relentless, and the thought of their insidious reach sent a shiver down my spine. As if reading my worries, a post I'd come across cautioned about "loose ends" that needed to be tied—a reminder that the organization had a long memory, and I was hardly an exception. I leaned back in my chair, rubbing my temples. I had to find allies, but who could I trust? My thoughts flickered back to Dylan. Although I hadn't opened to him yet, he was proving to be a supportive force. Maybe he could help in ways I hadn't considered. After all, there was safety in numbers. With morning creeping into the edges of my consciousness, I finally allowed myself to close my laptop, the weight of the past still heavy on my chest. I needed rest. But rest wouldn't come easily. As sleep beckoned, uncertainty and paranoia threaded through my mind, forcing adrenaline to keep me alert.

Once the sunlight poured into my room the next morning, I made a promise to myself: today would be about action. First, I decided to reach out to Dylan. Grabbing my phone, I typed out a quick message.

"Dylan, do you want to meet up later? I could use some advice on a project."

With that sent, I moved on to my next task—creating a plan for how to delve deeper into The Black Serpent's world without being ensnared. My head spun with ideas and leads, but the most pressing question remained: who could serve as an informant? A few hours later, I received a reply.

THE BLOOD PACT

"Sure! Just finished classes for the day. Want to meet at that café downtown? I'll buy your coffee!"

A smile tugged at my lips, and I agreed. The café was a quaint little spot tucked between a bookstore and a thrift shop, perfect for clandestine meetings. I made my way there, the cool breeze invigorating and clearing some of the fog clouding my mind. As I arrived, the scent of freshly brewed coffee wafted through the air, mingling with the earthy smell of old books from next door. Dylan was already there, a steaming mug cradled in his hands, his eyes tracking me as I approached.

"Hey! I got us a table in the back," he said brightly, gesturing to a corner away from the chatter of the crowd.

"Thanks for meeting up," I replied, taking a seat across from him. "I really need to talk."

"Everything okay?" His smile faded slightly, replaced by genuine concern.

"I'm just... dealing with some stuff," I admitted, weighing the risk. "And I think I might need your help."

"Absolutely! What's going on?" He leaned forward, earnestness radiating from him.

I took a deep breath, the weight of my words pressing against my chest. "It's about my past. There are some things I need to unravel, and I want to protect myself. But I might need some inside knowledge." Dylan's brow furrowed. "Inside knowledge? What do you mean?"

"The Black Serpent," I finally said, the words falling from my lips like a pebble dropping into still water. "I think they're trying to find me."

His expression shifted from curiosity to alarm in an instant. "The Black Serpent? You're serious?"

"Yes. There were messages. I can't explain all of it yet, but I need to know what you know about them," I said, urgency threading in my voice.

Dylan paused, seemingly weighing the implications of what I'd shared. "I've heard of them. They used to have more influence around here, but it seemed like the police began cracking down a few years ago. Still, they can be formidable," he said, his voice low. I nodded, feeling the gravity of his words. "I think they might be making a comeback, or at least trying to reclaim their territory. I can't let them drag me back into that life. I don't even know who to trust."

"Okay, so what do you want from me?" Dylan asked, leaning closer, his expression resolute.

"I think I need your help gathering intel. You mentioned a few contacts in the past; maybe you could introduce me?" I looked him squarely in the eye. "But it must be discreet. I can't afford to attract attention."

He nodded slowly, serious. "I'll help. But we need to be careful about how we approach this. I don't want to put you in more danger."

"Agreed," I said, relief flooding me to have someone in my corner. "I'll research whatever I can too. I just need to stay a step ahead."

Dylan smiled faintly. "We'll figure it out together. Just let me know what you need from me, and we'll take it one step at a time." Our conversation naturally shifted toward lighter topics, the normalcy of it felt refreshing amidst the cloud of apprehension swirling around us. But behind each shared laugh, I could feel the undercurrent of tension. The storm was still out there, looming larger than I wanted to acknowledge. Once we finished our coffee, we talked about potential resources and leads. Dylan had a knack for

THE BLOOD PACT

connections, and we brainstormed a list of people he could approach discreetly. As he spoke, I couldn't shake the feeling that we were stepping onto a precarious tightrope, one that could tip either way at any moment. As we wrapped up, I felt a sense of impending inevitability. "Thanks for being here, Dylan."

"Always, man. Just remember, you're not alone in this," he replied, his smile warm and reassuring.

As I left the café, the world outside felt alive with possibilities. The sun hung high in the sky, the warmth of it a balm against the unease curling in my stomach. With every step, I solidified my resolve. My past was not going to dictate my future. I would uncover the truth of the shadows that lingered just out of sight, and I would do it on my own terms. That evening, back in my dorm room, I plunged once more into online research, scanning forums and articles about The Black Serpent's known associates, their activities, and rumoured hideouts. I jotted down a few leads, highlighted names I'd read about elsewhere, and began formulating a plan to follow through with Dylan's contacts.

As the clock ticked toward midnight, my phone pinged with an incoming message. I opened it with a wariness that had become second nature.

"You can't run from this, Ryan. They will find you. You know better than to think you're safe."

I felt my heartbeat quicken as I read the words, the chill creeping up my spine stronger than ever. I scrolled back through the entire thread of messages, the sense of menace thickening with every encounter.

"**Who are you?**" I typed back, a small part of me desperate to draw out the sender.

No response came. I felt as if I was standing at the edge of an abyss, peering into the uncertain depths beneath. Turning my phone face down, I tried to regain my bearings. I needed clarity. And above all, I needed a way to counter the encroaching darkness. Tomorrow would bring new opportunities, new alliances—and hopefully—some answers. In that moment, I closed my eyes and focused on the flickering resolve within. I would rise to meet whatever shadows awaited, and I would not back down. My phone buzzed on my bed. I didn't even have to check the number to know who it was.

"Get out now."

The message was simple. Direct. Terrifying. I didn't have time to process it. Panic surged through me, making my heart pound. Without a second thought, I grabbed my jacket and headed out the door, feeling as if I were escaping a trap that was about to snap shut. I moved quickly through the dorm, the corridor echoing with the distant sounds of laughter and music that felt alien to me now. My footsteps were muffled by the carpet, but every sound felt like an alarm, every shadow an unseen threat. Once outside, the cold night air hit me like a shockwave; my breath came out in visible puffs. The campus seemed quieter than usual, as if everyone had disappeared, leaving only me to grapple with this growing sense of dread. I stood there for a moment, unsure of my next move. The message had offered no guidance—just a command to get out. I pulled my phone out again, scanning the screen for any new information. But there was nothing. No further instructions. Nothing that made sense. I needed to find out who was behind this. And why. Why now? As I contemplated my next step, a figure stepped out of the shadows, and I instinctively took a step back, my pulse racing. It was Dylan.

THE BLOOD PACT

"Just a heads up" His voice was calm, almost too calm, as if the night air didn't carry the same weight of urgency that pressed down on me.

His eyes were cold, calculating. It felt as though everything that had happened—the casual conversations, the probing questions—had been leading up to this moment.

"You need to stop digging," he said, his gaze piercing through me like he was seeing something I couldn't even fathom. "There's more at play here than you think. And I'm not the only one watching you."

I swallowed hard, my instincts screaming at me to turn and run, to disappear before it was too late. Yet, I remained frozen, waiting for the next move as if compelled by a force I didn't understand.

"What do you want from me?" I managed to ask, my voice steadier than the turmoil I felt inside.

Dylan smirked, the slight twitch of his lips revealing a stark seriousness lurking beneath the surface. "What do I want? I'm just here to make sure you stay... out of trouble. You're not the only one with a past, Ryan. Just remember that." His words hung in the air like an ominous warning, but I didn't know who he was warning me about. Was it him? Was it the people I'd left behind? Images flashed in my mind of the life I had tried so hard to escape—the incidents I thought were buried now creeping back like ghosts demanding recognition. As he turned to leave, he glanced back over his shoulder. "You might want to think about that text. Who's it really from, huh?" he said, his voice low, the insinuation clear. "You're not as invisible as you think." With those parting words, he vanished into the night, leaving me standing alone, more uncertain than ever before. The walls seemed to close in tighter, every breath feeling suffocating.

What the hell did he know? The anxiety coiled in my gut as I thought of that text message: "Protection." I wished I could dismiss it as mere paranoia, but the urgency of it clawed at my mind. A sudden chill danced down my spine. The environment felt charged—as if the very air around me was electric with danger. I looked around, but the campus was silent, as if holding its breath. An unsettling thought flickered through my mind: the weight I carried wasn't just mine anymore. Someone else knew my past, and it appeared they were equally determined to keep it in the shadows. As I turned to head down the path that snaked away from the campus, I felt it—the strings. They pulled at me, invisible threads tying my decisions to forces lurking just beyond my vision. Whoever was watching, though undetectable for now, was much closer than I wanted to believe.

With every step I took, the haunting words of Dylan echoed in my mind. This wasn't a simple case of paranoia; the world I thought I had escaped was closing in around me again. Each heartbeat felt like a countdown, and I had no idea how deep the rabbit hole went. But one thing was certain: I had to find out, and fast. As darkness settled over the campus, I pressed forward into the night, my senses heightened and my resolve hardening. I wasn't just running; I was searching—for answers, for safety, and for a way to reclaim my life from whatever shadows loomed ahead.

THE BLOOD PACT

Meeting Ruby

The night air was brisk, a refreshing contrast to the swirling chaos in my mind. I walked aimlessly, the campus grounds feeling more like a maze than the place I'd once hoped would be my sanctuary. As I made my way through the carefully manicured lawns and wide pathways, I couldn't shake the feeling that eyes were still lingering, watching from the shadows. After a few minutes of wandering, I ended up outside a small café nestled on the edge of campus. The warm, golden light spilling from the windows beckoned, offering a temporary refuge from the haunting thoughts that had clouded my mind. I hesitated for a moment before heading inside, the familiar scent of coffee and baked goods washing over me.

Inside, students huddled in clusters, engaged in hushed conversations and the occasional outburst of laughter. I spotted an empty table in the corner and headed toward it, eager to collect my thoughts over a cup of coffee. Just as I started to unwind, I felt a presence beside me.

"Hi there! Mind if I join you?"

I turned to see a striking young woman standing there, her long, wavy chestnut hair catching the light and accentuating her sun-kissed complexion. She had expressive green eyes that sparkled with a warmth that immediately put me at ease. Her smile was inviting, a genuine flash of enthusiasm that felt like a breath of fresh air.

"Uh, sure! I'm Ryan," I said, offering a shy smile.

"Ruby," she replied, sliding into the seat across from me. She wore a flowing, soft-pink blouse that added to her effortless charm. "I noticed you looked a little lost—figuratively or literally?"

I chuckled, a sense of comfort blooming in the pit of my stomach. "Definitely both. Just trying to figure things out, you know?" Ruby tilted her head slightly, her curiosity piqued as she leaned forward. "I get that. Sometimes, it helps to take a break and just breathe. Want to talk about it, or should we just enjoy our coffee in silence for a bit?" I hesitated. Part of me wanted to confide in her, to share the chaos and confusion swirling in my mind. But another part screamed for caution, reminding me of the shadows I couldn't quite shake off. Instead, I opted for something light. "Coffee sounds good. I think I could use a break." A smile broke across her face, and for a moment, I felt a sense of normalcy wash over me. Maybe this was what I needed—human connection, something raw and simple.

As we talked, I discovered Ruby was a psychology major, passionate about understanding the human mind. Her compassion radiated from her, making every word she spoke feel like a warm embrace. "I love helping people navigate their challenges," she said, eyes sparkling. "That's why I chose psychology. I believe everyone deserves support in their toughest moments." Her genuine nature resonated with me. I found myself opening more than I intended, sharing snippets of my experiences and the challenges I faced in transitioning to this new life. Ruby listened attentively, occasionally nodding, and her responses were thoughtful and insightful.

"Change can be daunting," she said, her voice soft yet firm. "But sometimes, it's the push we need to discover who we really are."

THE BLOOD PACT

Her words hung in the air, resonating within me like a gentle reminder. I felt a connection forming between us, something deeper than just a passing conversation. It was refreshing to talk to someone so genuine, someone who seemed to grasp the nuances of my struggles without needing to know every detail.

"So, what do you do for fun?" Ruby asked, shifting the conversation to a lighter note.

I smiled, feeling more at ease. "I like to read and stay active. I've been trying to get into running lately helping me clear my head."

"That's awesome! I love running too! It helps me think, especially when I'm stressing about classes," she replied, her enthusiasm infectious. "Maybe we can go for a jog together sometime? I'm always looking for someone who's up for a challenge!"

The idea sent a rush of mixed feelings through me. I wanted to say yes, to deepen this budding friendship, but the shadows of my past crept in, making me hesitate. Just as I opened my mouth to respond, Ruby's laugh rang out, cutting through my hesitation. And then I noticed it—the way her eyes lit up, her laughter contagious, the kindness that radiated from her. It was as if she had a way of making the world seem lighter, even in the face of uncertainty.

"Are you okay?" she asked, her expression shifting to genuine concern. "You looked a bit far away there for a second."

"Yeah, just... got lost in thought again," I admitted, forcing a smile. "Thanks for bringing me back."

She smiled softly, and there it was again—the warmth I found so comforting. I knew I didn't have to reveal everything; the connection itself was enough for now.

"If you ever need someone to distract you from those thoughts, I'm just a few steps away," Ruby said, her green eyes sparkling with sincerity. "I'm always around when you need that friend to help clear the air or to jog with you."

Sparks flew in the air between us, a connection I hadn't anticipated. In that moment, I felt a flicker of hope, a chance for something new amid the chaos of my life. Little did I know, as engaging as this new bond felt, it was only the surface of the currents swirling beneath—a thrilling yet perilous game beneath the calm facade of university life. As our conversation continued, I felt a renewal of spirit, a sense of promise. Ruby Smith might just be the unexpected light I needed in a world tainted by darkness. With each laugh, each shared thought, I could almost convince myself that perhaps this would be my fresh start after all. The hum of the café began to fade into the background as Ruby and I dove deeper into conversation. Each shared story, each burst of laughter added layers to the connection we were forming. I found myself captivated not only by her warmth but also by the depth of her understanding.

"So, you're a criminal justice major?" Ruby asked, tilting her head slightly, an eagerness igniting her eyes. "That must be fascinating! What's your focus?"

"It is," I replied, feeling a surge of passion at the mention of my studies. "I'm particularly interested in the psychology of criminals. Understanding what drives people to commit certain acts or how their backgrounds shape their choices fascinates me."

"Wow," Ruby said, her voice full of admiration. "You're like the bridge between two important fields! Combining psychology with justice can really make a difference."

Her enthusiasm for my passion was refreshing, and I found myself wanting to open even more. "I guess I've always been intrigued by the choices people make," I said. "You know, how sometimes a single moment or experience can lead someone down a dark path."

THE BLOOD PACT

"I completely agree," she said, her expression thoughtful. "That's what I hope to do one day—help people find healthier paths, even in moments of crisis. Everyone has a story, and it's so important to listen."

Her words resonated deeply within me, pulling at some of the insecurities I harboured. I recalled my own story, the choices that had led me here, how many times I had felt misunderstood.

"Have you ever thought about what you might want to specialize in as a psychologist?" I asked, eager to learn more about her passion.

Ruby's face lit up as she spoke, her enthusiasm coming alive as she talked about her dreams. "I really want to focus on clinical psychology, specifically in mental health. I think we're still breaking down so many stigmas surrounding mental health. I want to advocate for those who feel they have no voice." A wave of admiration washed over me. Not only was she smart and caring, but she was also deeply committed to making a difference. I felt a respect grow for her that was almost overwhelming. "That's incredible, Ruby. The world needs more people like you—dedicated, compassionate..."

"Thanks, Ryan," she said, her cheeks flushing slightly as her smile widened. "It's been a journey, figuring things out, but I feel so driven."

Just then, the barista came by to check on us, interrupting the flow of conversation. "Can I get you anything else?" he asked, his brow raised in curiosity as he glanced between us.

"Just the best mocha in the house, please!" Ruby replied with a bright smile, her charm infectious.

As the barista walked away, I took a moment to really look at Ruby. Her expressive eyes sparkled with life, and the warmth of her smile seemed to illuminate the small corner where we sat. I felt a protective instinct well up inside me, an urge to keep that smile on her face.

"Have you been at Horizon View long?" I asked, eager to learn more about her world.

"Just over two years," she explained, brushing a gentle hand through her hair. "I've met some amazing people, but it can be tough sometimes, balancing everything. Classes, volunteering, and just... life."

I nodded in understanding. The pressure to perform academically, alongside the hidden struggles I faced, was something I found all too familiar. "I get that. Sometimes it feels like there are just too many expectations to meet, you know?"

"Exactly!" Ruby exclaimed, her enthusiasm not dimming. "It's all about finding balance, but I think it's important to give ourselves grace. We're all figuring it out as we go along."

Her perspective was refreshing, and for the first time in days, I felt a flicker of hope. Maybe there were new paths to explore—paths that didn't just lead back to shadows of the past but opened doors to possibilities.

As we continued to share stories, I found myself leaning in, drawn into the orbit of her warmth. Ruby had a way of making the world feel less heavy. I wished I could hang onto this moment forever, but the reality of my life loomed just outside.

"Well, I should probably let you get back to studying or whatever else you have planned," I said reluctantly. "But I really enjoyed talking with you, Ruby. It was nice to escape for a little while."

"Me too, Ryan!" she said, her eyes sparkling with sincerity. "Why don't we exchange numbers? That way we can keep in touch. Maybe grab coffee again sometime or go for that run?"

The invitation was laced with potential, and I couldn't help but feel an electrifying excitement race through me. "I'd like that," I said, a genuine smile spreading across my face. As we exchanged numbers, the moment felt significant, as if I was crossing into a new chapter—one filled with promise and unexpected connections.

THE BLOOD PACT

"Take care, Ryan," Ruby said as she stood up, brushing her hair away from her face. "Remember, I'm just a text away if you ever want to talk or need a friend."

The words hung in the air, and as she walked away, I couldn't shake the feeling that something had just shifted in my life. The shadows were still there, lurking, but in the glow of Ruby's kindness, they seemed less daunting. With my heart lighter, I watched her disappear into the crowd, already counting the moments until I could see her again. Maybe this was my chance—a chance to forge connections and begin anew, regardless of the tangled threads of my past. As I left the café, the night unfolded before me, still fraught with uncertainty but now also imbued with a flicker of hope. One spark at a time, I would figure it out. The café door chimed as I stepped outside, the cool evening air wrapping around me like a comforting scarf. I took a deep breath, letting the moment settle. Ruby's laughter echoed in my mind, reminding me of the warmth and connection we had begun to build. I glanced at my phone, reading the message she had sent me moments after we exchanged numbers:

"Hey! So great to meet you today. Looking forward to our coffee (or run) soon! 😊"

A smile crept onto my face. I pocketed my phone and started to head back across campus, my thoughts swirling with possibilities. The day had felt heavy, but meeting Ruby had been like a burst of sunlight cutting through the clouds. I found myself meandering toward the student union, where a small group of students had gathered for an impromptu game of ultimate frisbee on the lawn. The energy was palpable—laughter, cheers, and competitive banter filled the air. My heart felt lighter just watching them, and I toyed with the idea of joining in. But before I could make my decision, I spotted Josh Williams, his tall frame easily identifiable even in the throng of students. He was tossing the frisbee with a few friends, his laughter ringing out above the rest. The moment I laid eyes on him, a twinge of hesitation washed over me. I knew how close he was to Ruby; they often studied together, and he was always there when she needed support. I wasn't sure how he'd take my growing interest in her.

As I approached, Josh spotted me, a wide grin spreading across his face. "Ryan! Dude, come join us! We could use another player!"

"Yeah, sure!" I replied, trying to push aside the knot forming in my stomach. I knew I had to navigate this situation carefully. Josh seemed to sense my hesitation as I joined the game, shortly finding himself beside me in the fray.

"Been a long time, huh?" he said, throwing me an easy smile as we jogged to position. "How's it going?"

"It's going," I replied, focusing on the game while trying to read the subtle cues in his expression. "Met someone today."

Josh threw me a sideways glance, his eyebrows dancing with interest. "Oh? Who?"

"Ruby," I admitted, allowing a small grin to break through.

The moment her name left my lips, I saw something shift in Josh's demeanour. The smile faded slightly, replaced by a more guarded expression. "Ruby, huh? She's great. Super smart. Always busy with her studies."

"Yeah, we bonded over psychology and stuff," I said, trying to sound casual while trying to keep a read on him. "She really cares about helping people."

Josh nodded, the hint of tension hanging in the air as he tossed the frisbee to a teammate. "She does... she's one of the best people you'll meet." I hesitated before probing further, wanting to understand what Josh was feeling. "You two are close, right? Friends?"

THE BLOOD PACT

"Yeah, we study together sometimes, and she's always been there for me," Josh said, his tone neutral yet tight. "I guess, um, I just hope it works out for you."

"Works out?" I repeated, uncertain of the underlying message. "What do you mean?"

"Nothing," he shrugged, his easy grin returning but not quite reaching his eyes, filling the silence with uncertainty. "Just... looking out for her, you know? She's special."

"Of course," I replied, trying to match his casual facade. "And I'm not trying to step on anyone's toes. Just making new friends."

"Right," he said, but the undertone of worry lingered in his voice.

As the game progressed, we played hard, running and jumping, chasing the frisbee as laughter and cheers filled the air around us. I tried to push aside the nagging feeling that I might be treading in sensitive territory with Ruby and Josh. But there was a spark I wanted to explore, and I wasn't going to hide in the shadows any longer.

After a particularly grand play that ended with a dramatic catch, the game finally wound down. Players began to disperse, satisfied with their exercise and camaraderie. Josh and I jogged to the sidelines, breaths heavy from exertion.

"Want to grab a drink?" Josh suggested, wiping sweat from his brow. "I owe you one for that catch."

"Sure," I replied, and in that moment, I felt compelled to address the tension. "Hey, about Ruby..."

"Yeah?" he asked, shifting his weight slightly, a flicker of apprehension crossing his face.

"I know you guys are friends, and I wouldn't want to come between that," I said, choosing my words carefully. "But I really do like her, man. I hope that's okay."

A long pause followed, and I could see Josh weighing his response. Regret flickered in his eyes, and then he nodded tightly. "I get it, Ryan. You won't hear me getting in the way. Just watch out for her, okay? She deserves someone who really sees her." In that moment, as the unspoken understanding settled between us, I felt a sense of relief. We were both advocating for Ruby in our own ways, and for now, that was enough.

"Thanks, Josh. I appreciate it," I said genuinely.

As we made our way toward the student union, I felt a strange mix of excitement and anxiety knotting in my stomach. Ruby had ignited something in me that I hadn't experienced in a long time. And as complicated as it might get, I knew I wanted to explore it—together with her, not against anyone.

"Hey, how about a group study session soon?" Josh suggested as we stepped inside. "Ruby, you, and I could tackle some of our coursework. I think it would be great."

"Count me in," I replied, inwardly bracing myself. This would be a chance to continue getting to know Ruby while keeping the lines of communication open with Josh.

With the transition of seasons on the horizon and new challenges ahead, I felt a renewed sense of purpose. As Ruby had said, we were all just figuring it out as we went along. But this time, I wouldn't face it alone. As we settled into a booth in the bustling student union, I could feel the caffeine buzzing through my system, heightening my senses as the conversations swirled around us. Josh grabbed us a couple of iced coffees, leaving me alone with my thoughts, and the lingering connection I felt with Ruby. The anticipation of seeing her again at the study session filled me with a mix of excitement and nerves. Would she remember our conversation fondly? Would she be open to the idea of something more? I hoped Josh's presence wouldn't complicate what was slowly

THE BLOOD PACT

blossoming between us. When Josh returned with our drinks, he plopped down across from me, oblivious to the storm of thoughts swirling in my mind. "So, man, how's life outside of the 'Ryan vs. the World' saga?" He chuckled, referencing the often-solo nature of my days on campus.

"Not too bad, actually," I responded, sipping my coffee. "Just trying to balance classes and figure things out, like everyone else." Part of me was tempted to confide more about my conversation with Ruby, but I hesitated.

"Have you had a chance to see any shows or events? I hear they're setting up for the fall festival soon," Josh said, eager to steer the conversation toward something livelier.

"The fall festival? I think I missed the notice," I said, recalling the small poster I had glanced at days earlier but had effectively forgotten. It seemed like the perfect opportunity to engage with more of campus life. "What do they usually have?"

"Food, music, games, the whole deal. It's a great place to meet people too," Josh replied, enthusiasm lighting up his voice. "You should check it out! Perhaps Ruby will go. You could ask her."

I felt my pulse quicken at the mention of her name, and my thoughts raced. The idea of attending the festival with Ruby sent a jolt of excitement through me, but I hesitated. Was it too soon? Would it come off as too forward?

"Yeah, I guess I could see if she's interested," I finally replied, trying to sound casual.

Josh smirked knowingly, clearly happy to play matchmaker in this budding connection. "C'mon, Ryan. Don't let that opportunity pass you by. Just be yourself. You've got this." His confidence was infectious, and for the first time that day, I felt a rush of boldness mixed with hope. Maybe I could ask Ruby out—maybe it wouldn't be so scary after all. As the conversation continued, we touched on classes, shared stories of professors who had challenged us, and laughed about past mishaps. I felt a strange sense of camaraderie growing between us, an understanding that stretched beyond the surface level of friendship. Yet, as entertaining as it was, my thoughts kept drifting back to Ruby, her quick smile and the way her eyes lit up when she spoke about her passions. After a while, our booths began to fill up with other students, and the chatter around us escalated. I caught sight of a little group off to the side—students clustered together around a table, and it hit me. One of them had to be Ruby.

"Hey Josh, is that Ruby's group over there?" I nodded toward the students, squinting slightly.

"Looks like it," he answered, leaning the opposite way to get a better view. "Want to go say hi?"

Panic surged through me. I wasn't sure if I was ready to confront her in the company of friends so soon after our private conversation. But at the same time, I yearned for that thrill of connection I had felt earlier. I just needed to muster enough courage.

"Sure," I said, my resolve returning. "Let's go."

We made our way over, the warmth of the bustling student union contrasting with the chill of uncertainty creeping down my spine. As we approached, Ruby looked up, her face lighting up as soon as she spotted us.

"Hey, Ryan! Hey, Josh!" she exclaimed, her voice brightening the atmosphere around us. "What are you guys up to?"

"Oh, just grabbing some coffee and thought we'd come say hi," Josh replied smoothly. "Thought we could join the fun."

I gave a small wave, unable to shake the slight bashfulness creeping up on me. "Hey, Ruby! What are you all working on?"

"Just finishing up some readings for my psychology class," she said, glancing back at her friends before turning her focus back to me. "Want to sit?"

"Might as well," I said, sliding into an empty spot across from her.

THE BLOOD PACT

As the conversation flowed, I learned about her friends and their plans for the fall festival. They spoke excitedly about food stalls and live music, but all I could focus on was Ruby's infectious energy. The way she laughed, her passion for everything she talked about—it drew me in, sparking an undeniable chemistry.

"Are you going to the festival?" one of her friends asked.

"Yeah, I was just talking about it with Josh," I chimed in, my heart racing as I seized the moment. "It sounds fun. Ruby, I was wondering if you'd like to go together—maybe catch a concert or something?"

The question hung in the air, time seeming to stretch as Ruby's eyes widened in surprise. My heart thudded in my chest as I awaited her response.

"Wow, that could be fun! I'd love to," Ruby said, her smile broadening. "I think it would be great to spend some time together outside of studying."

A rush of relief flooded through me, and I shot Josh a quick glance; he was grinning like an idiot.

"You should! You both would have a blast," he added, earning nods from Ruby's friends, who exchanged encouraging looks.

"Alright, it's a plan then," I said, unable to hide my grin. "We'll make it a group thing. The more, the merrier!"

As we finalized our plans, I felt the weight of uncertainty lift. This was what I'd been craving—a chance to truly connect with someone who seemed to see me, understand me, and perhaps even appreciate me in a way I hadn't experienced in a long time. Later, we departed from the group, the air buzzing with anticipation as Josh and I walked back toward our dorm. "You really nailed that, man!" he said, punching me lightly on the shoulder. "Ruby's going to be thrilled!"

"Yeah, I hope so." A sense of optimism blossomed within me. "I can't wait to see where this goes."

As night fell, we strolled through the campus grounds, illuminated by the yellow light of lampposts that stood like sentinels along the path. My thoughts remained consumed by the impending festival and the chance to explore this budding relationship with Ruby. The possibilities felt endless. Maybe this was just the beginning—of a friendship, an adventure, a newfound light in my life. And for once, it didn't feel like I was facing it alone. The days that followed were a whirlwind of anticipation and excitement. The festival was just around the corner, and I found myself counting down the hours. Each time I caught sight of Ruby in class, a warm flutter spread through my chest. We exchanged playful glances and small talk, but every time I envisioned our planned outing together, I felt a refreshing rush of possibility.

The night before the festival, I lay in bed staring at the ceiling, unable to sleep. My mind raced with scenarios—what if it rained? What if we ran out of things to talk about? What if, despite both of us wanting this, there was a spark that faded too quickly? The possibilities of what could go wrong loomed, but each anxious thought was met with a hopeful counterbalance, reminding me of the connection we'd already formed. I settled on scrolling through my phone, absentmindedly checking weather updates and the festival schedule. That's when I saw it: a social media post from Ruby, showcasing an array of vibrant fall colours cascading down campus. *Can't wait for tomorrow!* ◇◇ The caption was paired with a picture of her beaming in front of the multi-coloured leaves, and despite my unease, it filled me with a sense of warmth. She looked happy.

It was almost midnight when I finally drifted off, the sounds of the campus winding down like an echo, punctuated by the muffled laughter from late-night students still revelling in youthful enthusiasm. The next day, the sun broke through the clouds, casting a bright glow over campus. The festival was alive with the sounds of laughter, music, and the smell of sweet and savoury treats wafting

THE BLOOD PACT

through the air. My heart raced in rhythm with the thumping bass of a nearby performance as I made my way to the meeting point near the entrance. When Ruby arrived, she looked radiant, wearing a cozy sweater layered over a denim skirt and knee-high boots. Her hair flowed freely, catching the sun like spun gold. I was momentarily speechless as she approached, a beaming smile spreading across her face when she spotted me.

"Hey!" she exclaimed, her eyes sparkling with excitement. "You made it!"

"Wouldn't miss it for the world," I replied, my nervousness melting away as I returned her smile. "You look amazing."

She blushed slightly, a charming colour rising to her cheeks as she brushed a loose strand of hair behind her ear. "Thanks! I thought I'd go for 'fall vibes' today." The atmosphere around us buzzed as we navigated the bustling crowd together. We tried everything—from caramel apples to pumpkin spice lattes, and each bite was accompanied by laughter and playful banter. It felt effortless, like we'd known each other far longer than just a few days.

"Have you ever tried the corn maze?" I asked, pointing toward the sprawling field where other festivalgoers were darting in and out of towering stalks of corn.

"Not yet! Let's do it!" Ruby said, her eyes alight with enthusiasm. "I love mazes—it's always fun to get lost for a bit."

As we joined the line for the corn maze, I felt a sense of buoyancy about us—like we were embarking on an adventure together, navigating twists and turns both literally and metaphorically. With each step we took deeper into the maze, I couldn't help but wonder how many secrets awaited us, hidden within the husks of cornstalks and the laughter that echoed through the path.

"Okay, but here's the trick," I said as we entered the maze. "We must create a secret code for when we get separated. How about 'Pumpkin Spice'?"

Ruby laughed, her sound bright and infectious. "I love it! If I get lost, I'll just shout 'Pumpkin Spice!' at the top of my lungs!" The sun shone brightly overhead as we wandered through the crisscrossing paths of cornstalks, our playful navigation a dance between laughter and light-hearted guesses. Every now and then, Ruby would tug on my arm to indicate a direction to explore, and I found myself captivated not only by the vibrant colours of the maze but by the connection growing between us. Suddenly, as we turned another corner, we stumbled into a small clearing surrounded by the tall stalks. Turning to each other, we laughed together.

"Okay, maybe we did take a wrong turn," I said, feigning an exaggerated expression of confusion.

"Or maybe we're just in hiding," Ruby teased. "We can have our own little adventure here!"

As she struck a playful pose, pretending to be an explorer in the wild, I couldn't help but chuckle. The way she carried herself, with such vibrant energy, drew me closer. Moments later, we found ourselves sitting on a hay bale in the clearing, enjoying the quiet amidst the chaos of the festival.

"Do you ever get tired of it? The school, the studying?" Ruby asked, and I could see genuine curiosity in her expression.

I considered her question carefully. "Sometimes. I think everyone feels overwhelmed at times, you know? But days like today make it all worthwhile."

"That's true. It's nice to escape for a bit," she said, her gaze drifting toward the edges of the maze. "What do you do when you really want to escape?"

"I write," I admitted, surprised at the honesty spilling from my lips. "It helps me process everything. The chaos, the feelings..."

"Poems? Stories?" she pressed, leaning forward, genuinely intrigued.

THE BLOOD PACT

"Mostly short stories. I like creating worlds that I can escape into—places where I can say things I sometimes can't say out loud," I replied, feeling the weight of my words.

"That's beautiful, Ryan. I'd love to read some sometime," she said, her sincerity wrapping around me like a warm embrace.

"Maybe. I'm still figuring it all out," I said, a flutter of nervousness creeping back in. "But having met you, I feel more inspired than ever."

A fleeting moment of silence filled the space between us, a delicate pause where all the noise of the festival faded into the background. Ruby's smile softened, and I felt an undeniable spark in the air.

"Can I share something too?" she asked, her voice gentle yet earnest.

I nodded, intrigued. "Of course."

"I've always wanted to help people, you know? My mom is a therapist, and she's been such an inspiration for me," Ruby began, her eyes lighting up. "But I sometimes struggle with the pressure. It's like I want to make everyone feel better, but I forget to take care of myself in the process."

"You're so open and caring," I replied. "That's a gift, Ruby. But it's okay to put yourself first sometimes. You can't pour from an empty cup."

She smiled again, and I couldn't help but be captivated by the way she talked about her passions and the weight of her commitments. It made me want to know her deeper, to support her through whatever challenges lay ahead.

"Let's make a pact," I suggested, my heart racing. "To help each other find time for us while also supporting each other's goals. We can be each other's accountability partners."

"I love that idea," she said, her eyes sparkling with excitement. "Deal!"

Pride swelled through me as we shook on it—even in that playful gesture, I felt the shift as we ventured into uncharted territory, both as friends and perhaps something more. As we finally made our way out of the maze, the sun dipped toward the horizon, casting a golden glow over the festival. Laughter filled the air, and the evening lights began to twinkle to life.

"Where to next?" I asked, eager to continue our day of exploration.

Ruby grinned, her enthusiasm infectious. "I want to check out the live music! I heard there's a local band playing tonight." With that, we headed toward the stage, the rhythm of the drums echoing through the air, and I took a deep breath, feeling more hope for the future and excitement for what was unfolding between us. In that moment, all the worries about where this might lead dissolved into laughter, music, and the thrill of new beginnings. It was the perfect start to an adventure I never knew I needed until now.

The music from the stage became a backdrop to our growing connection as we navigated through throngs of people. We found a cozy spot on the grass, positioning ourselves close enough to enjoy the performance while still having room to talk. The local band was energetic, their melodies weaving through the air like the rich aromas of festival food. Ruby swayed slightly to the rhythm, her eyes sparkling as she enjoyed the music.

"You know," she began, turning to me, "there's something so exhilarating about live music. It feels like the energy of everyone around you just blends into this beautiful moment."

"I agree. It's like everyone's here for the same reason, sharing this experience," I replied, leaning in to catch her gaze. "It's infectious."

THE BLOOD PACT

A grin spread across her face, and in that instant, I felt an overwhelming urge to reach out and take her hand. I refrained, not wanting to rush things, but the moment lingered—full of potential, almost electric. We sat contentedly as the band played on, exchanging stories and laughter between songs. I learned about Ruby's love for classic rock, her passion for writing, and how she dreamed of traveling to music festivals around the world. In turn, I shared my own aspirations and the writers that had inspired me to create. As the sun began to dip below the horizon, casting a warm glow over the festival, the band shifted to a more intimate ballad. The atmosphere transformed, the world around us fading as we found ourselves lost in each other's presence.

"I absolutely love this song," Ruby said, her voice barely above the music. "It's about finding someone who feels like home."

I turned to her, captivated. "Yeah? What does that mean to you?" She smiled softly, her eyes glinting with a mixture of nostalgia and hope. "It means finding those connections that just click, you know? It's like when you meet someone, and everything just makes sense. The laughter, the conversations—it all feels like it's meant to be." Her words hung in the air, rich with meaning, and I couldn't help but feel that we were beginning to create a connection that could become something profoundly special. "I think I know what you mean," I replied, my heart racing. "I've felt that with you." Just then, the band transitioned into a more upbeat song, and Ruby jumped to her feet, pulling me up with her. "Come on! Let's dance!"

I laughed, caught off guard but quickly surrendered to the moment. The two of us moved to the rhythm of the music, our laughter blending with the sounds around us. I felt a sense of freedom as we twirled and spun, letting the joy of the music guide us. After a few songs, we found ourselves breathless and smiling, the exhilaration buzzing through us. We migrated back to our spot on the grass, collapsing in a heap, both of us giggling uncontrollably.

"Okay, that was fun," I admitted, trying to catch my breath. "I haven't danced like that in ages."

"Neither have I! It just felt... right," Ruby said, her expression unrestrained and genuine.

The night deepened, stars twinkling overhead, adding to the magic of the festival. As the music transitioned into slow ballads, the ambiance shifted once more. People began to pair off, swaying together on the grass, and I felt an urge to make my move.

"Hey, can I steal one more dance from you?" I asked, my voice almost a whisper against the lilting melodies.

"Of course," Ruby said, her eyes shining with a mix of excitement and surprise.

As we stood together under the starlit sky, I wrapped my arms lightly around her waist. She responded by placing her hands on my shoulders, electricity pulsing through us. We swayed slowly, lost in our own world, the warmth from our bodies mingling as we moved to the music, my heart pounding not just from the dance but from the growing closeness.

"It's funny," I said quietly, "how today started as just another ordinary day and turned into this incredible adventure."

"Right?" she replied, glancing up at me. "I wasn't sure what to expect, but I'm so glad I said yes to coming."

The song shifted to a softer tone, and in that moment, I couldn't resist any longer. I leaned in slightly, my breath catching as I prepared to say something meaningful. "Honestly, Ruby, I've really enjoyed today. You make everything feel more vibrant." Her gaze softened, and a slow smile spread across her lips—one that sent warmth spiralling through me. "I feel the same way. It's like I've known you

THE BLOOD PACT

forever." I gathered my courage, leaning in a bit closer, the world around us fading once more. "Can we take this moment and make it something more?" I asked, my voice barely a whisper. Her breath caught, and I could see the surprise wash over her, mingled with excitement. "You mean like...a date?"

"Exactly," I said, searching her eyes for any hesitation. "I want to see where this can go—if we can build on this."

She bit her lip, clearly considering my words. A flicker of uncertainty crossed her face, but it was quickly replaced with something more profound. "I would love that," she replied, her voice steady and full of sincerity.

At that moment, I felt a wave of relief combined with an exhilaration I had never anticipated. I gently brushed a loose strand of hair from her face, allowing the moment to linger. As the song came to an end, I took a small step back, catching my breath again. "I'm glad we're on the same page," I said, grinning from ear to ear.

"Me too," Ruby laughed, her cheeks slightly flushed under the glow of festival lights. "Now, let's see what else this festival has in store for us!"

With that, we dove back into the festivities, hand in hand, exploring food stalls, playing games, and laughing late into the night. Each shared adventure solidified the bond that was blatantly blossoming between us, a connection I was more than thrilled to explore. As the evening wound down and the stars twinkled above, I knew this was just the beginning of our journey together—a beautiful chapter unfolding in ways I could have only dreamed of.

.

R. STELLAN

Complications (Ruby)

A few days after the festival, I found myself sitting on the steps outside the campus library, my mind racing from everything that had happened in the last few days. Ryan Rossi, the mysterious transfer student, had somehow managed to weave his way into my thoughts in a way I couldn't explain. There was something about him—something beyond his striking looks and quiet intensity—that drew me in. It wasn't just curiosity anymore; it felt like a pull, an unexplainable force that made my heartbeat faster every time I saw him. But I wasn't the type to fall for someone I barely knew. I had to be cautious. I had to keep my distance. Still, the way his eyes met mine that day in the café, the way he smiled—like I was the only person in the room—haunted me.

"Ruby?"

My thoughts were interrupted as I looked up to find Carol standing in front of me, arms crossed with a teasing grin plastered on her face. I hadn't even noticed her approach; she always seemed to know when I was lost in thought.

"Hey, Carol," I replied, trying to shake off the lingering thoughts of Ryan. "What's up?"

"You tell me, "She said, raising an eyebrow as she settled down next to me. "You've been in another world for the last twenty-four hours. And I know you, Ruby. Something's going on. Something about him, right?"

I sighed, feeling the weight of it all settle deeper in my chest. "I don't know. I mean, I don't even know what to think. But when I saw him... it was like this weird connection. Like something clicked, but I can't figure out what it is. I haven't felt like this in forever." Carol tilted her head, her expression softening. "So, you're saying Ryan Rossi's got your attention?" I nodded slowly, heat creeping up my neck. "Yeah, I guess so. He's... different. There's just something about him. It's hard to explain." Carol fell silent for a moment, her gaze analysing mine with an intensity that made me uneasy. "You know, Ruby, I get it. He's a great guy, right? Quiet, mysterious, kind of handsome in that brooding way. But are you sure you know what you're getting yourself into?"

"What do you mean?" I asked, glancing over at her.

She leaned in slightly, lowering her voice as if to keep our conversation private. "I don't know. There's just something off about him. I've seen the way he moves around campus—like he's always looking over his shoulder. Like he doesn't quite belong here." I frowned, feeling a knot of unease form in my stomach. "What do you mean, 'doesn't belong'? He's just... a guy like anyone else, right?" Carol sighed, her eyes narrowing slightly. "I'm just saying, Ruby, you can't trust everyone you meet. I've been watching him, and there's something more to Ryan Rossi than what he's showing. You're a smart girl, and you know when something feels off. You're getting caught up in this, and I just don't want to see you get hurt." Her words hit me harder than I expected. The thought that Ryan might not be who he seemed was something I hadn't allowed myself to consider. But now, sitting here with Carol, I couldn't shake the memory of how he had looked at me in the quad—like he was keeping a secret, like he was hiding something even from me.

THE BLOOD PACT

I stared down at my hands, conflicted. "I don't know, Carol. You're probably right. I don't want to rush into anything. But when I'm around him... it's like I'm not myself. Like he pulls me in, and I can't resist. It's strange."

"Of course it's strange," Carol said, her tone firm. "Because you don't know him. You don't know what he's about, and that's the problem. You're falling for someone you know nothing about. What if he's not who he says he is? What if he's got a hidden agenda?"

I shook my head, trying to dislodge the growing doubts swirling in my mind. "You're being paranoid. He's just a guy. Maybe I'm overthinking it."

"Maybe," Carol replied, though there was no mistaking the concern etched across her face. "But promise me you'll be careful. No matter how intense things seem right now, trust your gut. If anything about Ryan feels off—if he starts giving you those red flags—I need you to step back. You can't let your heart make decisions for you when it comes to someone like him."

I swallowed hard, my heart pounding in my chest. I didn't want to admit it, but a part of me knew she was right. Something about Ryan felt like a puzzle I wasn't meant to solve, a mystery I wasn't prepared to get caught up in. Yet the other part of me, the one that couldn't escape the magnetic pull I felt toward him, was relentless.

"Okay," I said softly, my voice barely a whisper. "I promise. I'll be careful."

Carol flashed me a soft, knowing smile. "I'm just looking out for you. That's what best friends do." As we sat there, listening to the sounds of the campus bustling around us, I felt the weight of her words pressing down on me. I had always prided myself on trusting my instincts, on knowing when something was right or wrong. But with Ryan, it felt like I was playing a dangerous game—a game that could end in heartbreak if I wasn't careful. And yet, despite Carol's warnings, I couldn't shake the feeling that I was being pulled toward

Ryan. Somehow, our paths seemed meant to cross; no matter how hard I tried to resist, it felt inevitable. Later that day, the air in my dorm room felt thick with unresolved tension. I paced back and forth, my thoughts tangled. It had been a few days since I last heard from Ryan, but I kept replaying our conversations in my head—the way he looked at me, the intensity behind his eyes. It made my pulse race in a way I couldn't ignore. The sound of a knock at the door startled me from my thoughts. My heart skipped a beat, half-expecting it to be Ryan standing there, but when I opened the door, I found Carol again, this time with a small, amused smile.

"I thought I'd find you here," she said, stepping inside without waiting for an invitation. "You've been avoiding me all day."

I sighed, running a hand through my hair. "Sorry. Just a lot on my mind, you know?" Carol didn't miss a beat. "I know exactly what's on your mind. It's him, isn't it? Ryan Rossi?" Heat rushed to my cheeks, and I didn't try to hide it. Carol knew me better than anyone. "I don't know what's going on, Carol. I feel this... mysterious pull toward him. It's like he's magnetic or something." Carol sat down next to me on the bed, her expression softening. "Look, Ruby, I'm not saying you shouldn't feel what you feel. But you've got to be careful. I know you've got a big heart, and you want to see the best in people. But sometimes, people don't show their true selves right away. You can't let attraction cloud your judgment."

"Maybe," I murmured, my stomach sinking with doubt. "But it feels like there's something real about him. I just need to understand it. And I need to know if I can trust him."

Carol didn't say anything for a long moment, and when she finally spoke, it was in a low, serious voice. "Trust is earned, Ruby. Don't just hand it out because he looks at you like you're the only person in the room. You must be sure. And if you're not sure, you need to take a step back. Promise me you'll think carefully before jumping in too deep."

THE BLOOD PACT

"I promise," I said, though uncertainty gnawed at me. I didn't want to promise something I wasn't sure I could keep. For Carol's sake, I agreed—taking a step back felt like the right choice, even as it frightened me.

"Good," Carol said, finally standing. "Now, how about we go grab dinner? I think we both could use a distraction."

"Yeah, sounds good," I replied, forcing the knot in my stomach to settle.

As we left the room, a lingering unease clung to me like a shadow. I didn't know if I could keep my promise to Carol. I didn't know how long I could stay away from Ryan. But one thing was clear: if I was going to make it through this, I had to trust my instincts. And right now, my instincts were telling me to proceed with caution. Yet the heart has its own language, one I wasn't sure I could tame. The evening passed in a blur of noise and laughter as Carol, and I joined a small group of friends in the dining hall. Despite the bustle around me, I couldn't shake the feeling of being on the precipice of something significant with Ryan. I tried to engage with Carol and the others, but my mind kept wandering back to him—his mysterious gaze, his infectious smile. As we settled into a table with our meals, I felt the tension in the air shift when Josh, one of my classmates and a longtime friend, joined us. He was easy-going and always had a knack for lighting up the room with his banter. His charm was well-known, and he wove effortlessly in and out of conversations. But tonight, when his gaze met mine, I sensed something different. There was an intensity in his eyes, a flicker of something unspoken.

"Hey, Ruby!" Josh said, flashing me a bright smile as he settled into the empty seat next to me. "You've been a bit of a mystery lately. What's up with that?"

I offered a half-hearted smile, unsure how to respond. "Just busy with school and stuff. You know how it is."

"Yeah, but you seemed a bit lost today," he said, tilting his head slightly, studying me. "Is it Ryan? I heard you two had a good time at the festival."

My stomach twisted at the mention of Ryan's name, and I could feel my cheeks heat up again. "It was fun, I guess," I admitted, trying to keep my tone casual. "Just hanging out and enjoying the music." Josh raised an eyebrow, a playful smile spreading across his face. "You 'guess'? Come on, Ruby! You two were practically glowing. What's going on there?"

"What do you mean 'glowing'?" I replied, forcing a laugh that didn't quite reach my eyes. "It was just a festival."

"Sure, just a festival." His voice was light, but I heard something deeper lurking beneath the surface. "But if you don't want to talk about it, that's cool. Just know that I'm here if you need someone to listen."

There was a shy sincerity in his words that made me pause. Josh had always been the kind of guy who made it clear he cared. But lately, I'd been so consumed with thoughts of Ryan that I hadn't even considered what Josh might be feeling. He changed the subject, but I could feel the tension stemming from where he sat beside me. It clung to the air, heavy with unspoken feelings.

Over the next few minutes, I watched as the mood of the table shifted. Carol engaged in light-hearted banter, but I could sense Josh's focus on me—a tangible weight that grew with each passing second. The laughter around us felt like a backdrop to the drama unfolding in my mind. After a while, Carol leaned closer, shooting me a knowing look and nudging me lightly with her elbow. "You, okay?" she whispered so only I could hear.

"Yeah," I replied, though I wasn't entirely convinced. "I think."

"Listen, I know we talked about Ryan earlier, but don't forget about the people who've always been here for you, too," she said, her voice low and smooth. "Like Josh. He's been there a long time."

THE BLOOD PACT

I kept my gaze on my plate, feeling a pang of guilt. Josh had been a good friend, always supportive, and yet I couldn't decipher what he really felt for me beneath the camaraderie. "I know he's a great guy," I mumbled, "but..."

"But what?" Carol pressed gently. "There's a connection between you two. Trust me, it's not just one-sided."

Before I could respond, Josh jumped back into the conversation, playfully interrupting our exchange. "Hey, Ruby! Last one to the dessert line buys the next round of coffee!"

"You're on!" I shot back, a competitive spirit sparking to life. We both leapt up from our seats, laughter spilling out as we raced across the dining hall, the group cheering us on.

But as we reached the dessert table, and I turned to grab my treat, I caught a glimpse of Ryan through the window. He was crossing the campus green, his head down, almost as if he was lost in thought. My heart tugged, pulling me toward him even as Josh stood at my side, waiting for me to make my choice.

"Ruby, focus!" Josh said, holding two cupcake options in each hand. "Chocolate or vanilla?"

"Um... vanilla?" I managed, still distracted by Ryan's presence. As I grabbed the cupcake and turned back, I saw Josh's expression shift—disappointment mixed with something unidentifiable.

"Are you coming to the game on Friday? It's supposed to be a big deal," he said, his tone lightly teasing but his eyes searching mine.

"Yeah, I'll be there," I replied, unsure of how to navigate the shifting dynamic. I could feel the pull between Ryan and Josh—two paths diverging before me, both promising yet fraught with complications.

As we returned to the table, a knot of tension wove itself deeper in my stomach. While Carol was laughing with the others, I caught Josh's eye again. He seemed momentarily lost in thought, as if weighing his words before speaking.

"Hey, Ruby," he said, voice a bit steadier than before. "Can we talk later? I think we should hash out things. Maybe away from all this noise?"

My pulse quickened. This wasn't the kind of conversation I had anticipated having tonight. "Uh, sure. Sounds good." He nodded, relief washing over his features as he turned back to the group. I could feel the undercurrents swirling around us, shifting the dynamics of our friendship, and I couldn't help but feel like I was standing on shaky ground. As the night wore on and the chatter continued, I knew I had to prepare myself for whatever Josh wanted to discuss. His feelings, whatever they were, were framed against the backdrop of my turbulent thoughts about Ryan. I could sense that I was navigating some treacherous emotional waters, and the stakes felt higher than I had anticipated. Later that evening as I crawled into bed, the weight of the day hung heavily on me. I closed my eyes, but the image of Ryan and Josh collided in my mind, creating a whirlpool of confusion. I felt torn between the unexpected connection I had formed with Ryan and the comfort of a longstanding friendship with Josh, who possibly desired more.

I was left with only one certain thought amidst the chaos: I needed to figure out what this all meant before the pieces of my life started to fall apart. As I laid in my bed, the shadows of the evening danced across the walls, and the familiar hum of campus life continued outside my window. The weight of uncertainty settled heavily in my chest. I tossed and turned, trying to sort through my feelings for Ryan and the unspoken tension with Josh. I eventually drifted into a restless sleep, riddled with dreams of fleeting glances and lingering touches, images of both Ryan's enigmatic smile and Josh's earnest gaze swirling in my mind like a storm—each one vying for my attention. Morning came too quickly, the sunlight spilling through my window and drawing me into the reality of another

THE BLOOD PACT

day—a reality where decisions loomed like dark clouds. I stumbled through my morning routine, my mind still clouded with uncertainty. As my thoughts shifted to Ryan, my heartbeat quickened. I had to confront my feelings, but now Josh's emotions weighed on me, too.

After a long day of classes, I found myself wandering the campus, aimlessly drawn toward the quad. The air felt electric as I stepped onto the familiar grass, and for a moment, I entertained the hope that Ryan might be here, that maybe fate would bring us together again.

Just as I was about to turn back, I caught a glimpse of him across the quad, leaning against a tree, head slightly bowed over a book. I hesitated, my heart racing as I considered my next move. Should I approach him, or would that only complicate things further? Before I could decide, a voice broke through the noise of my thoughts. "Hey, Ruby!" It was Josh, jogging over to me with a smile that didn't quite meet his eyes.

"Josh!" I replied, forcing some cheer into my voice. "What are you doing here?"

"I was just about to grab a coffee. Want to come with?" he asked, his tone casual but his gaze betraying a hint of seriousness.

I glanced back toward Ryan, who was now flipping through the pages of his book, seemingly oblivious to the world around him. "Um... yeah, sure," I said, feeling a sense of relief as I stepped away from the gravity of my feelings for Ryan, at least for the moment. As we walked towards the coffee shop, Josh fell into step beside me, his demeanour brightening the air between us. "So," he began, glancing sideways at me, "you've been a bit distracted lately. Everything okay?" I sighed, the weight of the chat I knew we needed to have hung over me. "I guess I've just had a lot on my mind. Everything feels... complicated."

"I get that," he replied, his smile fading slightly. "But you know you can talk to me about anything, right? Especially with all this about Ryan."

His words hung in the air as we reached the coffee shop. I ordered a cappuccino, and once we got our drinks, we stepped outside to sit at a nearby table under a shading tree.

"Thanks for coming with me," Josh said, stirring his coffee thoughtfully. "I know the last few days have been hectic, but I wanted to talk to you about how you've been feeling, especially regarding Ryan."

I took a deep breath, turning the cup in my hands. "It's just... I don't know how to explain it. There's something about him that feels magnetic, but at the same time, it scares me. I thought I was overthinking it, but..."

"But?" He leaned forward in his chair, his expression earnest.

"But then there's you, Josh. You've always been a constant, a good friend," I admitted, feeling a mix of guilt and confusion churn in my stomach. "And it seems like I keep comparing you two."

"Comparing me to Ryan?" he asked. "What makes him so special?"

"It's not that simple," I began, but he was already shaking his head, a frown forming.

"Okay, but what is it that you feel for him? Is it serious, or is it just a crush?"

I paused, swallowing hard. "I don't know. I really don't. There's something deeper, but I can't put my finger on it. It's like he has this way of looking at me that makes me feel... I don't know, seen?"

"So why does that bother you?" Josh asked, a hint of frustration sneaking into his voice. "It's like you want to dive headfirst into uncharted waters with him. What makes him worth risking everything?"

THE BLOOD PACT

I sighed heavily, feeling the emotions swell in my throat. "Because it feels like there's potential. But with you, things are comfortable. Solid. You're my friend, and I know you. I'm afraid of losing that if I choose to explore whatever this spark is with Ryan." Josh looked at me, his expression softening. "Ruby, I admire your heart. But can you see where that leads? You don't have to choose right now. Just... don't forget the people who care about you while you sort this out, okay?"

"I know," I whispered, feeling tears pricking at the corners of my eyes. "I just wish I could figure it all out without hurting anyone."

"You won't hurt me," he reassured me softly, but I could tell that beneath his calm demeanour, his emotions ran deeper than he let on. "Just be honest with yourself."

Suddenly, Ryan's image flickered at the edge of my thoughts, and with that fleeting moment of temptation, the fear of risking something with Josh settled back in. "It's just so unclear to me, Josh. I wish I had the answers." Josh took a sip of his coffee, his brow slightly furrowed. "It's okay to not know," he said slowly. "But I need you to be open about your feelings. If it's Ryan you want to focus on, I can handle it. Just tell me."

"Just like that?" I murmured, still caught up in the chaos.

"Yes, just like that. Life is too short to live in confusion. Just don't forget about us," he said, a steely resolve underlining his words.

I looked down at my coffee, contemplating everything unfolding before me. I appreciated Josh's honesty, and yet, every passing moment felt unbearably heavy. "I'll try to be honest," I finally replied, knowing I owed him—and myself—that much. The rest of the afternoon passed in blurry conversation, marked by laughter that felt bittersweet. As we wrapped up our coffee break, I could feel the urgency of choices pressing in on me from all sides—Ryan's pull against Josh's comfort, the tangled web of friendship and budding romance. Once we returned to campus, I spotted Ryan again, this time seated on a bench, apparently lost in thought. With each step toward him, my heart raced. The conversation with Josh echoed in my mind, reminding me to be honest, to explore my feelings.

"Hey!" I called out, my voice catching in the cool air as I approached. I caught Ryan's gaze, and the warmth of his smile enveloped me as he looked up.

"Ruby!" he replied that same spark igniting in his eyes. "I was hoping I'd see you here."

As I took a seat beside him, I wondered whether I was heading into brave new territory or opening a door to something unpredictable. The tension from earlier still lingered in my mind, but for now, I focused on the potential before me—not just with Ryan, but with myself.

"Can I join you?" I asked, craving the comfort of connection.

"Of course," Ryan replied, his expression shifting from curiosity to something deeper.

As we started to talk, I felt the vast uncertainty ahead stretching out before me, but with it came a flicker of hope. Maybe in understanding both Josh's and Ryan's feelings, I could carve out my path in this tangled emotional landscape. And somehow, no matter what confusion lay ahead, I had to believe that I would find my way through it all. As I settled onto the bench beside Ryan, a surge of comfort enveloped me—a welcomed reprieve from the whirlwind of emotions crashing around in my mind. The sun diffused through the leaves above us, casting delicate patterns on the grass. I couldn't help but notice how easy it felt to talk to him, how each word that tumbled from our lips connected us a little more.

"So, what are you reading?" I asked, gesturing to the book resting on his lap.

THE BLOOD PACT

"It's some poetry," he replied, tapping the cover lightly with his thumb. "I find it helps clarify thoughts when chaos surrounds me." He looked at me, his expression serious yet playful. "Plus, I like trying to decode what profound meanings the poets had—or if they were just as confused as we are."

I smiled, feeling the ease between us growing. The conversation flowed as we exchanged thoughts about our favourite authors and the messy intricacies of our lives, the laughter and shared moments drawing us closer together. As I leaned in, eager to hear him recite a stanza from the book, I caught a flash of movement from across the quad out of the corner of my eye. I turned just in time to see Josh, seemingly absorbed in conversation with a group of friends, yet I noticed something different in his demeanour. He was standing a little too still, eyes locked onto us, and the playful lilt of his laughter seemed momentarily muted. A shiver ran down my spine, but I shook it off, directing my focus back to Ryan. He was animatedly reciting a poem, his eyes lighting up with each line. I felt a warmth spread through me—a connection that was drawing me in, making all my worries about Josh momentarily fade.

But unbeknownst to us, Josh lingered nearby, a storm brewing beneath his surface. Leaning against a nearby tree, he watched as Ryan animatedly discussed the meaning of the verses, that damnable spark in his voice drawing me in effortlessly. Each laugh, each moment of focus I shared with Ryan turned into daggers aimed at Josh's heart. With each passing second, Josh felt the green-eyed monster creep slowly inside him, clawing at the corners of his mind. He was used to being the centre of Ruby's attention; he'd always considered himself a safe harbour in her life, an anchor for her soul. Yet here he was, rendered powerless, overwhelmed by a growing surge of jealousy that he couldn't quite understand. What was it about Ryan that made me forget all else? Was it the ease of their interactions, the way she practically glowed when he spoke?

Something primal ignited within Josh, fuelling an urgent desire to stake his claim—to make Ruby see that he could be the one for her, that their friendship could transform into something more. He shifted slightly, adjusting his stance to get a better view. He caught another glimpse of that beautiful smile on my face, a lightness in my laughter that made his insides twist. The more he observed, the more he felt the underlying connection slip further away from him.

"Hey, Josh! You in there?" a friend nudged him, snapping him back to reality. "What do you think?"

Josh forced a smile, nodding absently as he turned away from us, his thoughts racing. "Yeah, totally. Just thinking..." His voice trailed off as he couldn't stop scanning the scene, torn between the loyalty he felt toward me and the growing envy that clouded his heart.

"Don't you think Ryan is a bit too much?" another friend mentioned, catching Josh off guard. "He seems a little too into Ruby."

"Yeah," he replied, trying to mask the rising tide of jealousy. "He's... interesting."

The dismissive tone crawled up his throat, and he hated how the words tasted. Each syllable was a cover for a deeper truth—a truth that might hurt our friendship. Yet he couldn't shake the need to assert his feelings. He needed to remind Ruby of who'd been there all along. As their laughter echoed across the quad, Josh turned back, eyes narrowing slightly. It was a silent determination burning behind his gaze; he wouldn't let Ryan steal what mattered most to him, not without a fight.

"Ruby!" he called, stepping forward with an air of feigned casualness. "Hope I'm not interrupting anything!"

Ryan looked up, his expression shifting to one of surprise mixed with curiosity. "Hey, Josh! Not at all—just sharing some poetry."

THE BLOOD PACT

Josh's heart raced as he approached, stealing my attention away from Ryan, a small victory that quickly morphed into tension. I felt a sudden shift in the air, a competition simmering just beneath the surface.

"Poetry, huh?" Josh said, forcing his smile wider. "Seems like you're really enjoying that."

"I am! You should join us," I said, my enthusiasm balancing on a tightrope.

"Sure," Josh replied, his voice steady despite the turmoil in his gut. "I've always liked poetry. Maybe you can share some of your favourites, Ryan?"

Ryan glanced between us, picking up on the slight shift in dynamics. "Definitely," he said, his easy demeanour still intact yet tinged with an awareness of the uninvited tension. I couldn't ignore it; it coiled around us, thick and palpable. The corner of Josh's mouth seemed to twitch, the mask of friendliness faltering for just a moment as he observed Ryan's assuredness.

"Awesome! So, what else—" I began before Josh interrupted, a flash of determination igniting in his eyes.

"Actually, Ruby, would you mind if we took a moment? Just us?" he asked, his voice layered with an urgency that surprised me.

My heart raced, feeling the weight of the moment. "Right now? But we were just—"

"I think it's important," Josh cut in, an edge sharpening around his words.

Ryan looked at me, a question in his eyes, and I caught the faintest hint of uncertainty on his face. I could sense both the protective urge that flickered in Josh's stance and Ryan's willingness to step back, his interest in me deepening.

"Okay... let me just..." I trailed off, glancing back at Ryan. "I'll be right back."

As I stepped away with Josh, I felt the tension mount. The shadows were deeper now—my heart pulled taut between the two of them.

"Listen, Ruby," Josh said, his voice dropping to a more personal tone once we'd moved a safe distance away from Ryan. "Can we talk about what's going on?"

"Sure," I replied, feeling a knot tighten in my throat. "What's on your mind?"

"I just... I need to know how you really feel about all this," he said, his eyes flashing with an intensity that took me aback. "Do you see potential with him? The way you look at each other?"

I hesitated, the truth bubbling just beneath the surface. "Josh, I—"

"Why him, Ruby?" he pressed, frustration boiling over.

"Because—" I stammered, taken by surprise. "It's complicated. I'm trying to figure it out. But I also value our friendship."

"Friendship..." he echoed, a bitter edge creeping into his tone. "It feels like more than that for me, Ruby. And I can't help but feel that you're getting swept up in it with Ryan."

"Josh, it's not just surface-level. I'm just as confused," I admitted, sensing the heaviness hanging between us. "But I don't want to hurt either of you."

"Maybe you need to make a choice," he said bluntly, the unfiltered urgency rushing out as he leaned closer, eyes fierce with emotion.

"Josh, it's not that easy!" I interjected, feeling the weight of his emotions hitting me like a wave.

"You can't deny it," he urged. "Just think about what you truly want."

THE BLOOD PACT

But as I gazed into his eyes—those familiar, warm eyes—I realized it was more than just friendship I'd taken for granted. And in that moment, Josh's simmering jealousy burned brighter, hinting at the raw intensity of his feelings for me that had now been laid bare. What had begun as a simple conversation about poetry had twisted into something entirely more complicated, and I was left teetering on a precipice, feeling the weight of the choices looming ahead. In that moment, I found myself trapped in a storm—a tempest of emotions, desires, and inevitable decisions that I could no longer ignore. Later that evening, the dining hall was buzzing with activity, the din of laughter and chatter creating a symphony of college life. I sat with Carol at our usual table, my pasta untouched as I wrestled with the knot of emotions swirling within me. She leaned in, concern etching her features as she took a sip of her drink.

"Ruby, you've got to talk to me. What's going on with you and Ryan? You seem so drawn to him," she urged, her voice barely rising above the noise.

I sighed, pushing my plate away. "I know it's complicated, but there's something about him that just pulls me in. It feels like there's this connection I can't explain." Carol nodded, her eyes sparkling with excitement. "But what about Josh? He's been into you for ages, and you two have this great friendship. Are you willing to risk losing that?"

I glanced across the dining hall, my stomach tightening as I saw Josh at a nearby table, a dark cloud forming around him. He was angled toward Ryan, who was calmly eating his meal, completely unaware of the tension simmering just beneath the surface. I felt an immediate sense of foreboding.

"I don't know, Carol. I'd hate to hurt either of them, but I can't deny how I feel about Ryan." My heart raced at the thought of Josh's simmering jealousy bubbling over.

Before I could add more, I noticed Josh stand up, a storm brewing in his eyes. My breath caught as he strode over to Ryan's table, fists clenched by his sides. Carol's eyes widened, and I felt icy fear grip my heart.

"Ryan!" Josh's voice carried across the room, hard and loaded with accusation. The chatter around us fell silent, eyes darting toward the impending confrontation.

Ryan looked up, surprise flashing across his face. "Josh? What's the matter?"

"You know exactly what the matter is," Josh seethed, his face darkening. "You've been hanging around Ruby, thinking you can come between us. But I'm the better man for her—always have been."

My heart raced as I shot to my feet, my instincts screaming for me to intervene. "Josh don't—" But my warning came too late. Ryan studied Josh calmly, his brow raised in a mix of bewilderment and amusement. "I'm not trying to come between you and Ruby. She can choose for herself, Josh. This isn't a competition."

"Is that so?" Josh snapped, taking a step closer. The tension crackled in the air like electricity. "You think you can just waltz in and take her from me?"

In an instant, all semblance of composure broke. Josh swung at Ryan, landing a punch squarely on his jaw. My heart plunged into my stomach as Ryan barely flinched, his expression still calm. But the spark of anger ignited further fury within Josh.

"Josh, stop!" I shouted, but my words faded into the chaos.

With swift anger propelling him, Josh threw a second punch, this time harder, connecting forcefully with Ryan's nose. The sound of flesh hitting flesh echoed through the hall, and blood instantly erupted from Ryan's nostrils, staining his shirt.

THE BLOOD PACT

"Ryan!" I screamed, my heart racing. I willed my legs to move, propelling myself toward the two of them, urgency coursing through me as all eyes in the dining hall turned our way.

"Get off! What the hell is wrong with you?" I yelled at Josh, shoulder-checking him as I reached Ryan, panic flooding my mind.

Ryan held his hand to his nose, wincing slightly but still standing his ground, his gaze steady but weary. "It's okay, Ruby. I'm fine," he said, though the blood trickling down his lip told a different story.

"Fine? You're bleeding! What were you thinking, Josh?" I turned to him, fury igniting within me like a wildfire. "You can't just attack someone like that! This is insane!"

"Ruby, he's trying to steal you away from me!" Josh's voice rose, desperation colouring his words as he glared at Ryan, whose calm demeanour only infuriated him further.

"I'm not trying to steal anyone," Ryan said calmly, his tone saturated with patience. "Ruby needs to decide for herself who she wants in her life."

"Enough!" I shouted, the emotional whirlwind crashing around me, leaving me feeling raw and exposed. "This is ridiculous! Josh, if you can't control your jealousy and anger, I can't be friends with you like this. Not anymore."

Silence enveloped the dining hall as my words fell like stone. I could feel the room's gaze upon us, raw tension thickening the air.

"Ruby," Josh's voice dropped, pleading, as his expression faltered.

"I mean it," I said, shaking my head, my heart breaking but resolute. "This isn't how friends behave. I can't do this."

Tears pricked the corners of my eyes as I reached for Ryan, who looked momentarily surprised by my sudden declaration. "Come on, let's get you cleaned up," I said softly. He nodded, blood still trickling down his chin, but the determination in his eyes held a strength that made my heart race again. As I led him away, glancing back one last time at Josh, I felt a pang of sorrow for what might have been. I had made a choice—one that would change our friendships forever. The lines had been drawn, and the consequences were only just beginning to unfold. As I exited the dining hall, the gravity of my decision weighed on my shoulders, but I couldn't deny the small flicker of hope that accompanied my choice—a hope for growth, honesty, and perhaps, a love that had been waiting to be discovered.

Ryan

I leaned against the edge of Ruby's bed, the ice pack pressed firmly against my nose. The throbbing pain was a lesser offense to the chaos that lay within my mind. Already, I could see how quickly everything had spun out of control in the dining hall. One moment I was just trying to go through a normal day, and the next I had a punch thrown in my direction and a whirlwind of emotions threatening to consume me.

And it was all because of Josh. The rivalry between him and me was the least of my concerns; it was the secret gnawing at my insides—the life I was desperately trying to leave behind. Ruby stood a few feet away, her silhouette framed by the glowing light from the desk lamp. Her presence had a way of soothing me, but it also sparked an urgency. I didn't want to pull her into my life—the filthy, tangled web of ties and connections that came with my last name.

"Ryan, are you okay?" Her voice cut through the tension.

I hesitated, not sure how much to reveal. I could see the concern etched on her face, and it tugged at my heart. I wanted to shield her from the truth, to protect her from a past that I was trying so hard to escape. But as I looked into her eyes, I understood that I was only building walls between us.

"Yeah, just..." I swallowed hard, the weight of my secrets closing in on me. "It's complicated."

"Complicated how?" she pressed, stepping closer, her brow furrowed with determination.

THE BLOOD PACT

I ran a hand through my hair, frustration surging through me. "Look, my family—my real family—they're not like yours. My father is... he's the Don of a crime family. The Famiglia Notturno. They've got long arms and deep roots in the wrong places. I never chose that life. I'm trying to sever those ties." Ruby's eyes widened in shock, and I could see her mind racing, trying to reconcile this new information. "The mafia? Ryan, I—"

"It's not something I'm proud of!" I interrupted, desperation in my voice. "My father, Dominique 'Dom' Giovannetti, has tried to groom me since I was a kid. His idea of protection was shaping me to step into his shoes, to take over when he finally decides to step back. But that's not who I want to be. I just want a simpler life—freedom from all the expectations and the darkness that comes with the family name."

"Your mother..." she started softly.

"Passed away when I was nine," I confessed, the pain of that memory rolling through me like thunder. "That loss left me with my father, and all he wanted was to prepare me for a life I've fought to reject. He thinks he's protecting me, but he doesn't see how it binds me. The more he pushes, the more I want to run."

Ruby stood there, processing my words, and I could practically see the gears turning in her head. "What happens if you refuse? If you walk away?"

"Walk away?" I scoffed, allowing the bitterness to seep through. "It's not that simple. My father would see it as a betrayal. He's been building something for years—untouchable power—and I'm supposed to be his successor. He wants me to step into the role of capo, but I can't do that. I won't. I'd rather be in a life where I must worry about exams and jobs instead of dealing with criminals and blood debts."

Ruby stepped closer, reaching out to touch my arm gently. "You don't have to face this alone. You don't have to fight it by yourself."

"I'm trying," I said, my voice thick with emotion. "But there are consequences. If I push back against him, I risk drawing attention. If the Famiglia feels threatened, then it could put you at risk, too. They don't just let go; they retaliate. I can't let my choices endanger you."

"Then let me help you," she urged. "We can figure something out together. You're not just running away; you're fighting for your own life."

Fighting for my own life. The words resonated like an echo through my mind. I never thought of it that way. But how could I trust her with this? How could I bring her into the world I was trying so hard to escape?

"Ruby," I started, but she shook her head.

"Just listen. If I'm going to care about you—if we're going to be something—I can't be kept in the dark. I want to know your truth, no matter how messy or complicated it is."

"Believe me, it's complicated," I replied, my throat tightening. "But not sharing my past means pushing you away. And pushing you away is the last thing I want. But my secrets—they've built a wall around me. If they come crashing down, they could take us both with them."

She paused, her gaze steady, and there was a spark of understanding. "Then let's bring them down together." The gravity of her words settled in me, igniting something that burned brighter than fear. In that moment, I saw a flicker of hope, a chance to be freed from the shackles that my past had placed on me. Perhaps sharing my truth didn't condemn me; perhaps it invited vulnerability, connection, and even strength.

"I never imagined finding someone like you would be so complicated," I admitted, my heart racing at the thought of letting my guard down.

"And yet, here we are," she said, her voice softening. "Let's take this step by step. Share what you can. We can figure it out as we go."

THE BLOOD PACT

Could it be that simple? Or would my history drag her down into the depths of a world I had spent years trying to escape? As I looked into her eyes, I couldn't help but think that maybe, just maybe, she was right.

"Okay," I said finally, a measure of resolve forging within me. "Let's talk. But promise me that you'll stay safe in this. Promise me you won't put yourself in harm's way."

She smiled, and it felt like a weightlifting ever so slightly. "I promise. But you need to promise me to be honest—completely honest—from this point on."

"Deal," I said, a tentative smile breaking through my earlier doubt.

Taking a seat next to her, I felt the distance between us close. The air was thick with anticipation as I began to share the story of my life, the secrets that had shaped me—and the ties I was determined to sever forever. I took a deep breath, feeling the weight of my past bear down on my shoulders as I prepared to lay it all out before Ruby. The room was small, yet it felt expansive in that moment, almost suffocating under the gravity of what I was about to share.

"Okay, let's start at the beginning," I said, forcing the words out as if they were stumbling over one another. "My name is Ryan Rossi. But it wasn't always that way. I was born Ryan Giovannetti, son of Domenico Giovannetti, the Don of the Famiglia Notturno."

Ruby's eyebrows shot up, and I could see the questions forming in her mind, but I pressed on, not giving her a chance to interrupt. "I changed my name when I left—it was my way of trying to escape. I thought if I severed ties, if I adopted a new identity, maybe I could find a normal life. I spent years running from the shadows of my past, trying to carve out something resembling normality... but it's hard to outrun blood." I paused, the memories flooding in, each one a dagger of sorrow. My mother's laughter, the warmth of her embrace before she succumbed to a violent world that engulfed our family. My father had always tried to shield me after her death, but his idea of protection was twisted with expectation; he didn't just want to shield me from danger—he wanted to groom me for the life he had defined for me.

"After my mom died, my father's pretty much all I had left," I continued, my voice trembling slightly. "He raised me in that world—a world of loyalty, crime, and legacy. I never chose that life, Ruby. I watched him climb the ranks, the power growing around him like a noose tightening around our family's neck."

"Ryan," Ruby whispered, her eyes softening with understanding.

"I'm not looking for sympathy," I replied hastily, but my tone lacked conviction. "My father tried to protect me as best he could, but in the end, he only became a puppet master—shaping me into something I resent. When I was old enough to realize that I didn't want anything to do with that life, I left. I thought I could break free. But now, it feels like the past is catching up to me."

"You've talked about your father wanting you to take over," Ruby said gently. "What happens if you refuse?"

I looked away, my heart racing. "He won't let me go that easily. The message I received just a few hours ago—it was a reminder of how intertwined our lives are. It said—" I hesitated, my throat tightening. "It said, 'You can't outrun the blood in your veins, Ryan. It's time to come home.' It's a grim ultimatum, a grim reminder that no matter how far I run, my family's legacy is always waiting for me, ready to drag me back." Ruby shifted closer, her eyes reflecting empathy and determination. "What do you want, Ryan? What does home even mean for you anymore?" I sighed, the weight of her question pressing upon me. "Home was supposed to be the life I imagined away from my father's influence—the freedom to be myself without the constraints of the mafia's iron grip. I want to build a life that doesn't end in bloodshed or betrayal, but I feel like every step I take toward that life pulls me back to where I started."

"But you're not just running away; you're fighting for something better," she said, and there was strength in her words. "You need to stand your ground."

"I want to," I admitted, the tremor in my voice betraying the hope I tried to suppress. "But the pressure is mounting. I can feel the walls closing in. It's like I'm being squeezed in a vice, every day growing tighter. I don't want to drag you into this darkness, Ruby. You deserve a normal life."

"But you're already in this darkness, Ryan. Running won't change that. You need to confront it," she urged, passion lighting her eyes. "You say you don't want me to get hurt, but you can't just push me away. I want to help you. We can figure this out together."

The thought of involving her in my struggles sent a chill down my spine. Yet, I could see it in her eyes that she wasn't going to back down. "You don't understand—this isn't just about my past. My family won't hesitate to find and eliminate anyone they see as a threat to their power, including you."

"I won't be a victim," she shot back, fire and defiance in her voice. "If we're going to be together, we need to be honest about the risks. I refuse to let fear dictate my life or our relationship."

I took a moment to gather my thoughts, feeling the gravity of her words sink in. Maybe the shadows of my past were going to loom over us, but I couldn't allow them to dictate my future or hers. If I was going to confront my father, it had to be on my terms, and I would need every ounce of courage to do it.

"Okay," I said, determination edging into my voice. "If you're steadfast in this fight, then I need you to be ready for whatever comes. There's a darkness waiting, and I refuse to let it swallow you whole."

Ruby nodded, her expression resolute. "Together, remember?" As we locked eyes, I felt a surge of hope mingled with fear. She was right there beside me, ready to stand her ground, and in that moment, I knew I had to fight—not just for myself but for us both. The stakes had never felt higher, but I was no longer alone. Together, we would take one step forward, even if that step meant staring into the abyss of my past. The air around us hummed with tension, a mixture of fear and determination. I could see the fire in Ruby's eyes—a spark that reminded me of everything I wanted for my life, everything I wanted for us. My heart raced as the moment stretched between us, and suddenly, all the doubts I had harboured melted away. I could no longer ignore the chemistry that had built over days—weeks—between us. It was a force pulling me closer, urging me to take that leap I had so long avoided. In the shadows of my past, I had forgotten what it felt like to be drawn to someone, to want someone so fiercely that the world around me faded away.

I shifted forward, the space between us shrinking until I could feel the warmth radiating from her skin. Bringing my hands to her face, I cupped her cheeks, grounding myself in the moment. Our eyes locked, and I saw my reflections in hers: vulnerability, trust, and a fierce yearning for something genuine amid a backdrop of chaos.

"Ruby," I breathed, my voice barely above a whisper. There were no more words left to say, no more explanations needed.

I leaned in, closing the gap completely, and kissed her deeply. It was the kind of kiss that ignited a thousand sparks—a collision of emotions, a blend of fear and hope. The warmth of her lips against mine consumed me, grounding me in the moment when everything else seemed uncertain. She responded instantly, her hands finding

THE BLOOD PACT

their way to my hair, tugging me closer as if she could erase the distance, I'd put between us for so long. It was intoxicating, this connection we shared. Fighting the shadows of my past with the light she brought into my life felt like the only way to reclaim what I had lost. As we broke apart, we were both breathless, caught in a world that belonged solely to us. I rested my forehead against hers, letting the warmth of the moment cascade over me.

"I need you to understand," I murmured, my voice shaky with emotion. "This is a dangerous game I'm playing, and I'm terrified of what my family might do. But being with you... it feels right. It's the first time in a long time I've felt something other than the weight of my past."

Ruby looked up at me, her expression fierce and unwavering. "I can handle it, Ryan. I know this isn't just about us. It's about fighting for a future—together. I will support you, no matter how dark it gets. You're not alone in this." Her words wrapped around my heart like a lifeline, tethering me to a hope I hadn't dared to dream. In that moment, I knew whatever challenges the world threw our way, we could face them together. Each kiss we shared reinforced our bond, a promise that we wouldn't let the shadows dictate our future.

"I want to fight for us," I said, conviction surging through me. "But we need a plan. I need to confront my father, to show him that I'm done living in the shadows. I won't take his place, and I won't allow him to dictate my life anymore."

"I'm with you," she said fiercely, her eyes shining bright. "Whatever it takes."

We sat there, our foreheads touching, the warmth of hope mingling with the reality of the challenges ahead. I resented the life I'd been handed, and for the first time, I felt empowered to change it. With Ruby beside me, I was ready to step into the light, confront my past, and carve out a future that was truly mine.

"Let's start planning," I said, pulling back slightly to meet her gaze. "I'll need your strength through this."

"Together," she affirmed, a gentle smile lighting her face.

The world faded, and for a moment, everything felt perfect. Little did I know that the path ahead would be fraught with dangers, but with Ruby by my side, I felt ready to face them all. The weight of our kiss lingered, electrifying the air around us. As I let go of Ruby's hands, my mind raced with new possibilities. No longer was I just a man running from the ghosts of my past; I had someone to fight for, someone who had become my anchor in a stormy sea.

"To confront my father, I'll need information—something I didn't have before." I leaned back slightly, my mind racing. "I need to know what he's planning, what his next move is. If he knows I'm looking for ways to end this, he won't just wait for me to come to him. He'll come for me, and probably for you."

Ruby nodded, her expression shifting from supportive to thoughtful. "We should start by gathering intel. Maybe there are people at the edges of your father's world who want to help you. Those who are disillusioned with how things are run. The mafia is always shifting—there are bound to be some who feel trapped, just like you." I could feel the spark of determination growing in me. It was true—my father had made enemies over the years. Allies turned into enemies in a heartbeat when ambition clashed with loyalty. "You're right. With the right information, I can figure out which players are worth reaching out to."

"The longer you wait, the more danger you put yourself in," Ruby pointed out, her brow furrowed as she considered the implications. "You shouldn't have to do this alone. I can help."

"Ruby..." I began, wanting to protect her from the potential fallout, but she cut me off.

THE BLOOD PACT

"Don't," she said firmly. "You're not shutting me out again. You need to understand that I'm not afraid of this life. It may be dangerous, but I want to fight alongside you, with you, for you"

I looked into her eyes, where the fierce determination burned bright. She was so unlike anyone I had ever known—so full of strength and resilience. "All right. But we must be smart about this. We can't go rushing in without a plan."

"Let's start by figuring out who might be willing to help you," Ruby suggested, her mind already working a mile a minute. "Do you have any contacts from your past that would be willing to talk?"

I sighed, the memories flooding back: old friends turned reluctant enemies, a web of loyalties that twisted like a serpent. "There's one person I could reach out to who might have valuable information—Luca. We were close when I was still involved. He moved here a couple of year before me. He's always been wary of my father's methods, but he feared for his life as much as I did. It's been years since we spoke, but if anyone knows how to navigate these waters, it's him."

"Then let's find him," Ruby urged, her resolve igniting mine. "We can figure out a way to contact him without raising too much suspicion."

I nodded, feeling the purpose settle in my gut. However, the darker implications of my past shadowed my thoughts. "But if I reach out to Luca, there's a risk. If my father catches wind of this, it could backfire terribly. He's always had eyes and ears everywhere."

"Then we'll be careful," Ruby said, determination colouring her voice. "But you can't allow fear to paralyze you. You must take that chance. We both do."

"Alright, we'll plan. But we need a safe way to communicate—no calls, no obvious messages. If he senses I am planning something, it'll raise alarms," I replied. "The last thing I want is for my father to pressure Luca before we can even meet."

"We could use a burner phone," Ruby suggested, her eyes lighting up with the idea. "We can set it up so we can communicate without it being traced back to you. I'll help you get one. We just need to be discreet."

"Good thinking," I said, impressed by her quick thinking. "We'll make it work. But we need to keep a low profile until we have more information. For now, let's head out. I'll grab what we need, and then we can find a way to contact Luca."

As we gathered our things, a sense of urgency began to form—a tangible feeling of movement toward reclaiming my life. My heart raced; I could no longer afford to hide in the shadows. I had to face my father's world on my terms, and with Ruby's courage by my side, I felt fired up.

"Let's go," I said, determination flooding my voice. Together, we stepped into the unknown, ready to carve our own path against the darkness threatening to engulf us.

As we made our way out, I couldn't shake the feeling that a storm was brewing on the horizon. But for the first time in years, I didn't feel alone facing it. With Ruby's fierce loyalty beside me, I was ready to challenge fate.

Unwanted Attention

The sun was dipping below the horizon as Ruby and I emerged from the convenience store, the night air crisp and tinged with the scent of impending rain. I clutched the burner phone in my pocket, its weight a reminder that our plan was set in motion, but an unsettling fear tightened in my chest—an all-too-familiar sensation. After everything that had happened in recent weeks, I had finally moved out of the cramped dormitory at the university. The space had become stifling, filled with the whispers of anxious students and the haunting echoes of past events. I found a small apartment in Horizon View, a modest place that felt like a refuge, but even here, I couldn't shake the tension that clung to me, especially with my father living thousands of miles away in Italy. The distance didn't matter; his reach felt ever-present.

"Are you sure about reaching out to Luca?" Ruby asked, glancing sideways at me as we walked. "I know he was a friend, but how well do you trust him now?"

I chewed my lower lip, considering her question. "Luca was loyal, but loyalty can shift quickly. Just because there's an ocean between me and my father doesn't mean he can't touch my life here. I'm not convinced."

"Then we'll be cautious," she replied, her eyes glinting with determination. "We'll reach out, but we won't put our trust in anyone but each other."

Just as I opened my mouth to respond, headlights sliced through the dimming street behind us. I turned to see a black SUV approaching, moving faster than the other cars on the road. My pulse quickened as it slowed down near us, engine rumbling ominously.

"Ryan?" Ruby sensed my tension and stopped beside me, her eyes wide.

I grabbed her wrist gently, leading her into the shadows of a nearby alley to create some distance. The SUV came to a stop several yards ahead. My heart raced, anxiety clawing at my gut.

"Keep an eye out. He's here somewhere," a low gravelly voice called out from the vehicle—Marco's voice, sending chills down my spine. "Ryan wouldn't miss a chance to show his face, especially after all this time."

I clenched my jaw. My past—the very thing I thought I could manage—was crashing back in, just as I feared. Marco was looking for me here in Horizon View, and the sense of safety I had felt in my new apartment evaporated.

"I need to get out of here," I muttered, adrenaline flooding my senses. "We can't stay any longer."

"What about your apartment?" Ruby whispered, her voice barely above a thread in the tense silence. "They'll know where to find you."

"I'll have to go underground for a while. I can't let them use you against me. You're too important," I replied, my mind racing to formulate an escape plan.

"Ryan, you can't just leave! It's dangerous!" she insisted, her face etched with concern. "I won't let you go through this alone." We navigated the dark streets toward the West End, the weight of uncertainty heavy on my shoulders. I pulled out the burner phone, my hands trembling slightly as I dialled Luca's number. I had kept his contact saved for emergencies, never imagining I'd need him under such dire circumstances.

THE BLOOD PACT

After a few rings, he answered, his voice cautious. "Who is this?"

"It's me, Ryan." I responded.

"Ryan? What's going on?"

"I need to talk to you. It's urgent," I replied, trying to mask the urgency in my tone.

"Where?" he asked, a hint of reluctance in his voice.

"Let's meet at Finn's Café in an hour," I suggested, knowing it was a spot we both knew well.

There was a pause before he responded. "Fine. But I can't promise you anything."

"Just trust me, Luca. I need your help."

Another pause, then he reluctantly agreed. "I'll be there." Ruby was sitting across from me in the dimly lit booth, her fingers nervously tapping the tabletop as we waited. "You're sure about this?" she asked, her brow furrowed with worry.

"I have to be," I replied, rubbing my forehead. "If Luca knows something, we can't just ignore it."

The next hour felt like a lifetime, filled with tension and anxiety swirling between us. When Luca finally arrived, he looked uneasy. His eyes darted around as he approached our booth, and he slid in across from me, his expression cautious. I could feel Ruby's eyes on him, assessing him as we prepared to dive into this unsettling conversation.

"Luca," I started, leaning forward. "I need to know what you know about my father and the Notturno. It's all connected, and I can't face it alone."

He hesitated, studying me for a moment, then glanced at Ruby. "You brought someone with you?"

"Ruby, she's with me," I said, a protective instinct rising in my chest. "She's part of this now. We need to know everything."

Luca sighed, the weight of unspoken secrets hanging in the air. "Your father—he's a dangerous man. What he's involved in... it's more complicated than you think."

"Complicated how?" Ruby chimed in, her voice steady.

"Do you know about your mother?" Luca asked, looking at Ruby first, then shifting to me. "There are things you don't know—things she wanted to protect you from."

"Protect me? But she died when I was nine. How could she protect me?" I felt my heart drop further down the rabbit hole. "What are you saying?"

His gaze shifted, guilt etched across his features. "The accident... it was staged. She faked her death to escape the grip of Dom."

My eyes widened, astonished. "What?!"

"I know it's hard to believe," Luca said, his voice sincere. "But your mother wanted to get out. The Notturno was consuming her, and she thought it was the only way to keep you safe."

I blinked, grappling with the weight of his words. "But how?"

"Your mother is alive," Luca revealed, his eyes intense. "I'm in contact with her. She's been strategizing, waiting for the right moment to make a move. She wants you to step in as heir and overthrow Dom and the Notturno."

The words hit me like a punch. I had thought my life was a cage of abandonment and loss, but now it felt like a carefully crafted game that I had unknowingly been a part of. "But why? How can I be the heir? I don't even know what that means."

"Because she believes you have the strength to rise above this. You've been moulded for this moment, Ryan. The messages you've been receiving—those weren't from Dom. They were from me, working under your mother's guidance. She had to communicate secretly to protect you."

THE BLOOD PACT

I leaned back, trying to absorb everything he had just revealed. Ruby was watching me intently, her thoughts a whirlwind behind her calm demeanour. "Ryan, this is huge," she said softly. "Are you sure you want to go down this path?"

"I don't have a choice," I replied, resolve hardening within me. "If there's any chance my mother is alive... I must know the truth."

Luca nodded, sensing the determination in my voice. "You'll have to reconnect with your mother. There's so much she wants to tell you. But we'll have to be careful about how we approach this. Dom cannot know that she is alive."

"What about the Notturno?" Ruby asked, realizing the danger that loomed over us.

"We'll gather allies. I'll help you—your mother's connections run deep. She's been preparing for this; the plan to take down Dom and the Notturno was always in motion, but it needs you to step up." Luca paused, his expression serious. "This isn't just about survival anymore. It's about reclaiming your identity."

As the gravity of his words settled, I realized this was a turning point. I could no longer run from my past. I had to confront it, armed with newfound knowledge and a purpose.

"Okay," I declared, my voice steady. "I'm ready. Let's do this... together."

Ruby reached over, squeezing my hand in solidarity. "We'll figure it out. You're not alone in this." Luca looked between us, a flicker of approval crossing his face. "Good. Together, we'll face whatever comes next." The atmosphere in Finn's Café crackled with uncertainty, the flickering overhead lights casting shadows across our determined faces. I couldn't shake the feeling that we were on the edge of something dangerous yet necessary.

"Alright, we need a plan," I said, sitting up straighter. "How do we approach my mother? How can we make contact without putting her at risk?"

Luca leaned in, eyes sharp and focused. "I have a secure way to reach her. But you need to be prepared for the possibility that she may not be the same person you remember. Living in the shadows can change a person."

"Change how?" Ruby asked, concern etched on her face.

"Her priorities, her mindset. The choices she made to protect you might have left scars. But regardless, she wants to see you," Luca replied. "You need to stay resilient. Emotions will run high."

I nodded, swallowing hard. "What's the first step?"

Luca pulled out a small notebook, flipping it open to a page filled with scribbles. "This is the encrypted communication method we're using. I'll send her a message, something subtle that she'll know is from me. We'll set up a meeting place, somewhere safe." He met my gaze. "But Ryan, you need to be ready for whatever happens. This isn't just about finding her—it's about confronting your father."

"Dom won't take this lightly," Ruby added, her voice steady. "We'll need backup, allies. If things escalate, we won't be able to do this alone."

"Exactly," Luca agreed. "I have contacts within the underground network who might be willing to help us. But it's risky. We need to know who we can trust, and who might inform Dom."

"Let's start by reaching out to your contacts then," I urged, feeling a surge of adrenaline. "The sooner we get the ball rolling, the better." My heart raced at the prospect of finally uncovering the truth.

Luca hesitated, then began jotting down a list of names. "These people have varying degrees of loyalty to the Notturno. Some may have their own agendas, but if we play our cards right, we can leverage their trust." As Luca outlined the names, Ruby leaned back, deep in thought. "What about your mother's past associates? She might have someone who can help."

THE BLOOD PACT

"You're right," I replied, remembering the whispers of old friends my mother used to mention—names lost to me, shadows of my childhood. "We'll look into any connections she might have left behind."

"Good," Luca said, then glanced at me, a flicker of uncertainty crossing his expression. "Just remember—if we proceed, there's no going back. You'll have to fully embrace your role in this."

I took a deep breath, the weight of his words settling over me. "I'm ready for that. I want to know the truth, no matter what it takes." Ruby nodded her agreement, her expression determined. "Then let's get to work." Luca quickly finished his notes, scribbling down a plan for communication and the names he thought might be pivotal in our journey. "I'll reach out to my contacts and see who's willing to meet. We should aim to reconnect within the next few days." As we continued strategizing, the café buzzed around us, but I felt like I was in my own world, the noise fading into the background. Each step we took toward unveiling the truth felt like a heartbeat—a rhythmic promise that we were moving forward, together. After the meeting, we left the café, stepping onto the bustling streets. The air was cool, but my thoughts were ablaze with possibility.

"Where do we go from here?" Ruby asked, leaning closer as we entered a quieter side street.

"First, we make sure we're safe," I said, glancing over my shoulder as the shadows stirred with every passing light. "I can't let Dom find out what I'm planning. We need a safe house, a place to regroup."

"I know a couple of places that might work," Ruby suggested. "Friends of mine are off the radar. They won't ask questions."

"Perfect. Let's go," I replied, my heart pounding in anticipation.

As we moved through the dimly lit streets, weaving in and out of the crowds, I couldn't shake the impending sense of danger that lurked behind us. It was a reminder that even as we embarked on this journey toward the truth, every step brought us closer to confrontation. Finally, we reached Ruby's friend's place—a small apartment tucked away in a rundown building. We climbed the narrow staircase, the walls adorned with makeshift graffiti and faded posters.

Once inside, Ruby introduced me to her friend, Ivan, a lanky guy with a quick smile and wild hair. "Hey, Ruby! Who's your friend?" he asked, eyeing me curiously.

"This is Ryan," she replied, "We're in a bit of a predicament, and we need a safe place to lay low for a while."

Ivan's brows knitted together in thought. "You got it. My place is your place. Just no trouble, alright?"

"Thanks, Ivan," I said, grateful for the support.

As night fell, we settled into the small apartment, the atmosphere thick with anticipation.

"Now that we're safe, what's the next move?" Ruby asked, pouring us each a glass of water.

"We wait for Luca to make contact with my mother," I replied, trying to remain collected despite the storm brewing within me. "But I think we should start preparing. If Dom finds out about us, we need a plan to protect ourselves."

"I've got some ideas," Ruby said, her determination igniting. "We can gather more intel about Dom and the Notturno. Figure out who his closest allies are, where he operates."

"Right," I replied, feeling the edges of my world sharpen. "If we can understand his moves, we can respond accordingly. Information is power."

THE BLOOD PACT

The clock ticked softly in the background as we turned our focus to filling in the blanks—gathering information, piecing together the connections, edging closer to the truth about my mother and the power I was meant to claim.

But with every plan made, shadows lingered closer, reminding me that time was of the essence, and danger was always just a heartbeat away. As the hours melted into the night, the city outside continued its rhythmic hum, but inside Ivan's small apartment, our focus remained sharp. I leaned against the wall, surrounded by remnants of old band posters and dusty furniture, feeling the weight of the plan we were about to execute. Ruby's phone buzzed as she scrolled through her contacts, her face illuminated by the soft glow of the screen. "I have a few people I can reach out to for intel on the Notturno," she said, her brow furrowing in concentration. "They might know more about Dom's operations, who his allies are—anything that could help us."

"Yes, let's do that," I replied, my heart racing at the thought of finally uncovering the truth about my father and the shadowy world he inhabited.

After a flurry of calls and messages, Ruby finally put her phone down. "Okay, we'll fortify this place, and I'll set up meetings with a couple of my contacts. We need to make sure we're not exposed before we meet your mother." I nodded, urgency settling in. "And we need to prepare for our meeting tomorrow night." Just then, a notification chimed from the old laptop Ivan had set up for us. Ruby and I both turned toward the screen, my heart pounding as I read the message that had just arrived.

"It's from Luca!" I exclaimed, leaning closer to the screen. He was our link to my mother, the connection I desperately needed.

"Ryan, I've been able to reach your mother. She agreed to meet us at the abandoned church at the edge of town tomorrow night. It's crucial that you're careful—Dom's people might be watching."

Hope surged through me, but it quickly gave way to concern. "What if it's a trap? What if they're just waiting for us?"

Ruby's expression was fierce, undeniably unwavering. "We can't let fear paralyze us. If we don't go, we might lose the only chance we have to find her." I took a deep breath, weighing the stakes. "You're right. We can't back down now." My mind raced with the implications of the meeting. "We need a solid plan. What do we do when we get there?"

"We can scope out the area first, see if anyone is watching," Ruby suggested. "If things look clear, we go in slow. If it feels off, we retreat."

I nodded, appreciating the methodical approach. "All right, then. We also should investigate using some kind of signal—something to alert each other if things go sideways." We spent the next hour brainstorming different contingency plans, drawing on our instincts and experience. I could feel the adrenaline coursing through me, a mix of fear and anticipation pushing me forward.

"Let's also consider how we'll handle Dom. If he finds out we're onto him, we need to be prepared," I noted, my voice steady. "No more running. It's time to confront him."

"Yes," Ruby said, her eyes bright with resolve. "If we get the chance to draw him out, we'll take it. But we must be smart about our approach."

With plans in place, the night wore on, each passing moment heightening the sense of urgency. The clock ticked steadily, a reminder that time was slipping through our fingers. Eventually, Ivan poked his head into the room, a mild curiosity evident on his face. "How's it going in here? Need anything?"

"We're good, just finalizing plans," Ruby replied, her tone clipped but polite.

THE BLOOD PACT

"Alright. Just let me know if you need anything," he said before retreating to his corner of the apartment.

Once we were alone again, I turned to Ruby. "I'm glad you're here with me. I couldn't do this alone." She met my gaze, a fierce determination flashing in her eyes. "Neither could I. We're in this together, Ryan. Every step of the way." As the night deepened, I felt the reality of the impending confrontation settle over me like a shroud. The church lay ahead, a space where secrets and truths would collide. What if everything I believed to be true was a manipulation? But beneath the fear loomed a growing conviction—I wasn't just preparing for a reunion; I was stepping into my place within a legacy filled with darkness and uncertainty. We kept vigil over the night, strategizing and reinforcing our resolve, fortified in the knowledge that whatever awaited us in that church, we would face it together. As the shadows grew longer, the weight of what lay ahead pressed down on us. I glanced at Ruby, who was still skimming through her contact list, her expression focused. I admired her intensity; it was a reminder that she was in this fight with me, wholly invested.

"Got anything?" I asked, breaking the silence that hung thick in the air.

"Charlie is willing to meet us tonight," she replied, her voice low but excited. "He's a friend from school, and his dad is a criminologist for the Horizon View Police Department. He has some insight into the Notturno's movements and Dom's recent activities."

"Let's do it," I said, feeling my heart quicken at the thought of gathering more intel. "Where are we meeting him?"

"Just a few blocks away at The Rusty Lantern," she answered, her fingers flying over her phone as she arranged details. "It's a safe spot. We can keep our heads down and not attract too much attention."

"Should we head out now?" I asked, already feeling the pull of urgency. Every moment counted, especially as the sun dipped lower in the sky.

"Yes, let's go," Ruby said, her determination infectious. She tucked her phone away and stood, her posture shifting to one of readiness.

We exchanged a glance that seemed to communicate everything—our fears, our hopes, and our shared resolve. Together, we made our way to the door, quietly slipping into the darkened hallway. The street outside was buzzing with life, but our steps were careful and deliberate as we navigated through the maze of the city. We kept our voices low, discussing our strategy for the meeting with Charlie.

"I'll handle the initial conversation," Ruby suggested as we approached the bar. "You can stay alert for anything unusual."

I nodded, appreciating her decisiveness. "Sounds good. And remember, if anything feels off, we walk away." We arrived at The Rusty Lantern, its flickering neon sign casting a ghostly glow over the entrance. Inside, the bar was dimly lit, filled with the low murmur of conversations and soft music wafting through the air. I could see a few familiar faces—people who had also learned to navigate the undercurrents of the city. We found a booth in the corner, one where we could easily observe the crowd while remaining somewhat hidden. Ruby's phone buzzed almost immediately after we sat down.

"Charlie's here," she said, her voice steady but a hint of excitement lingering in it. "He's at the bar."

I scanned the room, spotting a man in his late twenties with a friendly demeanour. Wearing a worn leather jacket and sporting tousled hair, he seemed both approachable and earnest. I watched as he turned, spotting us in the booth before making his way over.

"Ruby! Ryan!" Charlie greeted, sliding into the seat across from us. "Thanks for meeting me on such short notice."

"Of course," Ruby replied, her demeanour shifting into professional mode. "We need to talk about the Notturno and Dom, specifically—what's he planning?"

THE BLOOD PACT

Charlie leaned in closer, lowering his voice. "I've been talking to my dad since you reached out. He's been keeping tabs on the Notturno, especially lately, and he suspects Dom is up to something big."

"What kind of something?" I asked, my stomach churning with anxiety at the thought of my father's name being dragged into this.

"Dom's been laying low," Charlie said, glancing around to make sure no one was listening. "But my dad thinks that's a strategy. He believes Dom is gathering resources and alliances. It's likely he's looking to make a significant move soon, but we don't know the details."

"Resources?" Ruby echoed, her eyes narrowing. "What are we talking about here?"

"From what I've gathered, there's a shipment coming into the docks somewhere next week," Charlie explained. "It's rumoured to include a mix of arms and other supplies. Dom's planning something, but I can't figure out exactly what yet."

"Is there a way to observe this shipment without getting caught?" I asked, my mind racing as I considered the possibilities.

"Maybe," Charlie replied thoughtfully. "If you can get someone to plant eyes on the docks, you could see what's going down. But you need to be careful; Dom's not someone who plays nice."

"That's an understatement," Ruby added, crossing her arms as she thought through the implications.

I felt the tension mount, a knot tightening in my chest. "If we can delay his plans even just a little, it might buy us time to figure out what he's really after."

"I'd recommend being there to gather evidence. If you can spot something suspicious, you might be able to use it against him later," Charlie suggested.

We discussed the details further, plotting out our next course of action. I could feel the weight of it all—this was no longer just a personal affair; it was growing into something larger, something entwined with my family's history.

"Thanks for the intel, Charlie," Ruby said, sincerity in her voice. "We'll keep in touch. After we gather more information, we may need your help."

"Anytime," he replied. "Just be careful. I don't want to see you guys in over your heads."

As Charlie finished his drink and got ready to leave, I couldn't shake the unease settling in my chest. Dom's looming threat felt ever more real, and the uncertainty only heightened my resolve. As we stepped out into the night, I could see Ruby's determination mirrored in my own. We were on the edge of something unavoidable, and I was ready to confront whatever awaited us. Tomorrow would change everything.

THE BLOOD PACT

Confronting the Past

The morning light spilled into Ivan's apartment, breaking through shadows that lingered from the restless night. I felt a mix of exhaustion and anticipation, a gnawing awareness that the day ahead would be pivotal. Today was the day I would confront the ghosts of my past—and find my mother. Ruby was already awake, her phone buzzing with messages from her contacts. She flipped through them with practiced ease, her brow furrowed in concentration. I admired her focus but sensed the weight of everything we were about to undertake.

"Luca has checked in again," she said, glancing up. "He's confirmed the meeting at the church tonight, and he assured me he'll be there waiting for us."

"Good," I replied, my heart racing. "But we still must ensure he's not followed. Dom's connections run deep."

We spent the morning reinforcing our plan, making calls, and testing different scenarios for what could unfold once we reached the church. Each rehearsed line felt like a lifeline to clarity amid the chaos. I had to convince myself that whatever happened, I was ready to face the truth. As the clock ticked closer to evening, the interactions were charged with an unspoken tension. The weight of what we were about to undertake loomed large.

"Ryan," Ruby said suddenly, breaking my reverie, "we need to be prepared for your mother's reaction. We don't know how she'll feel after all this time."

"Right," I nodded, anxiety gnawing at me. "What if she's afraid to become involved again? Or worse, what if she thinks it's too dangerous?"

"Then we reassure her," Ruby replied firmly. "That you're here, that you want to protect her just as much as she wants to protect you."

With that, we gathered our things and headed out. The streets buzzed with the usual cadence of life, but I felt disconnected from it all—as if a bubble of tension surrounded me, leaving the rest of the world muted. As we walked toward the church, each step echoed with uncertainty. I replayed memories of my mother—the sound of her laughter, the way she used to comfort me whenever I felt lost. Would she even recognize me now, after all this time?

"Are you okay?" Ruby asked gently, noticing my clouded expression.

I nodded, forcing myself to smile. "Yeah. Just... thinking." The church loomed ahead, its crumbling façade a stark contrast to the vibrant life around it—a remnant of the past, reminding me how far I had come and how much I yearned to uncover the truth. We reached the entrance, a heavy wooden door that creaked as I pushed it open. Inside, the air was cool and musty, the quite broken only by the soft sigh of the wind as it filtered through stained-glass windows. Dust motes danced in the slanting shafts of light, creating an ethereal atmosphere that belied the weight of our purpose.

"Let's check for any escape routes," Ruby suggested, her voice barely above a whisper.

THE BLOOD PACT

I nodded, our instincts kicking in as we moved silently through the dimly lit pews. The church felt like a time capsule, frozen in moments of both despair and hope, steeped in the secrets of many who had passed through. Finally, we made our way to the front, scanning the space for signs of anyone waiting for us. The altar, once hallowed ground, now became a focal point of our unease.

"Nothing looks out of place," Ruby observed, her eyes trailing over the surroundings. "But we should remain vigilant."

Just then, the door creaked open, and a figure stepped inside—a woman cloaked in shadows, her eyes darting around, searching.

"Mom?" I called tentatively, my heart pounding as I stepped forward, hope blooming in my chest.

She stopped, her gaze fixing on me with a mixture of disbelief and recognition. For a moment, time stood still. I saw the resemblance—the familiar features, the intensity in her eyes, but she looked different, marked by years of hardship.

"Ryan?" she whispered, her voice trembling. "Is it really you?"

Before I could think, I crossed the distance between us, wrapping my arms around her. The weight of all those lost years pressed down, an overwhelming mix of relief and longing clawing at my heart.

"I thought I'd never see you again," I murmured, my voice thick with emotion.

She pulled back, her eyes brimming with tears. "I wanted to protect you. I had to stay away... for your safety."

"What do you mean?" I asked, trying to comprehend her words. "Why did you have to stay away?"

A shadow of fear crossed her face. "Because your father—Dom—he doesn't know I'm alive. I believed if I stayed hidden, I could protect you without interference from the Notturno." The revelation hit me like a punch to the gut. "He has no idea. You've been living in hiding this whole time?"

"I had to," she said, her voice breaking. "Dom is dangerous, Ryan. He wouldn't just come after me; he would use you against me. I thought by keeping away, I could keep you safe."

"But living like this... it must have been so hard," I said, bitterness creeping into my voice. "I've spent my whole life believing you were gone."

"I thought I was protecting you by disappearing," she said softly, reaching for my hand. "You were just a child. I couldn't let you be dragged into that world. I had to sacrifice everything, myself for your safety."

Ruby stood silently, a witness to our moment. I could feel her presence, but this was between my mother and me—two people caught in the wake of the past, grappling with the pain of separation.

"So, what now?" I asked, my voice steadying. "Now that we're together, we can't just go back to hiding. If Dom doesn't know, that's our chance."

"We need to be smart," she replied, a hint of resolve sparking in her eyes. "I can't let him find out about me. If he does, he'll come for you both."

"We'll protect each other," I assured her, the weight of her sacrifice igniting a fire within me. "We can face this together. You don't have to hide anymore."

She looked into my eyes, searching for the truth in my words. "But we need to plan. We can't just dive into this unprepared." I nodded, feeling the tension in the air shift slightly. "Luca is watching outside, keeping an eye out for any threats. We can go over everything now, think it through carefully." I turned to Ruby and looked at my mother, "This is Ruby, she has been my strength these past months. Ruby, this is my mother, Judie."

"I'm so happy you have a companion to find comfort in all this, Ryan." While she looks at Ruby.

THE BLOOD PACT

"We find comfort and strength in each other." Ruby smiled and extending a hand towards me.

As we began to discuss our next steps, there was a sense of unity that had been absent for so long. We were on the precipice of reclaiming a lost bond, a bond worth fighting for against the shadows that loomed over us. The stakes had never been higher, but now, with my mother seated beside me, I felt a surge of determination. Whatever lay ahead, I would confront my past and the darkness that came with it, together with the one person who mattered most. As we settled into seats on the worn, wooden pews, the atmosphere crackled with unspent emotions. My mother—the woman who had been nothing but a distant memory for so long—was finally here. I could see the exhaustion etched on her face, the toll that years of hiding had taken.

"Why did you come back now?" I asked gently, trying to navigate the turbulent waters of emotion that surrounded us.

A flicker of uncertainty danced in her eyes before she replied, "I never stopped protecting you wherever you went, I went, Ryan. I thought I could stay hidden until it was safe to tell you the truth. But Dom's grip was tighter than I anticipated. I couldn't risk him dragging you into that world until I knew you were safe."

"What changed?" I pressed. "What made you decide to reach out now?"

"Because I learned Dom was getting closer," she said, her voice trembling slightly. "People have started to suspect something. I couldn't allow you to live in ignorance any longer. You deserved to know that I was alive and that I loved you all this time."

My heart raced as the weight of her words settled over me. It felt surreal to finally have answers, yet the dread of what was still lurking in the shadows loomed large.

"I spent years feeling abandoned," I admitted, the bitterness surfacing. "I thought you had chosen to leave me."

"I never chose to leave you, Ryan. Not a single day went by when I didn't think of you," she replied, tears glistening in her eyes. "I wanted to come out and just let you know I'm here, but every time I thought of it, I feared Dom's reach. It's a tangled web of deception, and I didn't want to put you at risk."

The realization that her love had been steadfast even in her absence softened the sharp edges of my anger. "What do we do now? What's the plan?" She took a deep breath, steadying herself. "We need to gather as much information as possible about Dom's activities. Luca is connected, and he can help us understand the extent of Dom's network. We must stay one step ahead of him." Ruby, who had been listening quietly, finally chimed in. "I can help too. I have my own contacts, people who knows the city. The more eyes we have, the better."

I nodded, grateful for her support. "That's a good point. We'll need to leverage any contacts we have. But we also must ensure that none of this reaches Dom's ears." My mother's expression hardened. "He's not just a threat; he's a predator. If he suspects I'm alive, or worse, that we're working together, he will stop at nothing to find us." The gravity of her words pressed down on me. I could feel the weight of the reality we faced—a reality that had haunted my childhood and shaped my fears.

"Let's meet with Luca, see what he knows. We can't be afraid to confront this," I said, trying to rally our spirits. "We've been living in his shadow for too long."

"Before we meet him, I need you to know something," my mother said, her voice dropping to a whisper. "Dom is not just manipulative; he's dangerous in ways you can't even imagine. The man I thought I knew became a stranger long ago. He will use anyone and anything to get what he wants."

I felt a chill run down my spine. "But you know how he thinks. You can help us understand his tactics, his next moves."

THE BLOOD PACT

"Yes," she replied, nodding. "I can help you anticipate his strategies. But you must promise me that you'll be cautious. Trust your instincts, and don't let your guard down—ever."

"We will," I assured her. "I won't let my emotions cloud my judgment. I just want to keep you safe."

At that moment, Ruby laid a hand on my shoulder. "We're all in this together, Ryan. We fight as a team." As the three of us shared a moment of solidarity, the previous tension began to ease, transforming into a sense of shared purpose. The reality of our situation still weighed heavily on us, but for the first time, we had a framework, a plan to reclaim our lives from Dom's grasp.

We stood and moved to the exit, my mother's steps tentative yet strangely empowered as she walked beside me. The air outside was crisp, a stark contrast to the weight that had filled the church. The sun was beginning to dip below the horizon, painting the sky in shades of orange and purple—an omen, perhaps, of the challenges yet to come.

"Let's head to Luca," I said, determination flooding my voice. "He should be waiting for us nearby."

As we approached the rendezvous point Luca had chosen, I felt a pulse of adrenaline. The stakes had never been higher, and yet, I could sense something shifting within me. I was no longer just the scared child left behind; I was a man ready to fight for the truth and the safety of those I loved. Moving forward into the unknown, I could feel my mother's presence beside me—a steadying force amidst the chaos. Whatever lay ahead, I now knew we would face it together. As we stepped into the street, the bustling sounds of the city filled my ears, yet they felt distant and muffled as if the world were enveloped in a fog. A profound sense of urgency tugged at my insides; I could almost feel Dom's presence lurking in the shadows, a spectre that refused to let go. We quickly crossed the street toward the small café where Luca had suggested we meet. Its worn sign creaked in the breeze, a familiar touch of comfort in a day filled with emotional upheaval. The more I thought about it, the more I realized that it wouldn't just be the three of us fighting this battle. Luca had his own motivations, and while I knew he could be trusted for now, I also needed to remain cautious. As we entered the café, the warmth enveloped us, contrasting starkly with the chill of uncertainty hanging in the air. We spotted Luca at a corner table, his usually confident posture giving way to an air of tension. He was already scanning the room, ensuring we weren't followed.

"Thanks for coming," he greeted us, gesturing for us to sit. "I have some information that might be crucial."

"Let's get right to it," I said, trying to mirror his urgency. My mother took a seat beside me, her presence both grounding and anxiety-inducing.

Luca leaned in closer, lowering his voice. "I've been keeping tabs on Dom's activities, and it looks like he's ramping up his operations. There are whispers of him making moves to consolidate power, and that means we could be in his crosshairs sooner than later." I felt my blood run cold. "What do you mean? Does he know about my mother?" Luca shook his head. "Not yet. At least, not that I've seen. But with the way things are heading, he'll start tightening his grip on everything. He'll want to eliminate any loose ends, and you and your mother are that."

"Then we need to act fast," my mother interjected. "He is not just after power; he's about control. If he thinks you're a threat, he will come after you—with no hesitation."

Luca nodded thoughtfully. "I suggest gathering as much information as we can about his recent moves. We need to know who his allies are and how we can exploit any weakness in his network. But I must warn you—this isn't just about gathering intel. He's dangerous, and he won't hesitate to retaliate if he senses anything."

THE BLOOD PACT

"I understand," I replied, feeling the weight of his warning. "We have to stay one step ahead."

"From what I've heard, he's been pressuring some of his associates into silence about certain operations. There's a private meeting happening tomorrow evening. If we can infiltrate that, we might gain critical insight into his plans."

"Is there any way we can get in?" Ruby asked, her keen mind already plotting possibilities.

Luca leaned back, a slight glint in his eye. "I have a contact who might be able to help—someone on the inside who owes me a favour. But we'll need to move quickly. If I approach them too casually, they might decline."

"We don't have much time, then," I said, my heart racing at the thought of finally gaining access to the information we needed. "Let's reach out to him right away."

"Alright," Luca agreed, his weariness replaced by a flicker of determination. "But I need you all to be careful. I don't want anyone to get caught up in this. If Dom finds out about any of us collaborating—"

"He'll use us against each other," my mother finished, her voice steady but laced with fear. "So, we remain in the shadows. No names, no details exchanged unless necessary."

Nods of agreement surrounded the table, and I felt a surge of hope mingled with anxiety. This was the first time in a long while I had a plan in place, a strategy to reclaim the life Dom had stolen from us.

"Let's meet back here in a few hours," Luca suggested, rising from his seat. "I'll have more details by then. Just keep your phones off and your heads low."

We all stood, exchanging hurried glances before Luca slipped out of the café. My mother turned to me, her eyes reflecting both concern and pride. "You're doing so well, Ryan. I know this is hard for you."

"It's hard for all of us," I said, a hint of frustration creeping into my voice. "But it feels different now. We're not running; we're fighting back."

The words held a weight I'd never encountered before. It felt liberating to embrace the idea of fighting back, but I was under no illusions about the challenges we faced.

"Let's make sure we're ready," I continued, focusing on the task ahead. "We need to strategize. The last thing we can afford is for Dom to catch us off guard."

For the next hour, we mapped out our options, scouring through potential escape routes and strategies. Every detail mattered, from the restaurants in the vicinity to the alleys we could use to stay hidden. It felt like we were engineering a plan for a heist rather than involving ourselves in a battle against the man who had wrought havoc in our lives.

As the café winded down and patrons started to file out, I felt my anxiety resurface. The weight of the impending confrontation was almost suffocating, yet I felt a flicker of resilience igniting within me.

"Hey," Ruby said gently, drawing my attention. "You're not alone in this. We've got your back—no matter what."

I smiled, grateful for her unwavering support. "I know. And I trust you both. Together, we'll face whatever comes our way." With a shared sense of determination, we exited the café, ready to confront the impending storm. And somewhere within me, I felt an ember of hope stirring, a belief that we could reclaim our lives from the

THE BLOOD PACT

shadows of the past. The streets outside the café were bustling as the evening crowd filled the air with a mix of laughter and chatter. Yet, an ominous undertone shadowed my thoughts, a reminder of the looming danger that awaited us. My mind raced with the plans we formed, each decision cascading into potential risks and rewards.

"Let's head to my apartment," I suggested, trying to maintain a sense of normalcy amid the tension. "We can set up our base there until we hear from Luca."

"Good idea," my mother agreed, glancing around as if expecting to see Dom lurking in the edges of the sidewalk, ready to pounce. Ruby fell into step beside me, her presence a reminder that I wasn't alone in this chaos.

As we walked, the atmosphere shifted. The sun dipped lower in the sky, painting the horizon with hues of pink and purple. I watched my mother closely, noting how the daylight seemed to lessen the lines of worry etched on her face. I wanted desperately to bridge the years we lost, but the reality of our situation pressed heavily on both of us. When we arrived at my apartment, I swiftly locked the door behind us, feeling the comforting weight of security settle over me. The small space felt cozy and familiar, but it also served as a reminder of how isolation had shaped my life. I quickly moved to set up a work area, laying out my laptop and survival gear—all items I had collected during the years when I felt the need to protect myself.

"Let's go over what we know so far," I said, pulling up notes on my laptop. "Luca mentioned a private meeting tomorrow night. We need to figure out how we can infiltrate that."

I glanced at my mother, who was kneeling by the coffee table, flipping through a worn notebook she had brought with her. "I kept records of some of Dom's interactions. It's not comprehensive, but it might give us insight into potential allies and weak points."

"That's perfect," Ruby chimed in, leaning in to study the notebook. "Any names we can work with?"

"I didn't track every name, but there are a few entries here," my mother said, pointing to scribbled notes. "These three have shown up repeatedly in different contexts. They could be key players in whatever plot Dom is concocting."

I grabbed a pen and started jotting down notes. "We can cross-reference these names with what we have on Dom's network. Each connection could lead us to an advantage or a way to gather intel without exposing ourselves." Hours slipped away as we pored over information and potential strategies. The tension between us began to ease as we shared stories, recalling mundane moments from the past that kept the spirit of hope alive. The deeper we delved into planning, the more connected we seemed to become, as if the years apart were finally being stitched together. As we finalized our strategies, the phone buzzed across the table, breaking the focused silence. My heart leaped into my throat as I snatched it up, hoping—yet fearing—it was Luca. I glanced at the screen. "It's him."

"Put it on speaker," Ruby urged, her excitement pulsing through the air.

I pressed the button and spoke, "Luca?"

"Ryan, I've managed to get in touch with my contact," he said, urgency spilling through the phone. "We're in luck—there's a way for you to get into the meeting, but it's risky."

"Tell us what we need to know," I replied, leaning closer to the phone, my focus sharpening.

"Okay," he said, lowering his voice. "The meeting is at one of Dom's front businesses—a bar that he uses for these kinds of gatherings. You'll need to go as employees. My contact can get you three in as part of a new floor team."

"Employees?" I echoed, glancing at my mother and Ruby, whose expressions were a mix of surprise and determination.

THE BLOOD PACT

"Yeah. I told him you could handle yourself, but he insists on having you all look discreet—nothing that would draw attention. We must move quickly; he'll be finalizing the arrangements tonight, and it might be your only chance."

"Great. What do we need to do?" Ruby asked, excitement evident in her voice.

"Show up at the bar tomorrow afternoon, two hours before the shift starts. I'll arrange for you to meet him in the staff area. He'll brief you there. Just be careful—Dom will have eyes everywhere."

"Understood." I took a deep breath, adrenaline coursing through me. We needed to do this; it was a leap into the unknown—but it was our chance to disrupt Dom's plans.

Once I ended the call, we shared a moment of silence, the weight of our choices sinking in.

"My heart is racing," Ruby admitted, breaking the stillness. "But this could be what we need to take him down."

"I know," I said, my mind trying to absorb the rapid changes. "But we must stay composed. This isn't just about getting into the meeting; it's about gathering information and getting out safely."

My mother nodded, a flicker of determination sparking in her eyes. "We've come too far to back down now. This is our moment. We can't let fear dictate our actions." That night, we continued preparing. We gathered clothes that would blend in; simple black outfits that would work for the bar staff. We used the time to rehearse our cover stories—who would be who, how we would communicate discreetly, and escape routes if things went sideways. As I laid in bed later that night, doubts crept into my mind. What if we were caught? What if Dom was already onto us? Would we be risking everything for fleeting intel? But like before, a determination washed over me—a reminder that I wasn't just a boy lost in his past anymore; I was a man reclaiming his future. With the dawn's first light breaking through the curtains, I steadied my breathing. Today was the day we would challenge the darkness head-on.

THE BLOOD PACT

Shadows of Loyalty

The morning arrived too quickly, sunlight stretching through the curtains and shattering the early shadows. I lay in bed, staring at the ceiling, thoughts racing with the weight of what awaited us. It was impossible to shake off the anxiety clinging to my skin, but I felt something else rising within—a fierce determination kindled from the depths of my being. I turned toward the kitchen seeing my mother, who sat with her notes spread wide, furrowing her brow in concentration. The lines of worry etched on her face stirred a protective instinct within me—a primal urge to shield her from the storms ahead. I get up and walked to the kitchen. "How are you holding up?" I asked, breaking the heavy silence.

She sighed, glancing up at me with tired eyes. "Just preparing for whatever might come, Ryan. We must stay sharp." The moment hung in the air, palpable with tension. I leaned closer, my voice low and steady. "You and Ruby are my priorities. I'll do whatever it takes to keep you both safe." My words hung between us, a promise made from the depths of my heart. Just then, Ruby entered the room, her presence a bright flicker of light in the dimness. She wore a fitted black outfit, one that accentuated her resolve. I could see the concern etched on her features as she caught the tail end of my conversation with my mother.

"Ryan are you okay?" she asked, stepping closer, her voice wrapped in genuine concern. "I know this is a lot to handle, and I just want you to know—I'm here for you no matter what."

The tenderness in her gaze ignited a warmth in my chest. "I appreciate that, Ruby. But right now, it's my job to protect you both. There's something inside me... something about being a Giovanetti that's stirring. I can feel it." The words tumbled out, raw and unfiltered. The legacy of my family—a lineage woven with strength, both a blessing and a burden—was awakening within me. I'd been hesitant to embrace it, but today felt like a turning point. "I have to lead us through this." Ruby squeezed my hand lightly, her hands warm and grounding. "I know you'll find that strength, Ryan. I believe in you. Just remember, we're in this together." As we prepared for our mission, the tension crackled in the air. I slipped into my own black attire, somehow feeling different in the fabric as if it were a second skin, one that allowed my concealed resolve to seep through. I stood in front of the mirror for a moment, examining not just my outward appearance, but the fire igniting inside me. It was a fire lit by love and the need to protect those closest to me.

On our way to the bar, the streets shifted beneath my feet, every familiar crack in the sidewalk now marked by the threat we were facing. The bar itself was unassuming—dimly lit, with a flickering neon sign that read "Open." The atmosphere, however, thrummed with an undercurrent of danger, a reminder of what awaited us within. We crossed the threshold into the bar, the cacophony of laughter and conversations swirling around us like a tempest. But beneath that veil, I sensed the predator lurking, ready to strike. My resolve hardened. Dom wasn't just a figure from my past; he was a threat to the family I cherished. Everything inside me screamed to act—to protect.

THE BLOOD PACT

"Stay sharp, and keep close," I instructed Ruby and my mother, my voice low but firm. "We need to focus on gathering intel without drawing attention to ourselves."

Ruby nodded, her eyes wide with concern but filled with a determination that mirrored my own. "I'm right here with you." The hours unfolded as we busied ourselves amidst the clinking of glasses and hushed conversations. The weight of each task felt heavier, infused with the urgency of our mission. Every movement was calculated, and as the minutes ticked by, my gaze drifted repeatedly toward the entrance, waiting for Dom to arrive. And then he walked in.

Dom stepped through the door, flanked by a group of men who exuded power and menace. His laughter rang like a distant echo, laced with malice. There he was—the father figure turned adversary, his presence palpable and suffocating. The shadows crept closer, but rather than fear, I felt a surge of resolve course through my veins.

"Yes, loyalty means everything in this game," he proclaimed, raising his glass in camaraderie with his associates. "And anyone who thinks otherwise pays the price."

Those words settled like stones in my stomach. My loyalty had shifted—weaving itself into something fierce and protective, anchored to the love of my mother and Ruby. I was no longer the boy Dom once mentored, naive and trusting; I was forged in fire and prepared for battle.

"Stay close," I whispered to Ruby, my voice taut with urgency. "We need to hear what they're saying."

As we continued to serve drinks, every laugh and whispered word from Dom amplified my determination. Deep inside me, the Giovannetti blood surged, I felt the raw power of my lineage awaken. A new sense of fearlessness emerged, one that commanded respect and fostered leadership. I was no longer just Ryan; I was a protector, a guardian, and I would fight for those I loved.

As Dom switched topics, discussing shady deals and power plays, I felt Ruby's hand brush against mine again, grounding me. "I'm right here, Ryan," she whispered, her eyes bright with unwavering belief.

"Together," I responded, feeling that spark ignite within me anew. With Ruby by my side, my mother to protect, I knew that together we could face whatever darkness lay ahead. The shadows of loyalty might surround us, but within that darkness, I would emerge as a leader—a force for love and truth.

With every exchange I heard from Dom, my purpose crystallized. The path would not be easy, but I was resolute. I would rise to protect my family, to honour my heritage, and to reclaim our lives from the manipulative grasp of betrayal. As the minutes dragged on, I kept my focus on Dom and his group, a mix of unease and determination swirling in my stomach. I moved through the bar, serving drinks while keeping my ears tuned to the simmering undercurrents of their conversation. Each laugh and volley of words was laced with implications I knew were far more insidious than the surface revealed.

"I've got us covered," Dom boasted, his voice rich with confidence. "The shipment will come in next week. We'll have the city wrapped around our little finger before anyone knows what hit them."

I exchanged a glance with Ruby; her eyes widened slightly, revealing the gravity of what we were hearing. Dom was plotting something much larger than just a simple meeting. The thought prickled at the back of my mind. I had to find out what this shipment entailed and how it linked back to the Giovanetti family. Ruby leaned closer to me, her voice barely above a whisper. "We need to get proof—some sort of documentation to expose him. This isn't just about protecting our-selves; it's about stopping whatever he plans to unleash."

THE BLOOD PACT

I nodded, the gears in my mind whirring with possibilities. "Right. If we can grab something tangible, we can turn the tide against him." With renewed purpose, I scanned my surroundings. The bar was a labyrinth of shadows and light, filled with patrons lost in their own worlds, unaware of the storm brewing beneath the surface. I could feel the heat of adrenaline coursing through my veins. Dom's operation was a web of deceit, and we needed to penetrate its heart.

"Let's split up," I suggested, lowering my voice as I turned to Ruby and my mother. "I'll keep watch on Dom. Ruby, you can help me manoeuvre around, and Mom, stay near the bar but keep an eye on the back-office area. If you see anything unusual, let us know."

My mother hesitated, her concern evident. "Be careful, Ryan. It's dangerous to confront him directly, especially if you're alone."

"I know," I replied, stepping closer to emphasize the seriousness of the moment. "But we need to gather information. We can't hesitate any longer. This is about more than just us now; this hits at the very core of who we are as a family."

With a reluctant nod, she agreed. I could see the courage flicker behind her uncertainty. We had faced so much together; this was just one more step in reclaiming our lives. As we split up, the weight of the task ahead began to press heavily on my shoulders. I kept my gaze firmly trained on Dom, his charismatic facade almost disarming as he made jokes and passed drinks to those around him. Yet beneath that surface lay a predator—a man willing to do anything to maintain his control. Moments passed, and I knew that we had to act fast. The bar felt alive yet hollow—a place where fear and loyalty danced on a knife's edge. I moved into position, careful to blend into the background, my heartbeat matching the rhythm of the music pulsing through the room.

Suddenly, a figure moved toward my mother, someone I recognized by posture alone. It was one of Dom's enforcers, a hulking man named Tony, whose reputation for brutality preceded him. My heart raced as I observed the closeness of his approach, knowing my mother was vulnerable.

"Mom, watch out!" I hissed under my breath, but the words just barely escaped before he reached her.

"What do you want?" she said firmly, holding her ground even though her voice trembled slightly.

"Dominic wants you to deliver this," Tony said gruffly, tossing a small envelope on the counter in front of her. "You better not mess it up. Or else." Tony not recognising my mother.

As he walked away with an air of menace, my mother's hands trembled slightly, a pale reminder of the danger we were in. I felt a surge of protectiveness and a wave of anger wash over me. How dare he threaten my family? At that moment, the shadows of loyalty swirled into something darker—an oath to stand resolutely against the chaos.I signalled Ruby discreetly, and we shifted closer, focusing on my mother. "What was in the envelope?" I asked, urgency creeping into my voice. She opened it cautiously, revealing a series of photographs—unflattering images capturing someone being exchanged behind closed doors. I leaned in closer to inspect them, my mind racing. These were images that could unravel Dom's operations, clues leading to something larger.

"Looks like a meeting of some kind," Ruby whispered, studying the photographs intently. "Maybe it's tied to that shipment he was talking about."

"Let's head to the back office," I suggested, feeling the pulse of adrenaline under my skin. "If we can find any files or more evidence, we can turn these over to the authorities."

THE BLOOD PACT

We moved stealthily toward the back of the bar, our hearts pounding in unison. Just as we passed through the doorway, a noise erupted behind us—a glass shattering followed by furious shouts. I turned to see Dom's mood shift, his laughter dissipating, replaced by a storm brewing in his eyes.

"Get the hell out of my way!" he bellowed, striking fear into everyone around him.

The atmosphere thickened with tension, and I felt my throat dry up. Dom was no longer the affable figure I'd once known; he was a hurricane ready to destroy anything in his path. We had to move fast.

"Now's our chance!" I urged, pushing through the door with Ruby and my mother close at my heels. We slipped into the office, the darkness enveloping us as we pulled the door shut behind us.

Inside, stacked files littered the desk, accompanied by a computer glowing faintly in the corner. My fingers shook with anticipation as I rifled through the documents, scanning for anything that could serve as evidence against Dom.

"This one seems promising," Ruby said, peeling through a folder marked with a red stamp: "**CONFIDENTIAL**." The words sent a chill down my spine. Whatever secrets lay within could unravel everything.

"Keep an eye on the door," I instructed my mother as I leaned closer to read. "If Dom finds us in here… we need to be ready."

As Ruby skimmed through the contents, my attention drifted to the closed drawers. Steeling myself, I pulled one open and found a notebook, filled with names, dates, and disturbing details. It felt like a treasure trove of information begging to be uncovered. Suddenly, a loud bang resonated from the bar, followed by frantic shouting. The noises sharpened, and I could hear Dom demanding answers, fury lacing his voice. The stakes were escalating, and time was slipping away.

"Go, go!" I urged, heart racing in sync with the chaos outside.

"Just a minute!" Ruby insisted, peeling one more file from the stack.

"Now!" I shouted, pushing urgency into my voice. The shadows outside whispered danger, and in that moment, I realized the true meaning of loyalty—protecting my family, standing up against Dom, and fighting for a future untainted by the blood of betrayal.

As Ruby finally gathered the last documents, we made our exit, stealing one last glance at the darkened office. The shadows no longer felt ominous; they felt like the fuel that would ignite our fight. We emerged back into the bar, adrenaline surging as we navigated through the crowd, desperately seeking the exit before Dom's wrath descended upon us. I could feel the shadows closing in behind us, but I held tightly to the resolve shaping within me. Together, we would face the shadows of loyalty, armed with evidence and the fire of our convictions. We would reclaim our lives and dismantle the empire built on fear and deceit. With the stolen documents clutched tightly in Ruby's hands, we began to weave our way through the maze of bodies crowding the bar. The atmosphere was thick with drinks, laughter, and an undercurrent of tension that electrified the air. Each heartbeat was a drumroll of impending danger, propelling us toward the exit.

Suddenly, the loud crash of a chair upending shattered the duplicitous calm. I turned instinctively, anxiety clawing at my insides as I spotted Dom standing near the bar, frustration etched across his features. He was still unaware that my mother was alive, but he caught enough of the commotion to realize something was off.

"Where are they?" Dom bellowed, his voice reverberating through the bar. He demanded answers from those around him, his tone leaving no room for defiance.

"Ryan!" Ruby whispered urgently, her eyes wide with panic. "We need to get out!"

THE BLOOD PACT

"Now!" I snapped. I couldn't afford to let him figure it out. My heart raced as I grabbed Ruby's arm, pulling her close as Dom began scanning the crowd, his gaze turning hostile and determined.

Before I could think, I glanced around for an alternate escape, my eyes darting to the small window above the sink—just large enough for someone to squeeze through. "Stay close to me," I whispered. "I'm going to create a diversion." As Dom advanced, I hurled a nearby bottle at the wall, the glass shattering in an explosion of shards and liquid, drawing attention away from us. The crash echoed, patrons jumping in surprise, which bought us a precious moment.

"Get out!" I urged Ruby, shoving her toward the window. "I'll keep him busy!"

"Ryan!" Ruby protested, fear lacing her voice.

"Just go!" I insisted, channelling every ounce of my resolve into my words. Her hesitation stirred something within me—my need to protect us fuelled my courage. I needed her to get to safety.

With barely a moment's thought, Ruby grabbed my mother and together they climbed onto the counter, their movements hurried but precise. "Come on, Judie!" Ruby urged, desperation leaking into her voice. "You can do it!" Just as Ruby and Judie slipped through the window, I felt the tension in the air shift. Tony, Dom's right-hand man, was shaping up to confront me. The weight of impending danger prickled my skin as I turned to face him.

"Where do you think you're going?" Tony sneered, stepping forward, his bulk blocking any chance of escape.

"Stay away from them!" I shouted, fists clenched, adrenaline coursing through my veins. This was my family. I wouldn't let him touch them.

Instead of running, I lunged at Tony, the fight that erupted between us instant and furious. The brawl was physical, each of us using every advantage to overpower the other. For every blow he landed, I retaliated with defiance, fuelled by the knowledge of what was at stake.

"Dom will tear you apart for this!" Tony growled, attempting to grapple me to the ground. I twisted away just in time, my heart pounding with urgency.

While I struggled with Tony, I could hear Dom's increasingly agitated voice revealing itself in the background. "How did they get in?" He was scanning the bar, frustration creeping into his tone, looking for anything that could explain how his targets had managed to infiltrate his territory unnoticed. I ducked under Tony's swing, countering with a quick jab to his ribs. "You can't protect him, Tony!" I panted. "You don't even know where we are!"

"Ryan!" Ruby's voice broke through the chaos as she called out from the other side of the window, anxiety rich in her tone. "Please!"

"I'm coming!" I replied, but I needed to deal with Tony first.

The bar was a whirlwind of noise and chaos, patrons beginning to realize the severity of the situation as they darted toward the exits. I could hear Ruby urging Judie away from danger, the two of them making their way down the alley, but I knew I couldn't let Tony keep me from them. With a surge of strength, I threw a punch that connected solidly with Tony's jaw, sending him staggering back. I seized the moment and dashed toward the window, but Tony recovered quickly, lunging to grab me.

"Not so fast!" he snarled, but I ducked beneath his grasp, bolting for the opening. Through the glass, I caught a glimpse of Ruby leading my mother down the alley, the two of them just about to disappear around the corner.

"Go!" I yelled at Ruby, my voice cutting through the chaos. "Now!"

THE BLOOD PACT

I scrambled to my feet in the alley just behind them. My heart raced as I caught sight of Ruby and Judie ahead, but I could still hear Tony and Dom's men shouting behind me.

"Ryan!" Ruby cried, looking back with wide eyes. "They're coming!"

"Go!" I urged, urgency fuelling my words. "We need to run!"

I caught up with them. Together, we dashed down the alley, Ruby leading the way. I could feel the adrenaline pumping through my veins, but the looming chase brought a hard edge of fear. "We can't let them find us," I panted, glancing back at the bar. The threat was still hot on our tail, but the knowledge that Dom didn't know about Judie was a small comfort during the chaos.

"We need to find somewhere to hide," I urged, scanning the area for any sign of safety amidst the shadows of the night.

"Leo's place is a few blocks away. He'll help us," Ruby suggested, determination igniting in her eyes.

"Let's go," I replied, guiding them forward, the darkness of the streets looming around us as we made our way to the only refuge we had left.

As we navigated the streets, the tension hung heavy in the air, my thoughts racing. The weight of the stolen documents burned in Ruby's hands, a stark reminder of the battle we were fighting. If we could just reach Leo and strategize our next move, we might have a chance.

"Mom, stay close," I instructed, positioning myself protectively between her and any potential danger. The flicker of streetlights illuminated our path, but I couldn't shake the feeling that the shadow of danger lurked just behind.

With every step, hope intertwined with fear—daring to believe the tangled web of our lives could still be unravelled, one strand at a time. Together, we would face the dangers that loomed ahead, thwarting Dom's plans while safeguarding that which mattered most: our family. We dashed through the dimly lit streets, my heart pounding loudly in my chest, each footfall echoing my urgency. Ruby led the way, her expression a mix of determination and panic, while I kept a watchful eye on my mother, who trailed just behind us.

"Over there!" Ruby exclaimed, pointing toward an old brick building nestled between two larger structures. Its faded façade blended into the night, but that unassuming exterior signalled our best chance for safety...

We sprinted toward the front door, and I knocked urgently, feeling the weight of the world pressing down on me as I heard footsteps approaching from the alley behind us. The door swung open, revealing Leo, his eyes widening in surprise at the sight of us.

"What the hell happened?" he asked, quickly pulling us inside and shutting the door just as the distant sounds of raised voices and footsteps grew louder.

"we are being chased," I gasped, glancing over my shoulder as I leaned against the door. "We need to hide."

"Inside!" Leo motioned for us to follow him into the narrow hallway, his expression shifting from shock to grave determination. "We can talk in the back room."

We hurried down the corridor, the shadows deepening as we moved further inside. The faint smell of stale coffee and old books filled the air, a familiar scent that briefly calmed my racing heart.

"Leo, this is my mom—Judie," I said, introducing her, my voice laced with urgency.

"Nice to meet you, Judie," Leo said, shooting a reassuring smile, though his eyes betrayed his worry. "Let's get out of sight. You can explain everything in a minute."

THE BLOOD PACT

He led us to a small room at the back, lined with bookshelves and soft lighting, yet it felt anything but safe. Leo closed the door behind us, and for a moment, we stood together, catching our breath.

"What the hell is going on?" Leo asked, his voice barely above a whisper, urgency lacing every word. I could see the worry etched on his face.

"It's a long story..." I started, but the pounding of my heart drowned out my thoughts. My instincts screamed at me to focus on the immediate danger.

"Ryan, where's Dom?" Ruby asked, her voice shaking slightly. "He didn't follow us, did he?"

"Not yet," I replied, glancing around the room and assessing our surroundings. "But he knows we're here. Ruby, informed Leo about some of the details, just enough for him to understand our predicament.

We need to fortify this place as much as we can until we figure out our next move." Leo nodded, quickly moving to close the curtains and check the window. "I'll see if I can get my radio working. Might be able to alert the local enforcement. Maybe they can hold him off, give us time."

"Leo, we can't trust anyone," I urged. "Dom has people everywhere. We need to handle this ourselves."

"Ryan's right," Ruby interjected. "If we can expose him, we might stand a chance."

"Expose him? Do you have proof?" Leo asked, a hint of hope breaking through his apprehension.

"Yeah," Ruby replied, holding up the documents she had taken. "It's all here—his dealings, his connections. But if we want to make this work, we need a plan and time."

As Leo worked quietly at a corner desk, fiddling with an old radio, I took a deep breath and looked around the room. I could feel the closeness of the situation, the breaths of my family intertwining with the threat just outside.

"Okay, let's come up with a plan," I said, my voice steadying as I embraced this moment of clarity. "Leo, can we get to your laptop? We might be able to send this to someone who can help us. Someone who isn't bound to Dom."

Leo nodded quickly. "Yeah, in the main room. But I don't know how much time we have before he sends people looking. You need to secure this room while I grab it."

"Got it," I replied, and my focus sharpened. "Ruby, stay with my mom. I'll keep watch."

As Ruby positioned herself next to Judie, I felt a rush of protectiveness wash over me. I stepped toward the door, pressing my ear against it, straining to hear any sounds that might indicate the impending threat.

"Do you think Dom will come here?" Judie asked softly, her voice trembling slightly.

"I don't know," I replied, trying to mask my own worry. "But we can't let him find us—or you."

A tense silence filled the room, our breaths nearly synchronized in shared concern. I glanced back at Ruby, whose brow was furrowed with determination. In that moment, I could feel the weight of this mission bearing down on us, pressing against my conscience with an intense urgency. Just as Leo stepped away from the desk, ready to move into the main room, the sudden sound of pounding footsteps reverberated outside. My heart dropped.

"Leo!" I hissed, urgency choking my words. "Back to the door!"

He turned and rushed to my side, Ruby instinctively moving closer to Judie, her protective instincts kicking in.

"What do we do?" Ruby whispered, panic edging her voice.

THE BLOOD PACT

"We hold the door," I said, adrenaline spiking as I prepared for whatever was to come. "If they come, we need to make sure they don't get in here."

Just then, we heard raised voices outside, the unmistakable sound of men shouting.

"Search everywhere! They can't have gone far!" One voice carried through, full of anger and determination.

Dom was coming.

I shared a quick glance with Ruby, her eyes wide and determined. We were out of time.

"We need to act," I said, taking a deep breath, my brain already working to devise a plan. "Leo, is there another way out? A back door or anything?"

He nodded quickly. "There's a fire escape at the back. We can slip out through there if things get bad."

"Then we prepare to use it," I said, gripping the doorknob tightly. "I'll hold them off while you all make your way out. But we need to make it quick."

"No way!" Ruby yelled, stepping forward firmly. "We're not leaving you behind again. We stick together, no matter what!"

"Ruby—" I started, but she cut me off.

"You're not getting rid of me that easily, Ryan. We face this as a team."

"Ryan, listen to her," Judie said, her voice steady. "You know how much is at stake. We need to protect each other."

I took a moment, wrestling with my instinct to protect them. But deep down, I knew they were right. We had all entered this mess together. There was no way I could abandon them, nor would I want to.

"Fine," I relented. "We stick together. But if it comes to a fight, I want you, Judie, and Ruby to retreat through the back. Just make sure you're safe."

Leo nodded, urgency etched into his features. "I'll lead the way. Just keep them occupied as long as you can." The pounding outside grew closer, and my resolve solidified further. The stakes were higher than ever, and I wouldn't let fear dictate our actions.

"Here they come" I whispered as I braced myself against the door, muscles tensing as I prepared for the confrontation that awaited us.

We were more than just targets now. We were a unit, facing the shadows that sought to engulf us. Together, we would either find a way out, or we'd fight back with everything we had

A Test of Trust

The muffled shouts outside sent adrenaline coursing through my veins as I stood at the door, my hand gripping the handle firmly. The tension in the room was palpable, thickening the air around us as we prepared for the impending confrontation.

"Get ready," I murmured, my eyes darting between Ruby, Judie, and Leo. "We don't know how many of them there are."

Ruby nodded, her expression fierce but her grip on my hand trembling slightly. "We can handle this together," she said, her voice steady. I found reassurance in her strength, but doubt crept in as I imagined the worst-case scenario.

"Just remember," I said, gathering my thoughts, "if they get in, we retreat to the fire escape. Do not hesitate to run."

I could see Leo bracing himself behind us, ready to help block the door or stand in the way of whatever threat loomed outside. The sounds intensified, the footsteps drawing nearer, and with each moment, my heart hammered louder in my chest.

"Hey, Dom!" I shouted through the door, my voice cutting through the chaos. "You want to talk? Let's settle this like men!"

A brief silence fell over the crowd outside, and I could hear someone shifting. The door rattled slightly as they pushed against it.

"Roy," Dom's voice came back, smooth yet edged with menace. "You just can't stay away from trouble, can you? You think you can escape me? You brought this on yourself."

I felt Ruby's hand squeeze mine tighter as she readied herself for what was to come. "This isn't just about us," I called back, trying to buy some time. "You involved my family. You have no idea what you're getting into." There was a pause before Dom's next words slithered through the door. "I know exactly what I'm getting into. It's you who doesn't understand the game you're playing. It's too late to turn back now."

"Is this a game to you?" I yelled, my voice rising in frustration. "Because it's my life! And I've lost enough already!"

A dark chuckle echoed back, sending chills down my spine. "Life? We both know the only thing at stake here is loyalty. And yours is sorely misplaced."

"Loyalty?" I shouted incredulously. "You call terrorizing innocent people loyalty? That's not loyalty; that's tyranny."

Ruby shot me a worried glance, and I could see the fear in her eyes. I didn't know how long we could stall Dom or how many men he had outside. But I couldn't back down now. Not until I make sure my mother was, hidden from Dom's wrath.

"Enough of this," Dom called, his voice losing its calm façade. "You think you can just defy me? I'll show you what happens when you betray the family!"

The door shuddered violently as someone slammed into it from the outside, urgent thudding drowning out my thoughts.

"Leo!" I urged, shifting my body to block the door further. "We can't let them in!"

The door bucked again, and the hinges creaked ominously. I could feel the wood splintering beneath the relentless force, panic bubbling within me. Behind me, Ruby and Judie exchanged worried glances, understanding the stakes all too well.

"I can hold this for just a bit longer," Leo said through gritted teeth, his face a mask of determination.

THE BLOOD PACT

My heart raced, fear and anger swirling within me. "Dom, you're making a big mistake!"

"Am I?" he spat, eyes narrowing. "You've made all the mistakes, Roy. I gave you a chance. You didn't want it, so now... you'll pay for the consequences."

Just then, the door frame splintered, and I readied myself to push back, but I heard an unfamiliar noise—an engine revving. The moment shifted as a car screeched to a halt outside. The sound of doors slamming followed, and I could hear footsteps running toward us.

"Take cover!" I shouted, and we all ducked, instinctively huddling together in the corner of the room.

Dom's voice rose again, impatient and furious. "What now?" he demanded, clearly rattled. "Where did backup come from?"

"Ryan!" Ruby whispered urgently, and I caught her eye, realizing this was our chance to act. "What do we do?"

I kept my gaze fixed on the door, fighting the temptation to panic. "If they're here to contend with Dom, we need to be ready—" Before I could finish, the door burst open, slamming against the wall...

"Ryan! Get down!" Leo shouted, immediately grabbing my mother and Ruby and motioning toward the fire escape.

"Go! Get out of here!" he urged, pulling both toward the window.

But before they could exit, Ruby pulled back, her eyes wide as she registered the chaos unfolding. "No! I'm not leaving you!"

"Ruby!" I protested, desperation creeping into my voice. "You need to go with them! It's not safe here!"

"I won't leave you, Ryan!" she insisted, her voice filled with determination.

Leo's expression shifted, knowing the urgency of the moment. "You have to trust me!" he shouted. "Go now!" In a split second, Leo and my mother made their escape through the fire escape, moving undetected into the darkness of the alley below. I felt panic rise in my chest as I watched them disappear, but I knew they had to get away from Dom. The newcomers burst in with Dom on the forefront still hesitant, glancing between us and Dom, clearly unsure of their allegiance. With his back turned to me, I whispered urgently to Ruby, "We have to get out of here!"

"Not without you!" she replied fiercely, as if she could stand her ground against the chaos.

"Ruby, please," I pleaded, keeping my eyes on Dom's back, desperate for an opportunity. "If we stay, we'll both be trapped. Trust me!"

The tension in the room reached a boiling point as Dom's attention snapped back to us. He glared, his eyes narrowing dangerously. "You think you can defy me, Roy? You think you can just run away?"

"Dom, you don't own my life!" I shouted, trying to keep my voice steady despite the fear coiling in my stomach.

"This is my story, Roy," he replied, his voice low and cold. "And I'm not finished yet."

In that moment, as the darkness closed in around us and the stakes grew higher, I realized we had reached a point of no return. Trust would be put to the ultimate test, and we were on the verge of a battle that could change everything.

"Get ready" I whispered, adrenaline surging through me. "If it comes to a fight, we hold together"

"Keep your eyes on Dom" Ruby urged, voice firm. "We can't let him distract us"

THE BLOOD PACT

. "Where are they, Roy?" Dom demanded, stepping closer, each word dripping with menace. "I could hear four voices before I entered this room. You think you can shield them from me?"

"I don't know what you're talking about," I shot back defiantly, though my heart raced with the knowledge that my mother and Leo were safe for the moment; their presence gone like a whisper into the night.

Dom's eyes narrowed, anger flashing across his face, but I saw something else lurking beneath his bravado—a flicker of uncertainty. He was unravelling, and if I could hold his attention just a little longer, we might both have a chance to escape this nightmare.

"You think you can intimidate me? You think I haven't seen how you operate?" I pressed, my pulse quickening as I watched him weigh my words. "You're just another thug, hiding behind a mask of power."

His jaw clenched, fingers twitching as if he were resisting the urge to strike. "You think you're clever, don't you? You think your little games are going to protect you?"

"Protect me? No," I retorted, raising my chin defiantly. "But I'd rather stand here and speak the truth than live in the shadows of your reign. People talk about you, Dom. They know you're nothing but a coward who hides behind violence."

His face twisted in rage, and I could see the flicker of doubt in his eyes shift to fury. "You have no idea what lies ahead of you. You're so far past the point of no return."

"Maybe so, but I won't go quietly. I'll make sure everyone knows the truth about you. You think you can control me? You're mistaken. I'm not afraid of you anymore," I declared, feeling the spark of defiance rising within me.

Just then, a loud clatter erupted from outside, drawing his attention. My heart pounded in my chest as I glanced at Ruby, who stood beside me, seemingly just as taken aback by the commotion.

"Dom, they're coming!" one of his men shouted, stumbling through the door and clearly shaken.

"Who? Who's coming?" Dom's eyes gleamed with a furious edge as he spun toward the man, momentarily distracted from our confrontation.

"The cops! We need to move!" the man urged, urgency lacing his voice. "They're right outside!"

The tension shifted like a tide as Dom's face twisted with rage. "This isn't over, Roy. You'll pay for this," he spat, backing away slightly and throwing a glance toward the door.

In that flashing moment of chaos, I saw our chance slip past us. "Now, Ruby, let's go!" I shouted, sensing the urgency swelling around us as I grabbed her hand and pulled her toward the exit. With Dom still preoccupied by the sudden turn of events, we hurried toward the back staircase. I could hear the commotion of footsteps merging with the city night air as adrenaline surged through my veins.

"Where's your mom and Leo?" Ruby asked, keeping pace with me, her voice laced with growing urgency.

"They're safe! They got out the fire escape!" I replied, though I wasn't entirely sure if that was true. The thought invigorated me, pushing us to move faster. "We have to trust they've made it."

Despite my words, I felt a knot of fear twist in my stomach. If Dom caught a whiff of their presence—if he figured it out before it was too late—he could hunt them down. I couldn't let that happen. We reached the bottom of the staircase, bursting into the cool night air just as the sounds of chaos intensified behind us. I could see the flashing lights of police cars illuminating the street, flickering like beacons of hope against the darkness.

"We need to get out of sight," Ruby muttered, scanning the street for any possible escape routes. "Where could we go?"

THE BLOOD PACT

"Allies," I said, practically breathless as we moved cautiously toward a nearby alley. "We need to find someone who can help us before Dom realizes what's happening."

"Right," Ruby nodded, grateful for the steady presence during the overwhelming chaos. "We can't let him corner us, and we definitely can't let him know we're looking for backup."

We ducked into the alley, shadows pooling around us as we pressed against the brick walls, our breaths coming fast and shallow. The sirens wailed nearby, and the tension outside was palpable—a growing storm on the horizon.

"How did everything go so wrong?" Ruby asked, her voice barely above a whisper. "I thought you could reason with him."

"Me too," I admitted, surveyed the alleyway dotted with flickering neon lights from nearby businesses. "But Dom doesn't work from logic. He works from fear, and we've just kicked over a hornet's nest."

"We have to regroup," Ruby said, her expression resolute. "We need to figure out our next move."

Just then, I heard another shout from down the street. "Dom! They're getting away this way!" My heart dropped as the realization hit me—they weren't just coming for Dom; they were coming for us too.

"Let's move!" I urged, taking Ruby's arm and leading her deeper into the alley, adrenaline coursing through my veins as we pressed onward.

Each step echoed the urgency within me, and I remained focused on finding our way to safety. I was determined to find Leo and my mother again, and we would stop Dom and his empire of fear once and for all. As we made our way through the maze of alleys, I silently vowed that I would no longer be a pawn in Dom's game. I would fight—not just for my freedom, but for the truth, for my family, and for every life he had destroyed. Tonight, had changed everything, and as we vanished into the shadows, I knew it was only the beginning. We navigated through the labyrinth of alleys, the distant shouts and blaring sirens echoing around us. The city was alive with chaos, but it was a cover—a boon in our desperate escape. Each turn we took felt like a step closer to safety, and yet each corner held the lurking spectre of Dom's anger, his men, and the police.

"Where do we go from here?" Ruby asked, glancing back at the street as we stopped momentarily. Her eyes were filled with a mixture of determination and fear.

"There's a bar down the road owned by an old friend of mine, Jake," I replied, trying to recall the route in my mind. "He's reliable and knows how to handle situations like this. If anyone has the resources, it's him."

"Is he going to help or sell us out?" Ruby pressed, her tone sceptical but understanding.

"Jake's a good guy. He won't turn us in—not after everything we've been through. Plus, he owes me a favour," I assured her, though I felt a pinch of doubt creeping in. In this life, allegiances could shift in a heartbeat, but I had to trust my instincts.

"Let's hope you're right," Ruby said, her eyes darting around as we moved forward again. "We can't afford to take any more risks."

We picked up the pace, moving deeper into the shadows of the alleyways. The chill in the air wrapped around us, a stark contrast to the heat of our racing hearts. I could hear pursuit growing closer, footsteps and panicked whispers blending into a dissonant symphony. I led Ruby to a narrow pedestrian passage that opened to the main street. From there, we could see the flickering neon sign of the bar, its inviting glow a stark contrast to the turmoil we had fled. I took a deep breath, scanning for any signs of danger. As we crossed the street, a surge of adrenaline coursed through me. We couldn't afford to hesitate—it was a race against time. We reached the bar's entrance, the heavy door creaking ominously as I pushed it open.

THE BLOOD PACT

The dimly lit room was filled with the murmur of conversations and the clinking of glasses, a welcome escape from the chaos outside. I quickly spotted Jake behind the bar, pouring drinks with his back turned. He was a burly man with a kind face, but in this world, kindness could be as fleeting as a shadow. I approached him, urgency lacing my voice. "Jake! We need your help—now." He turned, his brow furrowing as he took in my dishevelled appearance. "Ryan? What the hell happened?" His gaze shifted to Ruby, and I knew he could sense the tension in the air.

"Dom's coming for us. We need to lay low, at least until this blow over," I explained quickly, my heart pounding as I saw the flicker of recognition in his eyes.

"Dom? Has it really come to this?" Jake muttered, glancing around the bar as if the walls could listen. "I've always told you to stay out of that mess. But alright, you're in here now, you've got my protection."

"Thanks, man," I said, relief washing over me, though my mind still raced with thoughts of my mother and Leo. We needed to regroup, to plan.

"Here, this way," Jake said, leading us through a back door that led to a small storage room. He slid a box aside, revealing a hidden passageway. "This will lead you to the cellar. From there, you can slip out the back without anyone seeing you."

"Isn't that risky?" Ruby asked, glancing around nervously.

"Better than the alternative," Jake replied, his voice steady. "You think Dom won't send men in here looking for you? You've got to keep moving."

I nodded, accepting that this was our best shot. "Thank you, truly. We owe you."

"I don't need anything from you, but just make sure to stay safe," Jake replied, his eyes firm. "And you tell that bastard, I'm not afraid of him."

I gave him a grateful nod and stepped into the hidden passageway with Ruby close behind. The air grew colder as we moved through the narrow corridor, the sounds of the bar dimming behind us. As we emerged in the cellar, the atmosphere shifted again—this was a realm of shadows intertwined with the faint scent of aged wood and whispered secrets. We covered the distance in hurried steps, my mind racing with thoughts of finding my family. "We can't stay here long, Ruby. Once Dom realizes we're gone, he'll come looking—" Before I could finish my thought, a loud crash interrupted us from the main bar area above. My heart leapt into my throat.

"They're here," I whispered, panic rising.

We hurried toward the far wall, finding the back exit in plain sight. Pushing it open, we were greeted by the cool night air, but there wasn't time to revel in our escape.

"Which way?" Ruby panted, glancing around in confusion.

"Left! We need to find transport out of here," I urged, leading her into the alley beside the bar.

As we emerged back onto the street, I spotted a bus stop a few blocks away—our chance to blend in with the late-night crowd. I could hear shouting in the distance, men's voices rising sharply, and I felt the urgency intensify in my veins. We sprinted toward the stop, weaving through groups of people oblivious to the danger lurking behind us. My mind was racing with thoughts of my mother—would she be safe? Had Leo managed to stay clear of Dom?

But I couldn't dwell on those fears now. We had to keep moving, stay one step ahead. As we reached the stop, I glanced back, my stomach churning. "Keep your head down," I instructed Ruby, trying to keep my voice steady despite the rising panic. The bus arrived just as I spotted shadowy forms emerging from the alley behind us. My heart sank as I saw the unmistakable figures of Dom's men, their eyes scanning the crowd with predatory intent.

THE BLOOD PACT

"Now! Get on!" I urged, and we jumped onto the bus just as the doors swung shut behind us.

The vehicle lurched forward, and I risked a glance back at the figures fading into the distance, a wave of relief washing over me that quickly settled into a deeper anxiety. We were not safe yet.

"We need to find a way to contact my mom and Leo," I said, determination hardening in my voice. "We can't let Dom get to them."

"Agreed," Ruby replied, her eyes locking onto mine with an intensity that fuelled my resolve. "But we need to lay low for a while. We must figure out a plan, and fast."

With the bus rumbling beneath us, I leaned back in my seat, closing my eyes for a moment. I could still hear the chaos of the night echoed in my ears, but beneath it all, a fierce determination stirred within me. This wasn't over. Not by a long shot. We had escaped one battle, but the war was far from won. And I would do whatever it took to protect my family and take down Dom once and for all.

Breaking Point

The bus rumbled onward into the dark night, the city lights flickering past in a blur. I sat beside Ruby, the tension in the air thickening as myriad thoughts collided in my mind. Our escape was only temporary, and the question loomed like a shadow: how long until we were tracked down again?

"Where to now?" Ruby asked, her voice a mixture of exhaustion and adrenaline. "We can't stay on this bus forever."

"Let's head to my friend Mia's place. It's discreet and she knows how to keep a low profile." I needed to feel some semblance of control in this chaotic narrative that was spiralling around us.

Ruby nodded, clearly on edge but trusting my lead. I dug out my phone, my heart racing as I began scrolling through contacts. There was a mix of desperation and hope in my chest. Mia had always been reliable, but I needed to reach her before Dom's men caught wind of our whereabouts. As we approached a major intersection, I looked up from my phone, the muffled sounds of the bus fading into the background of my thoughts. The gravity of our situation pressed down on me. Dom was relentless—how long could I hold back the tides of his wrath? A thought struck me like lightning: what if he had already found my mom and Leo? It was a possibility I dreaded, but one I could no longer afford to ignore. My chest tightened, anxiety pooling in my stomach.

"Are you okay?" Ruby's voice cut through my spiralling thoughts, pulling my focus back.

"Yeah, yeah," I replied, but the uncertainty in my tone betrayed me. "Just... trying to figure out our next moves."

The bus slowed to a stop, and I could see the flickering neon sign of a diner—a landmark I knew was close to Mia's place. "This is our stop," I said, a wave of urgency washing over me. "We can walk from here." As we stepped off the bus, the cold air hit us, a stark reminder of the predicament we were in. We moved quickly down the street, sticking to the shadows, my heart pounding in time with my rapidly racing thoughts. Once we reached Mia's apartment complex, I knocked on the door with urgency, hoping against hope that she'd be home. I could almost hear the pounding of my heart in the silence that followed.

"Who is it?" came Mia's muffled voice through the door.

"It's me, Ryan! Let us in, please!"

A moment later, the door creaked open, and Mia peered out, her expression shifting from confusion to concern in an instant. "What happened? You look like you've seen a ghost."

"We've got trouble. Can we come in?" I pressed, my voice low but urgent as I ushered Ruby inside before Mia could respond.

As soon as we crossed the threshold, I closed the door behind us and let out a breath I hadn't realized I was holding. Mia's apartment was cluttered but inviting, familiar in a way that assaulted me with nostalgia but felt like a distant memory in the current context.

"What's going on?" Mia asked, her eyes darting between us.

"Dom's men are after us. We need a safe place to figure things out," I explained quickly, trying to condense the chaos of our situation into digestible pieces.

"What? Are you serious? How did you get mixed up with him?" She looked incredulous, her brow furrowed with concern.

THE BLOOD PACT

"Long story," I replied, running a hand through my hair, the weight of it all pressing down like a fog. "But right now, we need to phone my mom and Leo. I need to know they're safe."

Mia nodded, understanding flashing in her eyes. "I can help with that—but we need to stay quiet. If Dom has people looking for you, they might be tracking your phone." I grimaced. "Right. Can we use a landline or something? A burner phone?"

"Let me see what I can find," Mia said, her resolve firm as she led us deeper into the apartment.

I sank onto the couch, drumming my fingers against my knee, the anxiety coiling tighter and tighter within me. Ruby settled beside me, her expression a mask of concentration as she seemed to mirror my inner turmoil.

"Do you really think they're okay?" she asked, her voice barely above a whisper.

I turned to her, feeling the weight of my uncertainty. "I have to believe that they are," I replied, clenching my fists. "I can't let myself think otherwise." Mia returned moments later with a flip phone in her hand—a relic of the past, but perfect for our situation. "Here, it's untraceable. Dial your mom's number but keep your voice low."

I took the phone, my hand trembling slightly as I pressed the buttons. After a few rings, the familiar voice of my mother came through the line, and a wave of relief washed over me.

"Who is this?" she sounded worried, echoing my fears.

"Mom! It's me. Are you safe?" I asked, barely able to contain the urgency in my voice.

"Yes, we're fine. At least for now. We took the back roads after you left," she said, her voice momentarily calming the storm within me. "But we can't stay where we are. Dom's men are scouring the town."

"Hang tight. We're working on a plan, but you need to keep moving. Don't let anyone see you," I instructed, my palms sweaty with the gravity of the moment.

"I know what to do, sweetheart. Just be careful. I love you."

"I love you too," I replied, swallowing hard at the lump in my throat. I hung up, my heart pounding once more as fear clawed at my insides.

"We've got to figure this out," I said, turning to Ruby and Mia, who were waiting for the next move. "If Dom's men are out there... He'll try to draw us out."

"What do you mean?" Ruby asked, her eyes wide.

"He has everyone in his pocket—the police, the gangs—he'll find a way to make us come to him," I said, pacing the small living room, my mind racing. "He's ruthless; I've seen what he's capable of. We need to keep our heads low until we can get everyone out of the city."

Mia stepped closer, her expression grave. "But if Dom finds out where you've gone, he'll retaliate. He won't stop until he has you."

"Then we'll make sure he doesn't find out," I said, resolve hardening in my chest. "We go on the offensive. We can't let him dictate how this plays out anymore."

"Are you sure you want to confront him?" Ruby asked softly, uncertainty flickering in her gaze. "What if it goes wrong?"

I met her eyes, the gravity of my choices weighing heavily on me. "Staying hidden isn't going to help us, nor my mom and Leo. We must face him—I have to face him. This is the only way to protect them." Mia crossed her arms, her frown deepening. "If you're going to go after Dom, you'll need allies. People who know his game."

"I have a few contacts," I said, taking a deep breath. "But it'll take time, and we may have to go fast if we want to stay ahead of him."

"Then let's start now," Ruby urged, her voice gaining strength. "No more running. Let's take back control."

THE BLOOD PACT

As I looked at Ruby, a fierce determination ignited within me. We were at a crossroads, and the choices we made now would determine not just our fate, but those of everyone involved. The resolve to fight back surged through my veins, spurred by the fear of losing everything I held dear.

"Alright," I said, my voice steady with conviction. "We get in touch with my contacts, plan our next steps, and we make sure Dom knows we're not backing down. It's time to show him what we're made of."

In that moment, the small room filled with a sense of newfound purpose—a coalition forged in resilience and defiance. The fear that once cornered me shifted into a blaring beacon of determination, and I knew that whatever lay ahead, I would face it head-on.

Dom thought he had the upper hand, but he hadn't seen the tidal wave of change coming. Together, we would rise, and we would reclaim our freedom—not just for ourselves, but for everyone trapped in the crosshairs of his reign. The weight of resolve settled over us like a thick blanket, and I felt the adrenaline coursing through my veins as I gathered my thoughts. "Mia, do you still have connections with anyone in the underground? Someone who can help us?" Mia nodded, her expression grim. "I might know a couple of people. There's Marcus, a fixer in the area—if anyone has intel on Dom, it's him. He's slippery, though. You'll need to approach him with caution."

"Then let's track him down," I said, gripping my phone tightly as anticipation rippled through me. "Do you have his number?"

"Yeah, I can dig it up," Mia replied, moving toward her cluttered desk to sift through a stack of papers.

Ruby leaned closer, her brow furrowed with concern. "What's the plan once we find Marcus? We can't just waltz in there and hope he helps us."

"No, we can't," I agreed, my mind racing. "But he's a businessman; if we offer him something tantalizing—a favour, information about Dom—we might make him listen."

As Mia rummaged through her items, I could feel the energy shifting in the room. The stakes were rising, and I could almost sense Dom's ever-present shadow lurking just beyond our sight.

"Got it!" Mia exclaimed, pulling a faded business card from the mess on her desk. She handed it to me. "Here's his number. Just remember—he plays hardball, and he won't hesitate to back out if he senses weakness."

I took the card, weighing my options. "We must be smart about this. I'll make the call and see if he's willing to meet." Mia glanced at the clock on the wall, her expression troubled. "But you need to be quick. The longer you stay here, the more risks we take. Dom's men could trace you back to this location, especially if he gets wind of your movements."

"Right." I turned toward Ruby, determination flashing in my eyes. "Let's move, then. We can't waste any more time."

Ruby and I gathered our things with frenzied urgency, steeling ourselves for the next phase of our plan. We shouldn't have to live in fear anymore; we had a chance to fight back and regain control. Once we were ready, I stepped outside the apartment, the cool night air hitting me like a jolt. The streets were quieter than before, the distant sounds of late-night traffic and muffled conversations blending into a dim chorus of normalcy that felt almost foreign. As I dialled Marcus's number, I felt a rush of nerves, but there was also an undeniable sense of purpose. I needed to suppress my fear to protect those who mattered most. The phone rang several times, and I wondered if Marcus was even awake or if he was already in hiding. Finally, he answered, his voice laced with a casualness that belied the precarious world we inhabited. "Who is this?"

THE BLOOD PACT

"Marcus, it's Ryan," I answered, my heart pounding. "I need to talk. It's urgent."

"Ryan!" Well, well, well, this is a surprise. You've made quite the name for yourself." There was a knowing edge to his tone. "But urgency doesn't always warrant civility. Speak your piece."

"Look, I'm in a tight spot. Dom and his men are after me and I need intel on him—anything you've got," I replied, trying to keep my voice steady despite the tension coiling in my gut.

There was a pause, and I could almost hear the gears turning in Marcus's mind. "Dom, eh? I'll admit, he's not someone you want to be tangled with. What's in it for me?"

"I can get you information about one of his shipments. Something valuable," I negotiated, hoping to leverage any back channel I could muster.

"Interesting..." he mused, the boredom in his voice fading. "Where and when can we meet?"

"Can you make it to the old docks by midnight?"

"Midnight? You're pushing it, Ryan. But it'll be done. You better have something worthwhile," he said sharply before hanging up.

I stared at the phone for a moment, the echo of his words lingering in the air. "He agreed," I said, my voice somewhat incredulous. Ruby nodded, but there was a warning in her gaze. "Just be careful. Even if he seems interested, he could have his own agenda. We can't trust anyone—especially in a situation like this."

"I know," I said, steeling myself against the doubt. "But we need this. It could be our ticket out of this mess."

As we began walking towards the docks, the silence weighed heavily, our breaths mingling with the mist rising from the pavement. Ruby fell into step beside me, the glow of streetlights casting soft shadows on her face.

"Are you sure you want to go through with this?" she asked quietly, glancing at me from the corner of her eye. "What if it goes south?"

"I must. For my mom and Leo... I can't let Dom hurt them," I replied, shaking my head, more to convince myself than her. "I refuse to let him dictate our fates any longer."

We approached the docks, the water shimmering under the moonlight. The rhythmic sound of waves crashing against the pier was the only noise, a stark contrast to the chaos swirling in my mind. Just before the hour struck, we made our way to a weathered old crate where Marcus had agreed to meet. Darkness enveloped us, casting shadows that seemed to ripple with unspoken threats.

"Keep your guard up," Ruby whispered, scanning the area cautiously.

Moments passed like hours, the silence stretching uncomfortably. Just when I began to wonder if Marcus would stand us up, footsteps broke through the quiet, and a figure emerged from the shadows.

"Ryan," Marcus called, his sly smile barely visible in the dim light. "You made it. And I see you brought company."

"Marcus," I greeted, keeping my tone neutral. "Let's cut to the chase. What do you know about Dom's operations?"

Marcus leaned against the crate, inspecting us with a calculating eye. "I can tell you that he's more aggressive than usual. He's looking for something—or someone—and he's not playing nice. He's got his hands in deals that could shake the very foundation of this town."

"Is he tracking my family?" I pressed, a surge of fear threatening to overwhelm me.

"Perhaps," Marcus said slowly, drawing out his words. "But I see you have something to offer, don't you? That valuable information you hinted at?"

THE BLOOD PACT

I swallowed hard, the gravity of our deal pressing down on my shoulders. "If I tell you what I know, you need to promise to give me something solid in return." He raised an eyebrow, intrigued. "Go on."

"Dom has a shipment coming in next week—a large cache of contraband and arms. If I give you specifics, you need to leverage that to help keep my family and Ruby protected. I need a guarantee."

Marcus regarded me with a coy grin. "You're learning fast, kid. But remember, in this world, trust is a rarity."

"I'm aware," I shot back, frustration bubbling beneath the surface. "But I'm willing to risk it for the people I care about."

"Fair enough," he replied, a glimmer of respect in his eyes. "I'll set up a distraction for you—a way to get your people out of town without Dom realizing. But it comes at a price."

I nodded, the stakes already set in motion. "What do you want?"

"Just a favour down the line—a little information here and there," he said, his smile widening unsettlingly. "Consider it an investment in future alliances. You'll owe me, and one day, I'll come knocking on your door."

"Fine," I replied, shaking his hand with a sense of finality, despite the lingering unease pooling in my stomach. "What's done is done."

Marcus pulled out a small notebook and began jotting down details. "I'll need specifics about the shipment, and then I'll make my move. You can take care of the rest. Just remember, Ryan—this city has eyes everywhere. Keep your head low." With that, he passed the notebook over to me. My heart raced as I reviewed the numbers and locations. It was risky territory, but I had to grip the reins of my fate firmly. I glanced at Ruby, who was observing quietly, and I felt an essential camaraderie strengthen between us. We moved forward, and as we turned to leave, I paused at the edge of the dock and glanced back at Marcus. "If you double-cross us, I promise you'll regret it." He chuckled softly, unfazed. "Now that's the spirit, kid. Just remember—this is a game, and only the sharpest players survive."

With that ominous reminder hanging in the air like an unseen storm, Ruby and I walked away, a world of uncertainty stretching before us. I had made a dangerous deal, but one thing was clear: it was time to confront Dom. Action was the only way forward, and I was done running. As the night deepened around us, I felt the weight of my choices bearing down heavily. The next steps we took could change everything. There would be no turning back. But I was ready to fight back. The time for hesitation was over. As Ruby and I stepped away from the docks, the sounds of the water lapping against the old pier faded behind us, replaced by the pounding of my own heart. The reality of what lay ahead threatened to drown me in fear, but the adrenaline of the night infused me with a sense of urgency.

"Did you get everything from Marcus?" Ruby asked, her tone steady, but I could see a flicker of anxiety in her eyes.

"Yeah, but it's going to be risky," I replied, glancing down at the notebook with Marcus's scrawled notes, full of details about Dom's operations. According to Marcus, Dom had a convoy of trucks coming in at a little past midnight tomorrow—a large quantity of narcotics. This was the information we needed to potentially leverage against him.

"We have to plan our next steps," I muttered, walking faster, the shadows of the alley nearly swallowing us. We headed toward Mia's apartment, which felt like our only sanctuary now, wanting to brainstorm before daybreak brought any additional complications.

Entering the apartment felt strangely comforting, the clutter surrounding us like an old friend. Mia looked up from her laptop as we stepped inside, her expression shifting once she saw the urgency etched across our faces.

"Did you find Marcus?" she asked, her brow knitting tightly.

"Yeah, we did," I replied, tossing the notebook onto the table. "He gave us intel about Dom's operations. We need to act fast. There's a convoy coming in tomorrow night."

THE BLOOD PACT

Mia picked up the notebook, flipping through the pages as she focused intently on the details. "This is big. If we can intercept that convoy, it could set us up to not only negotiate with Dom but also to throw him off balance."

"What do you mean by 'negotiate'?" Ruby interjected, her voice edged with concern. "What if he retaliates?"

"Look, we need leverage," I said, raising my voice slightly. "We can't just hide forever. If Dom feels cornered, he may become even more dangerous. This might be our one shot to hit back and create a distraction large enough for my mom and Leo to get out."

Mia nodded thoughtfully, absorbed in the implications of the plan. "We should be cautious. We need to gather a few more resources to ensure we're equipped to face him. I can tap into some contacts I have; they might know about any local movements or even have some intel on additional routes Dom might use."

"That sounds good," I replied, feeling a boost of hope. "Ruby, can you help us brainstorm on how to set up that distraction? You know how crowds react. Maybe we could create a scene that draws attention away from where we're waiting."

"Sure, I can come up with something," Ruby said, though a hint of doubt lingered in her voice. "But just to be clear, I've never dealt with anything like this before. I'll support you however I can, but I'm not as prepared for this kind of confrontation."

"That's okay," I assured her. "We all have our strengths. You're here to provide support, and your instincts—your insight—are invaluable. We're better together."

With a tentative smile, Ruby nodded. Our resolve strengthened, we articulated our ideas and constructed a plan that could leverage both the new intel from Marcus and the strengths we each brought to the table. As the hours flew by, we busied ourselves with logistics and communications. I managed to get Marcus on the phone again, updating him about our plans to intercept the convoy. He seemed intrigued and surprisingly pleased.

"I'll ensure everything goes according to plan," Marcus said. "Dom will not know what hit him. But remember, he has eyes everywhere. Stay sharp, and don't underestimate his ability to retaliate."

After the call, I sighed, running a hand through my hair. The weight of the looming confrontation felt heavier than before, but the allotment of tasks gave me a sense of control. The day dragged on as we made our final preparations. Ruby and Mia operated like a finely tuned machine, reaching out to different contacts and gathering the supplies we'd need for the operation. As the sun dipped lower, casting long shadows across the city, I couldn't shake the mix of anxiety and urgency stirring within me. This was the moment we had been waiting for, a chance to stand against Dom instead of running from him. When night finally fell, we gathered again, an air of palpable tension hanging between us. We shared our plans over a hasty dinner, excitement mingling with nerves.

"Okay," I said, breaking the silence as I placed the notebook in front of us. "When we get to the docks, we need to position ourselves strategically to intercept the convoy. Mia, how many contacts did you manage to line up?"

"Three solid ones—each of them has their own skill set," Mia replied, leaning closer to the notebook as she traced her finger over the details. "They're not all combatants, but they can assist in monitoring the perimeter and providing backup when we need it."

THE BLOOD PACT

"Good. Let's make sure they understand the plan," I nodded, my determination igniting as we prepared for the inevitable confrontation.

Ruby's eyes sparkled with a mixture of admiration and distraction. "I may not have experience in the underground, but I know our city. I can help us with general crowd control and distractions. I'll ensure we won't be on Dom's radar until it's too late."

"Just stick to the plan, and we'll be fine," I assured, feeling a swell of gratitude for Ruby's support. "Trust in each other. We know what we're up against."

As we finished our preparations, the minutes wore on slowly, each one taunting us with the possibility of failure. I glanced at the clock repeatedly, my heart hammering with anticipation. Finally, the time arrived. As we left the apartment and stepped into the cool night air, I instantly felt the weight of commitment upon my shoulders. Whatever awaited us, it was time to face it head-on. As we arrived at the docks, the moon hung high, casting the world in a silvery glow. The docks appeared eerily quiet, but the tension crackling in the air intensified as we neared the loading area. Mia pointed out our allies, who were already in position. "They're ready," she whispered, her eyes scanning the shadows.

"Good," I replied, positioning myself beside Ruby and Mia. "Once the trucks arrive, we'll execute the distraction. Ruby, I need you to be the one to trigger it."

"Got it," she replied, determination shining through her nerves.

The sounds of rumbling engines echoed through the night. A convoy of trucks appeared in the distance, headlights cutting through the darkness, drawing closer to our position. The moment had arrived.

"Now," I whispered, adrenaline hitting its peak.

As the trucks rolled to a stop, Ruby executed her plan. A series of loud fireworks erupted near the far end of the docks—a distraction meant to draw attention and divert the guards. The moment chaos ensued, the men began shouting, rushing toward the noise. We seized our opportunity, moving swiftly between the crates and shrouded in shadows, the element of surprise favouring us.

"Quick! We need to intercept before they regroup!" I urged, barking orders to my allies as we split into two teams.

With every ounce of my strength, I propelled myself forward, heart racing with the knowledge that we could finally strike back against Dom. We had come to reclaim our lives, to shatter the fear that had haunted us for far too long. Chaos erupted as Ruby's fireworks lit up the night sky, sending vibrant colours cascading over the docks. Guards scrambled, drawn away from their posts, and I took a moment to breathe as the adrenaline surged through me. This was our chance, but just as I was about to move, my phone buzzed violently in my pocket. I pulled it out, glancing at the screen. It was Leo.

"Leo?" I answered, half-shouting over the noise of the commotion.

"Hey! We've been trying to reach you. Where are you?" His voice was urgent, the sound of static crackling in the background.

"We're at the docks!" I replied. "What's going on? Is everything okay?"

"Not really. Judie and I want to join you. She's been talking about this moment for a while," Leo said, his voice nearly drowned out by the background noise. "She thinks it's finally time Dom finds out she's alive. She's ready to confront him, and she wants to help you take him down."

My breath caught. The implications of my mother's decision flooded my mind, a mix of excitement and fear thrumming through me. "Is she sure? This could get dangerous!"

THE BLOOD PACT

"She's more than sure," Leo reassured. "She believes that if we don't act now, we're giving Dom the upper hand again. She's been protecting you from the shadows, but she wants to fight alongside you. We're heading to the docks now. Just let us know where to meet."

"Okay, stay on the main road. We'll guide you in." I glanced around at Ruby and Mia, who were both tuning in to my side of the conversation. "I'll keep talking to you while we prepare here."

"Okay. Just be careful," Leo warned, and the call ended abruptly.

I turned to Ruby and Mia, who looked at me with wide eyes. "That was Leo," I explained, my voice steady despite the chaos swirling around us. "He and my mom want to join us. She's finally ready to confront Dom herself, now that we're about to make a move."

"Wow," Ruby breathed. "That's brave—dangerous, but brave. Do you think they'll be able to handle it?"

"I must believe they can. She's been laying low for too long, but this might be an opportunity to turn the tide." My heart raced at the thought of seeing my mother again, full of potential but tangled with the fear of Dom's retribution.

"Let's ensure they have a safe route to us," Mia suggested, her brow furrowed with concentration. "If they come in and get caught in the crossfire, it'll be disastrous. We need to create a larger distraction to cover their arrival."

"Right, right," I said, scanning the docks for an opportunity. "Ruby, can you help redirect attention? We might need something else to draw their focus."

"I can set off more fireworks," she said, clearly revved up by the chaos. "But I could also create a scene near that storage shed... something that looks bigger than it is."

"Do it," I urged. "Mia and I will keep an eye out for Leo and my mom. We need to know when they arrive so we can get ready for Dom's response."

Moments passed as Ruby darted toward the area she identified, her movements quick and focused. I turned back to my phone, the distinct sound of Leo's voice cutting through the chaotic atmosphere.

"Okay, we're nearing the docks now. Where do we go once, we arrive?" Leo's voice remained calm despite the urgency of the situation.

"Follow the road until you see a pair of red lights—those are our signal. Once you get close, we'll guide you in," I instructed. "Keep your eyes peeled. If you see anything suspicious or if Dom's men are nearby, don't engage. Just find a way to circle around until you hear from us."

"Understood," Leo replied, the line breaking up slightly. I could feel my heart racing; his willingness to join us could change everything.

"I just hope your mom knows what she's getting into," Mia said quietly, her gaze shifting to where Ruby was setting more fireworks. "This could be bigger than any of us anticipated."

"I know," I sighed, feeling the weight of uncertainty settle on my shoulders. "But Dom thought he could erase her. If she's willing to come back, we need to get in the right mindset to match that courage."

Just then, Ruby set off another series of fireworks, the explosive pops echoing through the air and filling the night with a cacophony of colour. I heard shouts from the guards again, voices raised in confusion and alarm.

"There it is! They're distracted," I said, glancing back at Ruby, who was grinning from the thrill. "Let's rally. Mia, keep an eye on the perimeter. I'll handle the front while we wait for Leo and my mom."

THE BLOOD PACT

Minutes felt like hours as the excitement of the night swirled around, and tension built among our group. I kept my phone close, staring into the dark expanse ahead while measuring each frantic heartbeat. Then, as if the universe had conspired to align our fates, I spotted Leo's car reflecting off the moonlight.

"There they are!" I shouted, feeling a rush of relief wash over me. "Everyone keeps your eyes open! We've got company!"

Leo parked quickly but cautiously, peering out into the darkness for signs of danger. I waved him in, gesturing for them to come toward us. As he and my mother stepped out, I felt a mix of joy and dread.

"Mom!" I yelled, rushing toward her as she emerged from the car.

She looked just as I remembered, strong and defiant, yet wearied by her time spent in hiding. "I'm not hiding anymore, sweetheart," she said, her eyes flashing with determination. "It's time Dom knows the truth."

"Mama, you shouldn't be here!" I exclaimed, echoing both relief and concern over her decision. "It's too dangerous!"

"No more running. Dom needs to understand that I'm back for good. We're stronger together," she said, her voice steady but laced with the undertones of anxiety.

"As long as we execute the plan, we'll minimize the risks," I reassured her, my heart swelling with pride.

Mia quickly stepped forward to introduce herself, her eyes wide with a mix of admiration and wariness. "I'm Mia. We're ready to move, but we need to be quick. The longer we stand here, the more risk we invite."

"Let's get into position," Leo said, urgency seeping into his voice as he glanced over his shoulder.

As we repositioned ourselves, I felt the weight of my family and friends beside me, standing together against the looming shadow that was Dom. The alignment of our spirits filled me with courage, a fierce conviction that we wouldn't be crushed by fear any longer. Steeling ourselves, we prepared for what lay ahead. Wherever the next moments would take us, we were no longer victims bound by the chains of the past. We were a united front ready to reclaim our lives and confront the monster that had haunted us for too long. With a heart full of hope, I took my place among them, ready to face the darkness together. The air crackled with tension as we regrouped. I could feel my muscles taut with anticipation as shadows shifted in the darkness, giving life to the fears lingering in my mind. We found our positions near the loading dock, hidden behind stacks of crates, our hearts pounding in rhythm with the distant sound of engines approaching.

"Everyone ready?" I whispered, scanning the faces around me. My mother, nodded resolutely, her eyes fixed on the approaching trucks.

"Stay close, and stay calm," I urged, hand resting on the aluminium box of tools and defence equipment we'd prepared. "Remember the plan."

The rumble of wheels grew louder. My palms felt clammy, but I steadied my breath, pushing aside the anxiety in favour of focus. I could see the faint outlines of men moving about, the unmistakable silhouettes of Dom's crew stepping forward to unload their cargo.

"There they are," Mia whispered, urgency threading through her voice. "We need to act fast."

As the trucks came to a halt, I caught sight of Dom stepping out, a figure cloaked in confidence, the very essence of intimidation. His presence radiated power, yet I felt something else mingling in the air—an unsettled energy that something monumental was about to unfold.

THE BLOOD PACT

"Now," I instructed, my voice a low growl as I gestured for Ruby to initiate her distraction.

With a swift motion, she set off a final, massive display of fireworks. The bursts lit up the night sky, blinding and stunning everyone for a moment—a perfect opportunity for us to make our move.

"Let's go!" I yelled, leading the way as we bulked forward, hearts pounding in unison.

Dom turned, startled, his crew caught off guard by the vibrant chaos erupting around them. I locked eyes with him, a fierce energy rising within me.

"Dom!" I shouted, stepping forward with purpose. "We know what you've been doing, and it's time this end!"

His eyes narrowed, and a smirk crept across his face, though his gaze flickered with uncertainty. "You think you can take me down now? You don't know who you're dealing with." Just then, from behind me, I felt a presence that made my heart leap and falter—my mother, Judie, stepping forward, her voice steady as she sliced through the tension.

"You're right, Dom. They don't know. But I do."

His eyes widened as if he couldn't quite believe what he was seeing. A rush of disbelief blended with recognition danced across his features.

"Judie? I thought you were dead!"

The air hung thick with disbelief. I could hardly breathe, the gravity of the moment leaving everyone momentarily frozen. For Dom, the realization must have hit like a freight train. But for us, this was the moment we had been waiting for—the confrontation that would unravel the web of lies he had spun around our lives.

"You made a mistake, Dom," my mother replied, voice quivering yet strong. "You thought you could erase me, erase us. But we're here, and we're not going back."

My heart raced as I watched the tension shift in Dom's demeanour, caught off guard by the appearance of a ghost he believed to be gone. It created an opening, one I couldn't let slip away.

"Your reign of terror ends tonight," I declared. "You've tortured us for too long. We're not afraid of you anymore!"

Dom's smirk faltered, replaced by rage as the moment shifted from shock to fury. "You think you can challenge me? You're all fools." As the tension in the air erupted, Dom lunged toward me, the fury in his eyes blinding. But before he could reach me, I barrelled through, facing him head-on. We collided, a wave of desperate energy spilling over into a chaotic brawl—shouting, fists swinging. In the melee, every second felt like an eternity, the world around us fading away. The struggle escalated, filled with rage and disbelief, as I grappled with memories of the past. I could see my mother hovering in the background, her gaze locked on Dom, reflecting years of pain. Suddenly, a noise cut through the whirlwind—a sharp clang of metal against metal. I glanced sideways just in time to see my mother, Judie, pulling a gun from her waistband, her hands shaking yet resolute.

"Mom, no!" I shouted, instinctively reaching out, but she held her ground, face flushed with emotion.

"Enough!" she cried, tears streaming down her cheeks, a mix of rage and heartbreak filling her voice. "You are done torturing us. It is done!"

THE BLOOD PACT

With a steady hand, she aimed the gun at Dom's chest, her voice gaining strength. "I've lived in your shadow for far too long." Time slowed as Dom's eyes widened, realization dawning too late. "Judie—" But the sentence was cut off by a thunderous bang that echoed over the noise of the night, resounding like a wave crashing against the shore. The shot rang out, and the world braced itself for impact. Dom stumbled back, shock filling his eyes, the arrogance slipping away as he fell to the ground—silenced forever by the very woman he had tried to obliterate.

My breath caught in my throat, and the frantic chaos around us halted. All that remained was the haunting sound of the crickets, the firework remnants dimming in the sky, and the echo of my mother's sobs as the reality of what had just transpired settled over us like a heavy fog.

"Mom..." I began, stepping toward her as the weight of the moment pushed against my chest.

"We did it," she murmured, both triumphant and grief-stricken, embodying the complexities of our shared history. "It's finally over."

In that moment, we stood there—together amidst the remnants of our past—and the future began to unfurl before us, filled with endless possibilities. The bonds of our family were both shattered and remade, forged anew in the fires of confrontation.

Dom was gone, but the battle for our lives wasn't quite over yet.

R. STELLAN

Choices Made

The night was still, a stark contrast to the chaos that had composed the moments prior. As I stood there, breathless and shaken, the echoes of gunfire reverberated in my mind like a haunting lullaby. Dom was gone—a dark chapter of our lives had closed, yet here we were, caught in the aftermath, unravelling the threads of what was, and apprehensively weaving the fabric of what could be. Ruby sidled up beside me, her face pale and eyes wide with disbelief. "I can't believe it's really over," she whispered, her voice almost lost in the heavy silence. "You... you know that was your mom who did that, right?" I nodded slowly, still trying to wrap my mind around the reality of the moment. My mother, the woman I'd thought I'd lost forever, had come back not just as a protector but as a warrior. The evidence of our fight lay in the dirt; the past had been a battleground, but now, in its quiet stillness, I felt an unprecedented weight settle on my shoulders.

"Are we really safe now?" I asked, my voice cracking slightly.

Judie stepped forward, her eyes seeming to pierce through the night as they reflected a mix of sorrow and fierce determination. "We can build back what he took from us. The shadows of our past won't haunt us anymore."

"Build back?" I echoed, incredulity colouring my tone. "Mom, this is everything. This changes everything."

"Exactly," she replied, her voice steady, comforting me in a way I hadn't realized I needed. "But we must make choices now. Choices that will define how we move forward."

I took a deep breath, the weight of the moment crashing down on me fully. I looked around at my friends, each of them grappling with their own understanding of the night's events. Mia was standing off to the side, looking between Judie and me, her brow furrowed in thought. Leo's expression was a mixture of concern for the future, the lines of youthful bravado beginning to fade as reality sunk in. It was then that the gravity of the choice I needed to make began to crystallize in my mind. I could either embrace this newfound freedom and the chance to rewrite our narrative or allow the remnants of fear and trauma to keep me tethered to the darkness.

"I've got to make a decision," I said, pulling everyone's attention towards me. "Not just for me, but for all of us."

"What do you mean?" Ruby asked, her expression softening, encouraging me to continue.

"I can't keep living in the shadows of what Dom built. We've lost too much already. I want to take control of our lives, shape our future instead of reacting to what's thrown at us. But... to do that, we need to act now."

"What kind of action?" Mia questioned, a hint of scepticism in her brows.

"A clean slate," I proposed, the words rolling off my tongue with newfound strength. "We can't just walk away and hope the remnants of Dom's empire will fade. They'll come for us. We need to destroy it from the roots."

Judie's gaze was piercing, analysing my resolve. "You realize what you're saying, right? The fight won't end simply because Dom is gone. His network won't just dissolve overnight."

THE BLOOD PACT

"A network I know how to navigate," I replied, thinking back to the threads of information I had absorbed while living in that world. "We can infiltrate them, pull apart the foundations he built, and rid ourselves of every threat hanging over our heads. It won't be easy, but it's what we need to do."

Leo stepped forward, reconsidering the situation with a contemplative frown. "But where do we even start? The list of enemies is long, and power vacuums create chaos. We might only escalate violence."

"Or seize the opportunity to reshape it," I countered, my voice gaining momentum. "Dom had the authority to keep us in fear, but what if we took that authority? We draw the line in the sand, inviting those who may be loyal to change rather than fear. We flip the script."

Silence enveloped us, each of my friends attempting to grasp the implications of my words.

"Are you sure you can do this?" Ruby asked, her eyes searching mine. "Are you ready to step into the role of leader?"

A moment passed as I wrestled with the depth of what that would require. "It's not just me. We have each other. I need every single one of you," I replied, feeling the electricity of possibility sparking in the space between us. "Together, we can turn this darkness into a source of light. We can reclaim our lives." Judie stepped forward, enveloping me in an emotional embrace. "You're right, Ryan. This isn't just about vengeance; it's about reclaiming who we are. We draw strength from each other now—not fear. I've hidden in the shadows for too long, and it's time to step back into the light."

With fervour rekindled, we stood as a new collective, each of us pulling from the well of our experiences, filling the void that had been left behind. This was about more than just tapping into power; it was about redefining who we'd become.

"Okay then," Mia said, steeling herself, the familiar fire in her eyes returning. "If we're doing this, we do it together. But it starts with gathering information first—learning who we can count on and who we need to watch out for."

"Ruby, can you tap into your contacts?" I asked without hesitating. "See if anyone's willing to turn against the remnants of Dom's crew?"

"I can try," she replied, her excitement palpable as her earlier worry transformed into resolve.

"We'll need a plan, though. A real plan," Leo added. "We can't just charge in blindly."

"No," I agreed. "We'll gather intel, assess our risks strategically. Every choice we make will lead us closer to the freedom we crave."

And so, with the remnants of the past fading into the darkness behind us, we no longer stood as victims but as warriors, poised to reclaim the future that had been stolen from us. Under the moonlit sky, we exited the scene of our fight, hearts ignited with purpose. It was time for choices to be made, and these choices would shape the course of our lives forever. We would define what came next—not just for ourselves, but for everyone still living in the shadow of fear. With each courageous step forward, we could almost sense the ground shifting beneath us, the very essence of our trajectories bending toward light. There was no turning back; there was only the promise of dawn breaking on the horizon. With the adrenaline still coursing through my veins, I gazed around at my friends, feeling a newfound sense of purpose crystallizing within me. We had survived the chaos of the night, but now it was time to thrive—and to do that, I had to embrace the mantle that had been thrust upon me. We were no longer just escaping a threat; we were forging our destiny.

THE BLOOD PACT

"Alright, everyone," I called out, gathering them all around as we huddled together under the dim glow of our flashlights. The night felt heavy yet charged with an energy that mirrored our collective determination. "We have a lot to discuss, and we need to be strategic in our moves moving forward."

Everyone turned their attention to me, eyes filled with a mixture of anxiety and hope. I took a breath, steadying myself. "First, I want to lay down our leadership structure so we're clear on where we're headed. From this day on, my mother, is stepping in as our matriarch." Judie stood tall, her presence resolute. "I'm honoured, Ryan. I'll do everything I can to protect this family and guide us through."

"Our informant and protector will be Mia," I continued, watching as her eyebrows shot up in surprise. "Her connections and quick thinking can help us gather essential information and protect Ruby while we establish our plans."

Mia nodded, a fierce determination in her eyes. "I won't let you down. I'll use every resource I can find to ensure we know what's happening in the city." I looked at Leo next, his expression serious and resolute. "Leo, you're my right-hand man. You're going to be responsible for gathering men who can fight alongside us against the remnants of Dom's network. We'll need strength and loyalty if we're going to crush what he built."

"Understood," Leo replied, a fire igniting within him. "I know a few people who owe me favours. I'll reach out to them—and see who among our past friends might be willing to join."

"Great," I acknowledged, my heart swelling with appreciation for his loyalty and commitment. "Finally, we need to establish a base—a stronghold where we can work from and make our plans. I've had my eye on an estate in Horizon View. It's secluded enough to keep us under the radar but spacious enough to house us all and build what we need."

Everyone exchanged glances, the weight of my announcement settling over us. "We can turn it into a command centre—a place where we can regroup, gather intel, and plan our next moves."

"What about funding?" Ruby piped up, uncertainty lining her voice. "Assets? The estate might not be cheap."

I nodded, acknowledging her concerns. "We'll have to pillage what's left of Dom's accounts. It's a risk, but we'll only be taking what was rightfully ours. I'm confident the networks he operated would have resources we can exploit—money, assets, information. We'll reclaim what he stole."

"Sounds dangerous," Mia cautioned, her brow furrowing. "Rushing into financial raids could put us in the crosshairs of his loyalists looking for revenge. We'll need a well-laid plan for that."

I lifted my chin, determination solidifying in my heart. "That's why we'll start off slow—gathering intel from the outside first, reaching out to those who have weights in the shadows, and hosting meetings to build a united front. I want you all to start with the connections you have while Leo rounds up fighters." As I spoke, the realization sank in that this was no longer just a dream; this was our reality, and it would take all of us to make it work. "In the end, we're not just warriors; we're community. We trust and rely on one another, and from that trust, we will become stronger than Dom ever was."

Silence enveloped the group momentarily—each of us absorbing the magnitude of the shift we were embarking on. If we worked together, I felt certain we could change the course of our lives. We had been victims for too long; now, it was our turn to be the authors of our own stories. Finally, Ruby stepped forward, her demeanour shifting to one of confidence. "Count me in. I'll start talking to whoever I can about the estate and what we need for repairs—there might be places we can scavenge for what we need." I smiled at her, and Leo's eyes shone with determination as he nodded, "And I'll begin reaching out. We'll have enough willing fighters soon enough." Mia's gaze shifted between us, then landed on my mother. "And you, Judie. What's your vision for us as matriarch?"

Judie took a moment, reflecting on the question as her eyes glimmered. "My vision is for us to be a family that can heal together. We need to move forward, learning from our past but not allowing it to dictate our future. We will create a safe-haven and a new legacy together."

"Exactly," I affirmed, feeling an invigorating wave of confidence surge through me. "This is just the beginning of our journey. We may be scared, but we're never backing down again. Together, we will break the chain of fear and claim our lives back."

With the night closing around us, we solidified our plans, each of us taking the first steps toward a new chapter. The stakes were higher than ever, but as a united front, I felt we could face whatever dangers lay ahead. Together, we would transform the remnants of fear into strength, and from the ashes of our past, we would rise stronger than ever. The choice was made; now we just had to follow through and forge a destiny of our own making. As the conversation wound down, I felt the weight of our plans settling over us like a mantle. It was a mixture of excitement and apprehension, a tightly woven combination that reminded me how far we had come—even when it felt like we were just on the edge of a precipice.

"Alright," I said, clapping my hands together to break the lingering tension. "Let's set a timeline. We'll meet back at Mia's apartment tomorrow night to assess our progress and discuss the next steps."

"Sounds good," Leo said, already pulling out his phone to jot down notes. "I'll coordinate with everyone I can think of. The sooner we get on this, the better."

"Make sure to choose wisely," I warned. "Dom had loyalists who may be lurking. Not everyone is going to want to jump ship."

Mia crossed her arms, her gaze contemplative. "We'll need a vetting process for anyone who comes forward. We can't afford any surprises."

"Good call," I replied, appreciating her foresight. "We need to establish trust before we build our ranks."

As the discussion intensified, I glanced at each of my friends, noticing the shifts in their demeanour. Ruby, typically the bubbly source of energy in our group, wore a serious expression, clearly stewing over the new responsibilities before us. I could see her grappling with the implications of her role as we began to carve out our identities and destinies. I placed a reassuring hand on her shoulder. "Hey, we're all in this together. You won't be alone. We've got your back—always."

"Thanks, Ryan," she replied, a small smile breaking through her hesitations.

Judie stepped in, her voice calm yet firm. "You all need not carry this weight alone. As matriarch, I'm here to guide us, to ensure we're not just building a fortress but a community. Our past has shaped us, but it doesn't define our future."

Critically, I reminded myself that our circumstances could either bind us or free us. Our stories were intertwined now more than ever. I felt gratitude swell as I looked around, appreciating the loyalty and courage radiating from each member of our makeshift family.

"Let's set up a plan for checking out the estate," I suggested, shaking off any lingering doubts. "Mia, could you put together a list of essentials we might need for the estate?"

"Absolutely," Mia nodded. "I'll take an inventory of what we have and what we might be able to salvage. I've got some contacts who might be able to help with repairs, too."

THE BLOOD PACT

"Perfect," I replied, feeling the sparks of enthusiasm ignite further. "Once we have our base secured, we can organize meetings to fortify our ranks. We'll strengthen our intelligence and prepare for any backlash."

As we wrapped up the evening, a plan began to take shape, bolstered by confidence and camaraderie. Our spirits lifted, and I felt the unmistakable bond tying us all together tighten. Before we broke off to head to our separate homes for the night, I needed to impart one last message.

"Whatever happens in the next few days, keep in mind that this isn't a solo mission. We're a team," I said, looking each of them in the eyes. "We're in this fight together. Whatever challenges we face, we face them as a family."

With that declaration hanging in the air, we began to disperse, the night cool against my skin as I ventured outside, breathing in the freedom that felt almost palpable. We had a long road ahead, but for the first time in a long while, I felt a sense of hope pushing through the darkness.

Mia's apartment was only a few streets away, a cozy space that had once served as a haven for our group during the quieter times. As I walked, I couldn't help but imagine how we could transform it into a hub of strategy, a headquarters where we could regroup and plan our next moves. The night sky was peppered with stars, reminding me of the infinite possibilities that awaited us. I took a deep breath, feeling the cool air fill my lungs—it felt refreshing, invigorating. It was a moment of clarity amid the chaos, where everything seemed to align, and I could almost see our future unfolding before me. Arriving at Mia's apartment, I pushed open the door and stepped into the familiar space. The warm glow from the lamps cast a soft light over the room, and I could already see the outlines of the others gathering. The couches would soon be filled with our laughter again, memories waiting to be made, even as we prepared for the fight ahead.

Mia was setting up her laptop on the kitchen counter, ready to draft our action plan. "Ryan, you're right on time. We've got to lay the groundwork if we want to hit the ground running tomorrow. Can you pull up some intel on Dom's assets?"

"On it," I replied, rolling up my sleeves as I joined her at the counter.

Judie entered next, carrying a box of snacks. "I thought we could use some nourishment as we plan," she said, a twinkle in her eye. "Even warriors need to eat."

"Thanks, Mom," I said, smiling at her. "Fuelling up is definitely a good idea."

As we dug into the snacks, we discussed strategy and plans, the atmosphere shifting from uncertainty to a dynamic hum of creativity and resolve. Every idea built upon the last, and with each passing moment, I felt the energy in the room shift to one of empowerment.

"Let's meet early tomorrow morning to scope out the estate," Leo proposed, his foot tapping on the kitchen tile with eagerness. "We can make a checklist of what we need while we're there."

"Agreed," Mia said, her eyes lighting up with enthusiasm. "And if anyone wants to join us in brainstorming repairs, I'll need extra hands."

The conversation flowed easily now, our minds working in concert as we began to piece together our future. Mistakes and failures from our past were weaving into our narratives, shaping our courage and resilience, but they would no longer dictate our course. As I looked around the room, a sense of pride welled within me. We were no longer just survivors; we were becoming architects of a new legacy—one built from the very ashes of our fears. With unity, we would take back our power. Together, we were bound for something greater than ourselves. And as midnight crept closer, I felt the palpable anticipation in the air—a collective hope that breathed life into our mission. Tomorrow would bring new challenges, but we

THE BLOOD PACT

were ready to face them together, unyielding and unbreakable. We gathered around the kitchen table at Mia's apartment, the air thick with anticipation. Ideas flowed freely as we divided up tasks, each of us eager to contribute to the transformation of the estate. I could feel the excitement radiating between us, a palpable force ready to launch us into action.

"Alright, team," Mia said, her voice cutting through the chatter. "Let's keep our focus on what needs to be done today. We'll head to the estate, take stock of the repairs needed, and start drafting a plan of action."

Leo pushed a stack of notes toward the centre of the table. "I did some digging last night. Here's an overview of the estate's layout and what we might encounter. Knowing what we're working with will save us time."

"That's fantastic, Leo!" Ruby exclaimed, rifling through the stack. "Let's prioritize our list based on what's most urgent. Safety first—if we're going to open this space, we need it to be secure."

"Agreed," I added, glancing at Mia. "We'll take photos and measurements today. Once we know what we need, we can reach out to local businesses for supplies and perhaps even some community volunteers."

Mia nodded, her enthusiasm infectious. "I'll coordinate the volunteers. I can reach out to my contacts and see who's willing to lend a hand." As we mapped out our plan, I felt a resurgence of hope. Each idea we shared built upon the last, solidifying the sense of community that had blossomed between us. I couldn't help but smile as I watched my friends become energized by the possibilities. Their faces seemed to shimmer with a kind of determination I hadn't seen before. After a few cups of coffee and a hearty breakfast, we finished our planning session and gathered our supplies: notepads, pens, camera equipment, and a toolbox filled with essential tools. As we headed out, the air felt vibrant, charged with anticipation.

Mia locked her apartment door behind us as we stepped out onto the bustling street. The morning sunbathed us in warmth, and I could feel the weight of yesterday's fears begin to lift. We were ready to embrace our new chapter, alive with potential. Arriving at the estate, I couldn't help but take a deep breath, soaking in the atmosphere. The building loomed before us, its chipped paint and overgrown grass a stark reminder of neglect, yet I saw beauty in its potential.

"This place needs a little TLC, but I can already picture it as a vibrant community space," I said, my excitement bubbling over.

"Let's divide and conquer," Ruby suggested, her gaze scanning the exterior. "Mia, you head inside and check the main rooms. Judie and I will start assessing the yard, and Leo can look at the structural integrity of the entryway."

"Sounds good. I'll take photos as I go," I replied, pulling my phone out of my pocket and snapping a couple of shots of the outside.

As we dispersed to our assigned areas, I felt a rush of purpose. We were no longer just individuals caught up in chaos; we had become a collective force, ready to turn despair into hope. Inside, I navigated through the dimly lit rooms, taking note of the peeling wallpaper and the dust that clung to every surface. Each creak of the floorboards seemed to whisper stories of the past, but I was determined to write new narratives here. Mia's voice floated from the kitchen. "It looks like the plumbing will need an overhaul and the electrical system might not be up to code. We can investigate hiring a contractor for those specifics, but in the meantime, at least we have a good start." I nodded, making a note in my phone. "Let's keep a detailed account of everything," I said, as I moved into the next room, envisioning how we could turn a neglected space into something beautiful—a meeting hub, a sanctuary.

THE BLOOD PACT

After a few hours of imaging possibilities and taking measurements, I walked back toward the main area, where I found Mia deep in thought, flipping through her notes.

"How are things looking?" I asked, joining her.

"Better than I anticipated," she replied, a smile brightening her face. "Once we get the repairs underway, I think we can create a great gathering space here—somewhere people can share their stories and form connections."

"When we're done, this will be a place of healing," I said, feeling a swell of pride in what we were building. "I can't wait to bring everyone together here."

Just then, Ruby and Judie entered, their laughter filling the space as they stepped inside, covered in dirt and grass clippings. "You won't believe what we found out there!" Ruby exclaimed, her eyes alight with excitement. "We could turn that overgrown patch into a beautiful garden."

"Yeah!" Judie chimed in. "Imagine what we could grow, what we could share with the community. Fresh herbs, vegetables... it could provide so much!"

Mia looked between them, her smile growing wider. "And that could also serve as a healing garden. A place for people to come together, to cultivate not just plants, but relationships and support."

"Exactly!" I said, catching their infectious enthusiasm. "Let's add it to the plan. A garden can be a powerful symbol of growth and revitalization, much like what we're doing for ourselves."

The day continued to unfold beautifully, each task bringing us closer to our goal. We took measurements, snapped endless photos, and created lists for materials we would need. The atmosphere was charged with creativity and collaboration, a reflection of our commitment to transform the estate into a beacon of hope for our community. As the sun began to dip below the horizon, casting long shadows through the windows, we gathered one last time in the main room. The dust and chaos felt familiar now, almost comforting, knowing that transformation was on the horizon.

"We made great progress today," I said, looking at each of my friends, grateful for their support and resilience. "I'm proud of what we're building together."

"Tomorrow, we finalize our list of materials and start reaching out to contractors and volunteers," Mia reminded us. "We're on the right track."

Ruby added, "And let's not forget to advertise the garden idea! We need to get the community involved." As night enveloped the estate, I felt a renewed sense of purpose. We weren't just reclaiming a forgotten space; we were breathing life into it, reinvigorating it with our dreams and hopes. This place would become our home—a sanctuary for healing, connection, and rebuilding our lives. Together, we forged ahead, united in our mission, ready to face whatever challenges lay ahead. With our hearts set on the journey before us, we left the estate that night, the stars twinkling above as if to remind us that even after the darkest hours, new beginnings awaited. As we went back to Mia's apartment, a comfortable silence enveloped us, the kind that comes after a fulfilling day of hard work and shared purpose. The streets were quieter now, the city winding down for the night. I stole glances at my friends, their expressions a blend of exhaustion and satisfaction.

THE BLOOD PACT

"I can't believe how much we accomplished today," Ruby said, breaking the silence. "It feels like we've already laid the groundwork for something incredible."

"Definitely," I replied, feeling the warmth of camaraderie wash over me. "And it's just the beginning. Tomorrow, we keep the momentum going."

Mia peered at me through the nighttime glow of the streetlights, her eyes gleaming with excitement. "We should all meet early to finalize our outreach plans and maybe even brainstorm some events once we're ready to open the place. I think it'll help to have something on the calendar to draw people in."

"Like a community launch event?" Leo suggested, his fingers drumming against his thigh. "That would get people excited and invested in the space. We could invite local artists, performers—everyone could contribute something."

"That's brilliant!" Judie exclaimed. "A festival, maybe! We could have art displays and storytelling sessions. It would showcase the talents of the community while inspiring others to get involved."

All my fears about reclaiming the estate faded as we exchanged ideas. I could picture it—the garden blooming, laughter echoing through the hallways, people gathering to share their experiences, to support one another. Once we arrived back at Mia's apartment, the evening air brisk with the promise of a new dawn, we kicked off our shoes and collapsed on her living room floor, still buzzing with energy.

"Alright, what's next on our agenda for tomorrow?" Mia asked, grabbing a notepad and pen from her coffee table.

I pulled out my phone, scrolling through our notes from the day. "We need to make sure we have a clear list of materials and tools needed for repairs. We'll also want to draft a message for local businesses and community volunteers." Ruby leaned back, her expression thoughtful. "And we should think of some engaging ways to present the vision for the estate to the public. If we can get people emotionally invested from the start, they'll be more likely to join us."

"That's key," I added. "We need to convey not just what we're trying to achieve, but why it matters. For many of us, this isn't just a project; it's personal. It's about rising from the ashes of Dom's shadow and creating something meaningful."

Mia nodded, furiously jotting down notes. "We can highlight personal stories, share our journeys of healing and growth, and make it an open call for everyone to contribute their voice. This space is going to belong to all of us." With every idea shared, the room grew warmer with excitement. We dove into our plans, mapping out the outreach strategy and brainstorming creative approaches to draw the community into our mission. Hours later, as we wrapped up our discussions, the exhaustion from the day's labour settled in. "I think we should call it a night," Mia suggested, yawning. "We've got a big day tomorrow, and I want us all to be fresh."

"I'm down for that," Leo said, stretching. "But let's not forget to create a calendar for the tasks leading up to this launch event. We'll need to be organized if we want it to be successful."

"Definitely," Ruby agreed. "And maybe we can set up a group chat to keep everyone updated and inspired?"

THE BLOOD PACT

As we crafted the group chat together, I felt a swell of gratitude. This wasn't just about the space we were reclaiming; it was a testament to the bonds that had formed among us. We were no longer isolated individuals fighting our battles alone; we were a unit, a support system. After hugs and well-wishes, I made my way home, the cool night air revitalizing me. I couldn't wait to dive into the plans for the estate, to witness the dreams we had for it flourish.

The next morning broke with vibrant sunlight spilling over the city, its warmth a promise of new beginnings. I had barely slept, my mind racing with ideas and possibilities, but I felt invigorated as I dressed and grabbed a quick breakfast. When I arrived at Mia's apartment, I found Ruby and Leo already there, a flurry of activity as they went over their notes.

"Morning! Ready for another day of planning?" Ruby greeted me, her eyes sparkling with enthusiasm.

"Absolutely! Let's tackle this," I replied, my heart full.

We soon settled around the table, poring over our notes and refining our outreach messages. Mia appeared shortly after, holding a steaming cup of coffee and a determined expression. "Alright, team. Let's make our impact felt today." With everyone on the same page, we finalized our materials list and drafted emails to send to local businesses. Ruby volunteered to handle the social media outreach, brainstorming hashtags and posts to create buzz around our project. As we worked together, I felt a deep sense of belonging. There was no longer any doubt about our mission. We were on a path toward healing, not just for ourselves but for our community—turning shared pain into collective strength. As the day progressed, we divided our tasks to ensure we covered all our bases. Leo took charge of the physical space, planning to inspect the estate and chat with contractors. Mia began reaching out to community organizations and artists to gauge interest in participating in our launch event.

Meanwhile, Ruby and I tackled the social media aspect, brainstorming ways to draw people in. We designed a flyer, capturing the essence of what we wanted to achieve—a vibrant space filled with support and love. We infused it with personal stories of our journeys, inviting others to join us on this bold new venture.

"Okay, I think we're ready to post," Ruby said, her excitement palpable. "This is going to get people talking!"

The response was swift and positive. Comments and messages began to flood in—encouragement, offers to help, people sharing their own stories of struggle and resilience. My heart soared.

With renewed energy, we continued to refine our plans, diving into logistics for the launch event. We discussed potential themes, activities, and ways to ensure everyone felt included—a warm welcome for all who sought solace within those walls. As the day waned and dusk settled in, wrapping the city in its embrace, we decided to take a break and reflect on the day's progress.

"I can't believe how far we've come in just a couple of days," I said, feeling a sense of pride swell within me. "We're really doing this."

Mia smiled, her expression a mix of elation and disbelief. "It feels like a dream, doesn't it? I never imagined we'd turn this place into something so beautiful."

"And we're just getting started," Leo said, leaning back against the wall, a relaxed grin on his face. "The best is yet to come."

As I looked around at my friends, I saw not only what we were creating, but also who we were becoming. Brave, resilient, and united—we were no longer bound by the past but propelled forward by hope and possibility. And in that moment, I knew we had finally stepped into a light that would guide us through whatever challenges lay ahead. Together, we were unstoppable. With renewed determination, we dove back into our planning, forging ahead, ready to combat any darkness that may try to creep back in. This was

THE BLOOD PACT

our time, our place to thrive. As I headed home that night, the stars twinkled bright in the sky, reflecting the light I felt inside. Tomorrow would bring more challenges, but we were prepared—we would embrace them as they came, together, ready to build the future we envisioned.

Paths Diverged

The sun rose on a crisp morning, painting the sky in shades of orange and purple. It was the first day of the week since our ambitious project began, and a sense of purpose filled the air. Yet, beneath the excitement, I felt tremors of uncertainty rippling through me. Today would challenge us differently than before—while we had made great strides together, it was time to confront the new realities awaiting each of us outside of our shared mission. Gathered at Mia's apartment, the four of us looked over our plans for the estate, enthusiasm crackling around the table. Mia was organizing our calendar of events, while Ruby, with her expressive green eyes shimmering with anticipation, checked her computer for updates on our social media posts. Leo sat deep in thought, sketching out potential layouts for the community garden. But as I glanced at everyone, I noticed that their faces held traces of apprehension. Each of us was grappling with our own personal struggles, the shadows of our pasts lingering just outside the periphery of our shared hope.

"Mia," I began, breaking the silence, "have you thought about how this project will change things for you? I mean, working on the garden and this community space... it's a huge commitment."

Mia looked up, her eyes wide with realization. "Honestly, I've barely even thought about it. I just know I need this. But... you're right. I guess I haven't considered what it all means for my life moving forward."

"Same," Ruby replied, her green eyes glistening even in the daylight. "After everything that's gone down, I'm not just taking on this project; I'm trying to reshape my future. It's all exciting, but... daunting too."

Leo scratched the back of his neck, glancing between us. "I think we're all feeling that pressure. This isn't just about the estate; it's about who we become in the process." The atmosphere shifted, the weight of our realities settling in. This was it—time to confront what lay ahead. We each had dreams and aspirations that were intertwined with this project but also separate from it.

"I want to do something meaningful," Mia said, her voice trembling slightly. "But I also must figure out how to balance my life—my job, my healing. I can't let this consume me."

I nodded, understanding her plight completely. "I want us to succeed and create something beautiful, but I also have my own responsibilities to face. Work has been more stressful than ever, and I can't help but wonder how much I can really manage. I need to find a way to protect my energy while still contributing." Ruby leaned forward, her eyes shining with emotion. "We all want to make this work. But if we're not careful, we might end up burning out... or losing ourselves along the way. It's important to check in with our-selves too, to establish boundaries."

"That's true," Leo replied thoughtfully. "We need to support each other, but we also need to recognize that we each have unique journeys to take. It's okay to be honest about our limits."

"I think we should all commit to weekly check-ins," I suggested. "A space where we can talk about how we're feeling and the expectations we have for this project—and for ourselves."

THE BLOOD PACT

With our emotions laid bare, we shifted our focus back to the estate's plan. "Alright, let's prioritize our tasks for the week," Mia suggested, her demeanour steadying. "If we can set concrete goals, it'll help keep us focused and grounded." We developed a detailed schedule that divided up responsibilities, ensuring everyone had a manageable workload and space to breathe. Leo volunteered to coordinate with contractors for the repairs, while Ruby took charge of organizing outreach efforts to engage the community and gather volunteers. Mia and I decided to work on setting up workshops and storytelling nights, where people could come together, connect, and share their experiences.

"What if we create a 'Vision Board' wall at the estate?" I proposed. "People can write down their dreams, their hopes for what this space should become. It would give everyone a sense of ownership."

"I love that idea!" Ruby exclaimed, her vibrant green eyes sparkling with inspiration. "It's a perfect way to get people involved and invested!"

As the hours passed, our spirits soared, buoyed by the sense of purpose that filled the room. The project felt more tangible than ever, yet I couldn't shake the realization that we would face many trials ahead—not just externally through the project, but also internally within ourselves. Mia struggled to balance her daily job with the demands of the estate. Late into the night, I would hear her typing furiously on her laptop, pouring over work assignments that loomed over her like a dark cloud. Each day, she seemed more tired, more distant. Ruby faced her own battles as well. The excitement surrounding the project was a double-edged sword—while it brought her joy, it also acted as a reminder of the challenges she was trying to escape. Late one night, her meticulous plans began to unravel into tears as she confronted her feelings of inadequacy.

"Why can't I just focus on the good?" she sobbed, her green eyes shimmering with unshed tears. "This was supposed to be a fresh start, but I feel so lost."

Leo's situations proved just as challenging. Juggling work and the demands of the project seemed to fracture his energy. He became withdrawn, consumed by thoughts that he could never be enough and that others were counting on him. And me? I felt the overwhelming weight of everything—the estate project, my job, and the lingering fears that lurked in every corner. I had promised to stay committed, but every time I faced the looming deadline of responsibilities, anxiety clawed at me.

Weeks passed, and finally, a turning point came one evening after a particularly tough day. It was just after we'd wrapped up a brainstorming session at the estate. The air was heavy, and our energy was waning. We ended up sitting together on the worn steps of the front porch, watching the sun sink below the horizon. The beauty of the moment contrasted sharply with the tension we had been carrying laughter echoed in the distance as neighbours strolled by, visibly enjoying their lives.

"What if we're trying to do too much?" Leo broke the silence, looking up at the clouds. "I mean, we never have a moment to just... breathe."

"I know what you mean," I replied, feeling the knot in my gut tighten. "But we keep pushing through because we believe in what we're doing. Maybe that belief is what we need to focus on."

THE BLOOD PACT

Taking a deep breath, Mia spoke up. "I think we need to acknowledge that we don't have it all figured out. And that's okay. We can still lean on each other while navigating this mess together." Ruby nodded, tears glistening in her expressive green eyes. "I don't feel like I'm enough sometimes. Like I can't keep carrying this weight. I want to succeed, but I'm scared." Silence hung in the air as we processed the vulnerability, we each shared. It took courage to voice these pressures, but as we did, I felt the shadows of self-doubt begin to dissipate, albeit only slightly.

"Maybe it's time for us to step back for a moment," I suggested gently. "Let's have an honest conversation about what we need from each other, what we can give, and how we can best support one another without losing ourselves."

With those words, the atmosphere began to change. We took turns expressing our fears, our dreams, and our struggles. We spoke of our individual paths diverging and converging—the intertwined journeys that coloured our lives.

"I think we each have to remember that it's a process," Leo said softly. "Healing, creating, building... none of it happens overnight. We can't put pressure on ourselves to do it all."

"Yeah. We must be gentle with ourselves," Mia added, her voice steady. "If we're going to make this project thrive, we must nurture ourselves too."

We wrapped our arms around each other, feeling the weight of support envelop us. It was a simple gesture, but it reminded us of camaraderie—a bond forged not just through the project but through the rawness of life itself. From that moment, it became clear: as our paths diverged into unique narratives filled with struggle and hope, we would always find our way back to each other. We were united by more than just a mission—we were bound by our shared journey toward healing, connection, and the type of growth that was real and authentic.

As we left the estate that night, the stars flickered brightly above us, illuminating the road ahead. We would face challenges, but armed with newfound honesty and understanding, we could navigate the turbulence of our diverging paths while keeping the spirit of community alive—together. As the days turned into a blur of planning and preparation, each of us wrestled with the diverging paths of our lives. The project at the estate took on a new significance; it was no longer just a shared endeavour, but a reflection of our individual journeys, fraught with challenges yet full of potential. Even as we committed ourselves to weekly check-ins, the realities of our lives loomed large. Mia struggled significantly in the days that followed. With her job demanding longer hours than ever, she often arrived at our work sessions visibly exhausted. Her once-bright enthusiasm began to dim; the laughter that had filled her eyes was replaced by worry lines and fatigue.

One particularly Gray afternoon, Mia dragged herself to the estate, her shoulders hunched and her usually vibrant presence muted. I watched her as she stumbled through our discussions, her thoughts half-formed and her smiles fleeting.

"Hey, Mia," I said gently during a break, stepping aside to catch her alone. "Are you okay? You've been looking, a bit... overwhelmed."

She sighed, running her fingers through her hair. "I wish I could say I'm fine, but I'm not sure how to handle everything. My boss has dropped another project on me, and I can't keep up with the demands at work. I know this estate work is important, but I can't just abandon my job either." Her voice trembled, and a lump formed in my throat. "You don't have to do everything on your own," I encouraged. "Remember our commitment to check in? We're all feeling the pressure. You're not alone in this."

THE BLOOD PACT

Ruby's struggles mirrored Mia's, but hers were more internalized. Her green eyes carried an ever-present flicker of doubt, a reflection of her ongoing battle with self-worth. One evening, as we prepared for a community outreach event, I caught her staring at her list of potential volunteers, her fingers trembling as she tapped the screen.

"Ruby," I said softly, drawing her attention. "You're doing a fantastic job with this outreach—truly. These connections you're making will help us cultivate a real sense of community."

She looked up, her gaze vulnerable. "Do you really think so? I'm terrified that I'm not doing enough. What if no one shows up? What if I've put all this effort in for nothing?" I stepped closer, meeting her gaze. "Even if no one shows up, that doesn't mean your efforts are in vain. You're building relationships, connecting with people, and that's invaluable. You're enough, Ruby. You always have been." A smile broke through the clouds of doubt in her eyes, and for a moment, the weight lifted. But it was fleeting. I could see the worries lingering just beneath the surface, waiting to resurface. As the project momentum built, Leo dealt with his own tumult. Admittedly more introverted than the rest of us, he often felt the pressure to maintain a façade of steadiness. However, one evening, the masks began to crumble. We had just finished a particularly exhausting day of labour, and I noticed him staring at a half-finished sketch of the community garden on a clipboard.

"Leo," I said, sitting next to him on the outdoor steps of the estate, "what's going on in that mind of yours? You've been distant."

He sighed heavily, glancing up to meet my gaze. "I guess I just feel the weight of it all. I want this to work, to be perfect, but I keep thinking... what if I mess this up? What if my vision isn't good enough, or what if I'm not enough?" I could see the tension in his shoulders, the frustration of unmet expectations tightening his brow.

"Leo, this isn't about perfection. It's about the process, the growth we experience along the way. You have incredible ideas; we wouldn't be where we are now without you." His expression softened slightly. "Thanks, I needed to hear that. It's just hard sometimes. I don't want to let everyone down."

"You won't," I assured him, feeling a glimmer of hope. "We're in this together, and we believe in you. We all want this to be a place of healing and growth, and that starts with being true to ourselves."

The following week, we gathered for our check-in, this time at the estate surrounded by the vibrant colours of new blooms pushing through the soil. The air buzzed with anticipation and possibility. Mia arrived first, looking slightly more rested, with a newfound determination sparkling in her eyes. Ruby followed, a spark of enthusiasm in her green gaze. Leo came in last, his expression pensive but present. When we convened, I could feel the energy shift as we truly leaned into our conversation.

"I think it's time for us to truly share what we need to keep moving forward," I suggested, trying to keep the tone open and inviting. "This project is important to all of us, but our individual well-being is too."

Mia spoke first. "I feel like I've been trying to balance too much and it's taking a toll on me. I need to be able to say no sometimes. I want to contribute fully, but I can't be everything at once." Ruby chimed in, her voice stronger than before. "I want to stop worrying so much about what others think of my contributions. I need to embrace the idea that I'm already doing enough, just by being here."

THE BLOOD PACT

With a commanding presence, Leo added, "I also need to free myself from expectations. I want to share my ideas, but I don't want to feel paralyzed by the fear of making mistakes. Maybe we should create a space where our ideas don't have to be perfect." I nodded, feeling the momentum build. "How about we have a brainstorming session where everything is welcome, no judgment? We can create an atmosphere where ideas flow freely and become a collective vision." In that moment, we all needed the same thing—a chance to let go of the pressure and engage with an open heart.

As we dove into the brainstorming session, we laughed and exchanged ideas, sketches of the community garden blending with discussions of upcoming events. The weight of our worries slowly lifted as we realized that we were creating something truly special, not for ourselves, but for the community around us. Mia found herself sketching designs for the garden alongside Leo, both their creative energies merging. Ruby's outreach ideas flourished into tangible plans as she pulled from her background in communications, infusing the project with creative marketing. In that moment, as ideas fluttered between us, I saw that despite our looming challenges, we had created a space where not only our project could thrive, but where we could also heal.

Days turned into nights, and before long, we were inching closer to the launch of our community garden. The project transformed from a mere dream into a liveable reality. The day of the big unveiling arrived basked in sunshine, the air fragrant with the scent of blooming flowers. The space buzzed with familiar faces and curious newcomers, each person adding to the tapestry of our initiative. Surrounded by friends, family, and new faces from our community, we gathered to celebrate what we had built together. And there, before everyone, each of us spoke openly about our journeys, acknowledging the struggles we faced to reach this beautiful moment.

With Ruby sharing her heartfelt words, her green eyes bright with emotion, Mia shining with a renewed spirit, and Leo's calm resolve alongside me, we spoke of challenges, commitment, and the hope that bound us. We concluded by inviting everyone to contribute their own visions to the Vision Board wall, creating a floral tapestry of dreams and aspirations that would continue to grow with us.

As the sun dipped below the horizon, casting golden rays across our gathering, I realized that we were no longer just a group of individuals working on a solitary project; we had forged a community—a living testament to resilience and connection. In that shared space of vulnerability and hope, our paths, though diverged, intertwined in ways we had never imagined. And as we stood together, surrounded by laughter and support, I knew we would face whatever came next, not just as teammates but as friends committed to nurturing joy and possibility. As laughter and joy filled the air, I felt a warmth enveloping each of us—a testament to the months of effort leading to this moment. Neighbours meandered through the estate, admiring the vibrant flowers swaying gently in the breeze, the community garden slowly coming to life. Underneath the surface, however, I sensed lingering uncertainties, shadows of doubt that we had yet to confront fully.

The celebration swirled around us, but my gaze wandered to Ruby, who stood slightly apart from the crowd, her expressive green eyes scanning the faces of the attendees. Sensing her unease, I approached her, noting the way she fiddled with a delicate bracelet on her wrist.

"Hey, Ruby," I said gently, drawing nearer. "You, okay?"

She turned to face me, a mixture of pride and anxiety reflecting in her gaze. "I just can't shake this feeling that I'm not doing enough. I mean, look at all these people showing up! What if I don't live up to their expectations?"

THE BLOOD PACT

"Ruby, you've done so much already," I reminded her, gesturing to the bustling garden. "This wouldn't be happening without your outreach work. You brought everyone here!"

"I know, but still..." she trailed off, her voice tight. "I'm terrified that I'll let them down. What if they don't see the value in what we've created?"

Before I could respond, Mia unexpectedly joined us, her bright smile cutting through Ruby's anxiety. "What's all this talk about letting people down? We're here celebrating what we've accomplished, right? You've been instrumental, Ruby!" Ruby's shoulders relaxed slightly under Mia's affirmation, but the shadow of doubt still lingered. "I prefer to work behind the scenes. This—being in the spotlight—it makes me uneasy." Mia smiled knowingly. "Then let's play to our strengths. You and I can focus on gathering stories about what this garden means to the community. We can showcase that in our next outreach campaign. Acknowledge all the voices behind this project." A flicker of hope came into Ruby's eyes. "You think that could help?"

"Absolutely! Every story adds another layer to this tapestry we're weaving together," I chimed in, my enthusiasm growing. "You are more than enough simply by being who you are. You're a vital part of this community, and your voice matters."

Ruby took a deep breath, the tension ebbing away as she nodded. "Thanks. I'll try to keep that in mind."

Meanwhile, I turned my attention to Leo, who was speaking with one of the neighbours, an older gentleman who seemed captivated by Leo's ideas for expanding the garden. Yet, I noticed how Leo's smile didn't quite reach his eyes. When the conversation ended, I approached him.

"Looks like you had a good chat there," I said, trying to draw him out.

"Yeah, he has some fascinating ideas about incorporating native plants," Leo replied, but his tone suggested that he was still wrestling with something deeper.

"You seem a bit distant. Everything alright?" I asked, searching his eyes.

He sighed, scrubbing a hand across the back of his neck. "I guess I'm just anxious. This event is amazing, but I keep cycling through what's next for us, what we're supposed to do after this launch."

"Don't let that overshadow today. We can only move forward one step at a time," I reassured him. "Just bask in what we've created together, and let's enjoy this moment. We'll figure out what comes next after we've celebrated our success."

Leo nodded, allowing a smile to break free. "You're right. For now, I want to soak it all in."

As the sun dipped into the horizon, I couldn't help but notice the closeness forming among our group. Families laughed, and newcomers shared ideas, creating a tapestry of voices around us. But as I watched, I also feared that beneath the surface of this celebration, the anxieties we had voiced in our earlier check-in would resurface. At that moment, someone tapped my shoulder. It was an older woman from the neighbourhood, Mr. Thompson's wife, her kind eyes twinkling. "You must be the mastermind behind all this," she said warmly, "Thank you for bringing this community together."

"No, it wasn't just me," I insisted, glancing back at my friends. "It was all of us—together."

Her gaze shifted to where Ruby, Mia, and Leo stood. She smiled knowingly. "I can see that. Each of you adds a special touch. It's the unity among you that makes it work. That's what community is all about." Hearing her words, I felt a sense of relief. Perhaps we had successfully crafted something meaningful beyond our individual struggles. We were learning and growing together—a community in every sense of the word.

THE BLOOD PACT

As evening set in, the sunset painted the sky in hues of gold and pink, the garden lit with strings of fairy lights. We gathered again, standing in a circle, our hearts brimming with gratitude.

"Before we end the evening," I began, addressing the group. "Let's take a moment to acknowledge everyone who came today. We're grateful for your support, your stories, and your trust in us. We want to continue making this garden a place for everyone—a space to share and to heal."

The crowd applauded, and I felt that spark of connection within the group. Mia took a deep breath and stepped forward, her eyes bright. "We invite you all to help us shape this garden further. Add your stories to our Vision Board starting next week. Let's continue to grow this community together!" The excitement buzzed around us, the culmination of our hard work shining brightly in that moment. Ruby stepped up next, her voice steady as she announced upcoming community events and initiatives we planned to roll out in the coming months. And then Leo spoke, sharing his vision of a space for art in the garden, a place where creativity and nature could intertwine harmoniously. "I want everyone involved; this is a canvas for all of us to paint our dreams on." Their words ignited enthusiasm, the crowd echoing their excitement. The worries we had felt just days prior dissolved into the background, replaced by a collective spirit of collaboration.

As the evening waned, we gathered around a fire pit, roasting marshmallows and recounting stories from our journey. Laughter mingled with the crackle of flames, and I looked around at my friends—each of us in a different space, yet undeniably connected through this shared experience.

"Let's make a promise," I suggested, my heart swelling with affection for the bonds forming. "No matter how busy life gets, let's carve out time to keep checking in with one another. To remind each other of our worth. We can't forget to support ourselves while we uplift our community."

Mia, Ruby, and Leo nodded, their eyes reflecting the flickering firelight. "Deal," they said in unison.

"Together," Ruby added, her green eyes sparkling with resolve.

And as the stars unfolded overhead, I felt an overwhelming sense of gratitude. This project—the community garden, the friendships we had forged, the struggles we had faced—had woven us into a tapestry far richer than any of us ever anticipated. Tomorrow would bring new challenges and discoveries, but for tonight, we were here, together. And that was enough.

THE BLOOD PACT

A Blood Pact

The sun had barely risen over the horizon, casting a soft, muted light that filtered through the curtains. I lay in bed, replaying the previous evening's revelry in my mind. The laughter, the warmth, the shared dreams of our community garden project; all of it felt euphoric and real. But with daylight came the awareness that beneath the surface of those connections lay unspoken truths, tensions, and unresolved fears. I got up and brewed a pot of coffee, seeking the comfort of its rich aroma to shake off the remnants of sleep. Today, I understood, would call for clarity and courage. As I poured a steaming cup and took a moment to breathe it in, I felt a tremor of anxiety rush through me. The promise I had made to check in with my friends wasn't just about fostering community; it was also about confronting some hard realities.

Later that afternoon, I arranged to meet with Ruby at a quaint café downtown. As I stepped inside, the scent of freshly baked pastries mingled with the sound of soft jazz, immediately calming my nerves. Ruby was already seated at a table by the window, her expression thoughtful as she looked out at the bustling street.

"Hey," I greeted her, sliding into the chair opposite her. "Thanks for meeting me."

She offered a small smile but didn't meet my gaze. "Of course. I was just thinking about last night. It was beautiful, but I still can't shake that feeling."

"I know what you mean," I replied, feeling the weight of our collective worries. "We've all faced challenges—family ties, expectations, even personal doubts. I think it's important for us to acknowledge those."

She nodded, her fingers tracing the rim of her coffee cup. "I come from a family where loyalty is everything. My parents... they expect me to not just be involved but to lead. The pressure sometimes feels suffocating. I want to make them proud, but I also want to carve my own path. Sometimes I wonder if I'm being true to myself or just trying to live up to their legacy." Her words resonated deeply. I understood the implications of loyalty and family ties all too well. "You're more than your family's expectations, Ruby. You have your own dreams and passions. The garden reflects your voice—a voice that deserves to be heard." Her green eyes sparkled with a flicker of understanding, yet there remained a cloud of uncertainty. "If only it were that simple. What happens if my choices don't align with their vision of what loyalty should look like? I fear they might see it as a betrayal."

A chill ran down my spine as the thought of familial loyalty resonated with my own history. The tension between family allegiance and individual desire had been a constant struggle in my own life. But I needed to encourage Ruby to fight her own battles, to stake her claim in this world.

"It's okay to have different paths," I urged. "You define what loyalty means for you. It doesn't mean abandoning your family but rather expanding the definition of love and support. You can be loyal to them while also being loyal to yourself."

A thoughtful silence hung between us before Ruby spoke again. "But what if my family doesn't understand? What if they see my independence as a threat to our bond?"

THE BLOOD PACT

"Then have that conversation with them," I suggested, feeling the urgency of our discussion. "Establish what that loyalty looks like with them—and remember, family is not just about blood; it's about support, understanding, and respect. You can create your own version of a blood pact, one that allows you to stay true to yourself while honouring your roots."

Just then, my phone buzzed on the table, disrupting the moment. I glanced at the screen and saw Leo's name. "Could we talk when you're free?" it read, followed by, "It's about the garden and something important." I felt a pang of concern as I turned my attention back to Ruby. "Looks like we're not the only ones feeling the pressure. Leo wants to talk." Her brow furrowed with curiosity and worry. "Do you think it's about the garden?"

"I'm not sure, but let's find out." I typed a quick response to Leo, agreeing to meet later.

As we finished our coffees, Ruby's expression turned serious. "Whatever he has to say, I hope it doesn't unravel what we've built. This garden..." she paused, "...it means everything to us."

"It does," I replied, my heart heavy with the weight of her fear. "But whatever happens, remember the blood pact doesn't just define our loyalties to our families; it also encompasses the bonds we've forged as a chosen family."

The ground felt unsteady as we walked towards the garden, where Leo awaited us. The sun dipped lower in the sky, casting elongated shadows that danced among the flowers and plants, vibrant reminders of the life we had nurtured together. As we approached, I felt the tension in the air—a prelude to a storm of emotions that might sweep through our trio. The implications of loyalty and our deeper connections loomed like clouds on the horizon, reminding us that blood ties could sometimes cut as deeply as any blade. The moment we reached Leo, I could see the urgency reflected in his eyes, a mirror of the swirling uncertainties we all shared. Whatever lay ahead, I knew we would confront it together, as a family built not just on shared lineage but on shared dreams, struggles, and unwavering support.

"Thanks for coming together," Leo began, his voice steady but edged with apprehension. "There's something we need to address."

I exchanged a glance with Ruby, her expression matching my unease. As the sun began to slip beneath the horizon, we braced ourselves for the revelations that could shift our course forever. Leo took a deep breath, his eyes scanning the garden before settling on us. "I know how much this garden means to all of us," he began, his voice steady but laced with tension. "But there's something we need to discuss. Something that could impact everything we've built." Ruby and I exchanged uneasy glances, the weight of his words hanging heavy in the air. "What is it, Leo?" Ruby asked, her voice barely above a whisper. He sighed, running a hand through his hair. "It's about the land. The owner wants to sell it, and there's a developer interested in buying. They're planning to turn it into luxury apartments."

A wave of shock and disbelief washed over me. The garden, our sanctuary, our shared dream, was under threat. "Is there anything we can do to stop it?" I asked, my mind racing with the implications. Leo nodded slowly. "There might be, but it won't be easy. We need to gather community support, raise funds, and present a strong case to the city council. We must show them that this garden is more than just a piece of land. It's a vital part of our community." Ruby's expression hardened with determination. "We've come this far together. We're not going to let it go without a fight."

THE BLOOD PACT

I felt a surge of resolve, a renewed sense of purpose. "Then let's do it. Let's rally everyone we know, spread the word, and make our voices heard." Leo smiled, a glimmer of hope in his eyes. "We'll need to work quickly. The developer is pushing for a decision within the next few weeks. But if we stand together, we can make a difference." As the sun dipped below the horizon, casting long shadows across the garden, I felt a sense of unity and strength. This garden was more than just a project; it was a symbol of our collective dreams, resilience, and unwavering commitment to each other and our community. In the days that followed, we threw ourselves into action. We organized meetings, created flyers, and reached out to local media. The community rallied behind us, their support overwhelming and heartening. Stories of how the garden had touched lives poured in, each one a testament to its importance.

Ruby, with her natural leadership skills, coordinated our efforts, while Leo handled the logistics. I focused on storytelling, capturing the essence of what the garden meant to us and sharing it with the world. Every evening, we gathered in the garden, strategizing, supporting each other, and reinforcing our resolve. As the deadline approached, tension and anticipation grew. We had done everything we could, but the outcome remained uncertain. On the day of the council meeting, we stood together, a united front, ready to fight for our dream. The council chamber was packed with supporters. As we presented our case, I felt a swell of pride and gratitude for the community that had come together in defence of our garden. We spoke passionately, each word a plea for the preservation of something beautiful and irreplaceable. When the council members retired to deliberate, the room buzzed with nervous energy. Minutes felt like hours, every second stretching the uncertainty. Finally, they returned, their expressions guarded.

"The council has reached a decision," the chairperson announced. "We recognize the significance of this garden to the community and the value it brings. After careful consideration, we have decided to deny the developer's proposal and preserve the garden."

A wave of relief and joy swept through the room. We hugged, cried, and celebrated, our dream saved by the power of unity and determination. As we returned to the garden that evening, under a sky filled with stars, I felt a profound sense of accomplishment. We had faced a daunting challenge and emerged victorious, our bonds stronger and our resolve unshaken. The garden, our sanctuary, stood as a testament to the power of community and the enduring strength of our blood pact. Together, we had not only preserved a piece of land but also a symbol of hope, resilience, and the unbreakable ties that bound us. As we basked in the glow of our victory, the gravity of our achievement began to settle in. The garden was safe, but the journey had only just begun. We had proven to ourselves and the community that together, we could overcome seemingly insurmountable obstacles.

The following weeks were a whirlwind of activity. We set to work improving the garden, with new plants, pathways, and community events. The garden became not just a place of beauty but a vibrant hub for our neighbourhood. It was during one such event, a garden festival filled with laughter and music, that Judie Giovanetti arrived. Judie, with her commanding presence, walked through the garden's entrance, her eyes taking in the scene. She paused, smiling slightly as she observed the people, the flowers, and the palpable sense of community. Ryan, who had been helping set up a booth, spotted her and excused himself. "Mom," he called out, his voice filled with warmth and respect. "I'm glad you could make it."

THE BLOOD PACT

Judie turned, her piercing hazel eyes softening as they met her son's. "I wouldn't miss it for the world," she replied. Her gaze shifted to Ruby, who was coordinating volunteers nearby. "And I see Ruby is keeping everything in order." Ruby approached, wiping her hands on her jeans, her smile genuine. "Judie, it's great to see you." Judie nodded, a subtle acknowledgment of the younger woman's efforts. "You've done an impressive job here, Ruby. The garden looks magnificent."

"Thank you," Ruby replied, her eyes sparkling with pride. "It means a lot to all of us."

Mia Carter, ever watchful and efficient, hovered nearby, her sharp green eyes surveying the area. She approached the group, nodding respectfully to Judie. "We've got everything under control here," she reported, her tone professional but warm. Judie gave a small, approving smile. "I'm sure you do, Mia. Your vigilance is always appreciated." As the festival continued, I found myself reflecting on the journey we had all been on. The garden had become a symbol of our collective strength and unity, a testament to our determination to build something beautiful and enduring. That evening, as the sun set and the festival wound down, we gathered in the centre of the garden. Judie stood beside Ryan, Ruby, and Mia, their presence a powerful reminder of the bonds we had forged. Judie raised her glass, her voice carrying a tone of solemnity and pride. "To the garden, and to all that it represents. May it continue to grow and thrive, just as we have."

We raised our glasses in unison, the moment a celebration of our shared journey and the promise of the future. As we stood together, under the canopy of stars, I felt a profound sense of connection and hope. The garden was more than just a place; it was a living embodiment of our dreams, our struggles, and our unwavering bond.

In that moment, I knew that whatever challenges lay ahead, we would face them together, as a family—bound not just by blood, but by the pacts we had made and the love we had nurtured. In the days following our victory at the council meeting, we fully embraced our roles at the estate, transforming it into a thriving headquarters. The once dilapidated mansion now stood as a testament to our dedication and hard work. The garden, nestled within the estate grounds, became a vibrant centre of activity and planning, reflecting our collective vision. As we settled into our new roles, each of us brought our unique skills and strengths to the forefront. Judie, with her sharp strategic mind, guided our decisions with an iron will be tempered by compassion. Ruby, with her warm and approachable nature, became the heart of our team, fostering connections and maintaining morale. Leo managed the logistical operations, ensuring everything ran smoothly. Mia, ever vigilant, oversaw security and intelligence, keeping us informed and protected.

One evening, as we gathered in the garden for a meeting, the atmosphere was filled with a mix of determination and camaraderie. The setting sun cast a golden glow over the flowers, the serene beauty belying the intensity of our discussions.

"Alright," Judie began, her voice commanding attention. "We need to address our next steps. The developer's threat may be behind us, but we can't let our guard down. We need to strengthen our community ties and expand our influence."

Ruby nodded, her green eyes filled with resolve. "We should host more events, bring the community together, and show them the positive impact we can have. The garden festival was a great start, but we can do more."

"I agree," Leo chimed in. "We should also look into partnerships with local businesses and organizations. The more allies we have, the stronger our position."

THE BLOOD PACT

Mia, ever practical, added, "We should also enhance our security measures. The estate is our home and our headquarters. We can't afford any vulnerabilities." As we discussed our plans, I felt a deep sense of pride and unity. Our headquarters wasn't just a place; it was a symbol of our commitment to each other and to our community. It was a place where dreams took root and grew, nurtured by our collective efforts. Over the following weeks, we set our plans into motion. We organized community events, forging stronger bonds with our neighbours and allies. We established partnerships with local businesses, creating a network of support that extended beyond the estate's boundaries. And we fortified our security, ensuring that our sanctuary remained safe from any threats.

The estate thrived, a bustling centre of activity and collaboration. The garden, now a verdant oasis, became a place of reflection and inspiration, where ideas bloomed, and friendships flourished. Our headquarters was more than just a base of operations; it was a living testament to our resilience, unity, and shared vision. As we stood together in the garden one evening, under a sky filled with stars, I felt a profound sense of accomplishment. We had transformed a dilapidated mansion into a thriving headquarters, a beacon of hope and strength for our community. And as we looked to the future, we knew that together, we could face any challenge and achieve any dream. As the sun set over the estate, casting long shadows across the garden, we gathered for another meeting. The twilight added a serene, almost magical atmosphere to our discussions, blending our resolve with a quiet sense of purpose.

"Now that we've established the garden and secured the estate as our base," Judie began, her voice calm but commanding, "we need to turn our attention to our broader objectives. We have the resources and the community's support, but we must remain vigilant and proactive."

Ruby, sitting beside me, nodded in agreement. "We should start by identifying potential threats and opportunities. The developer's attempt to buy the garden was just the beginning. We need to be prepared for whatever comes next." Leo leaned forward, his expression serious. "I've been looking into local politics and businesses. There are some influential figures who might either support or oppose our efforts, depending on their interests. We should reach out and build alliances where possible." Mia, ever the pragmatist, added, "And we need to keep an eye on any criminal elements that might see our success as a threat to their own operations. Our influence is growing, and that can attract unwanted attention."

Judie looked at each of us, her hazel eyes filled with determination. "We will handle this as we have everything else—strategically and together. Ryan, I want you and Ruby to lead the outreach efforts. Leo, you'll manage our local intelligence. Mia, continue to oversee security and gather information on potential threats." I felt a surge of purpose as I looked at my family and friends, each one ready to face the challenges ahead. "We've built something incredible here," I said, my voice filled with conviction. "And we will protect it, no matter what." Over the next few weeks, we expanded our efforts, reaching out to local leaders, businesses, and community organizations. Ruby and I attended countless meetings and events, building relationships and securing support. Leo's intelligence network provided us with valuable insights, helping us navigate the complex landscape of local politics and business interests.

THE BLOOD PACT

Mia's vigilance ensured that our operations remained secure, her sharp instincts and skills keeping us one step ahead of any potential threats. The estate buzzed with activity, our headquarters becoming a centre of planning and coordination. One evening, as we reviewed our progress in the garden, I couldn't help but feel a deep sense of pride. The estate, once a symbol of decay, had become a thriving hub of hope and resilience. Our garden, now a lush oasis, stood as a testament to our hard work and unity.

"We've made incredible strides," Ruby said, her eyes shining with excitement. "But there's still more to do. We need to stay focused and continue building our network."

"Agreed," Leo said, his tone serious. "I've identified a few key figures who could be potential allies or adversaries. We need to approach them carefully."

Mia nodded, her expression thoughtful. "And we should continue to fortify our defences. Our success makes us a target, and we need to be prepared." Judie, who had been listening quietly, spoke up. "We've come a long way, but we must remember that our strength lies in our unity. We face these challenges together, as a family. That's what makes us unstoppable." As we stood in the garden, surrounded by the fruits of our labour, I felt a deep sense of connection and purpose. The estate was not just our headquarters; it was a symbol of our collective dreams and determination. Whatever challenges lay ahead, I knew that we would face them with courage and resilience, guided by the bonds we had forged and the love we shared Our headquarters at the estate had become a vibrant hub of activity, a testament to our determination and the bonds we shared. As days turned into weeks, the garden flourished, and so did our sense of purpose. But with each step forward, the complexity of our mission grew.

One evening, as we gathered in the garden for another strategy session, the cool night air was filled with the scent of blooming flowers and the distant hum of city life. Judie stood at the head of the table, her piercing hazel eyes scanning each of us with a mixture of pride and resolve. "We've made significant progress," she began, her voice carrying the weight of leadership. "But we must remain vigilant. The threats we face are not just external. We need to ensure our unity and trust within this family." Ruby, sitting beside me, leaned forward, her expressive green eyes reflecting her determination. "We've built something incredible here. But we must be prepared for anything. We need to continue strengthening our alliances and our defences." Leo nodded, his demeanour serious. "I've been keeping tabs on potential threats. There are some figures in the local scene who might see our success as a challenge to their own interests. We need to be proactive."

Mia, ever the sentinel, added, "Our security measures are in place, but we should consider expanding our surveillance and intelligence operations. Information is our most valuable asset." I felt a surge of determination as I listened to my family and friends. "We've faced many challenges together, and we've come out stronger each time. Whatever comes next, we'll handle it together." The following weeks were a whirlwind of planning and action. We fortified the estate, implemented advanced surveillance systems, and expanded our network of allies. Our garden, once a symbol of tranquillity, now served as the heart of our operations, a place where plans were forged and decisions made. One afternoon, as I walked through the garden, I found Ruby sitting on a bench, her gaze distant. I joined her, the silence between us filled with unspoken thoughts.

"Sometimes it all feels overwhelming," she admitted, her voice soft. "But then I look at what we've built, and I know it's worth it."

THE BLOOD PACT

I took her hand, the warmth of her touch grounding me. "We've come a long way, Ruby. And we'll keep going, no matter what. Together." She smiled, a flicker of hope in her eyes. "Together." As night fell, we gathered in the garden once more, the stars above a reminder of the vastness of our journey. Judie stood, her presence commanding respect.

"We face many challenges, but we do so as a family. Our strength lies in our unity, our resilience, and our unwavering commitment to each other."

The words resonated with each of us, a reaffirmation of our purpose and bond. As we stood together, the garden a living testament to our efforts, I knew that whatever lay ahead, we were ready to face it.

R. STELLAN

Echoes of the Past

The estate was abuzz with activity, the hum of life and purpose masking the unease that had settled in the corners of my mind. Dom was gone, shot by my mother in a decisive act that had sealed my position as the new head of the Famiglia Notturno. But while his death had brought a semblance of stability to our fractured world, it had also stirred up a hornet's nest of resentment and vengeance. As I walked through the garden, the peaceful surroundings contrasting sharply with the turmoil within, I couldn't shake the feeling that we were living on borrowed time. Dom's network, though leaderless, was far from dismantled. They were out there, lurking in the shadows, plotting their revenge. I found Ruby in the greenhouse, tending to the plants with a calm that belied the tension in the air. "Hey," I greeted her, my voice betraying the weight of my thoughts.

She looked up, her green eyes filled with concern. "Ryan, what's wrong?"

"It's Dom's people," I confessed, running a hand through my hair. "They're not going to let this go. We need to be prepared for whatever comes next."

Ruby set down her watering can and walked over to me, her presence a balm to my frayed nerves. "We knew this wouldn't be easy. But we're not alone. We have each other, and we have a plan."

That evening, we gathered in the grand hall of the estate, the atmosphere heavy with anticipation. Judie, ever the matriarch, stood at the head of the table, her eyes sweeping over our assembled team—Ruby, Leo, Mia, and myself.

"Dom's death was a necessary step," she began, her voice steady and unwavering. "But it has unleashed forces that we must now confront. His network will seek retribution, and we must be ready."

Leo leaned forward, his expression grim. "I've been tracking their movements. They're mobilizing, and it's only a matter of time before they make their move." Mia, always the sentinel, added, "We need to strengthen our defences and gather intelligence on their plans. We can't afford any surprises." Judie nodded, her gaze settling on me. "Ryan, you are the head of this family now. Your leadership will be crucial in the days ahead. We must stand united and resolute." I took a deep breath, the weight of my responsibilities pressing down on me. "We'll face this together. We've overcome every challenge so far, and we'll get through this too." In the following days, we fortified the estate, implementing advanced security measures and expanding our network of informants. Mia's expertise in surveillance and intelligence was invaluable, her sharp instincts keeping us one step ahead of our enemies. Leo coordinated our efforts, ensuring that every aspect of our defence was meticulously planned.

Ruby and I focused on maintaining the morale of our team and the community. We organized events and meetings, reinforcing the bonds that held us together. The garden, our sanctuary, became a place of refuge and strength, a reminder of what we were fighting for. One night, as I patrolled the estate with Mia, we spoke in hushed tones about the looming threat. "They're getting bolder," she said, her green eyes scanning the perimeter. "We need to be ready for anything."

"I know," I replied, my voice filled with determination. "But we have each other. That's our greatest strength."

THE BLOOD PACT

The inevitable confrontation came on a stormy night, the rain lashing against the windows as we huddled in the war room, analysing the latest intelligence. Mia's voice crackled over the comms, her tone urgent. "They're here. Multiple vehicles approaching the estate. Get ready." Judie, always composed, directed us with military precision. "Positions, everyone. This is what we've prepared for." As the sounds of engines grew louder, I steeled myself for the battle ahead. The echoes of the past were coming for us, but we were ready to face them head-on. The estate, our sanctuary and stronghold, stood as a symbol of our unity and resilience. Together, we would defend our home and our family. The first shots rang out, the clash between past and present erupting in a storm of violence and resolve. We fought with everything we had, our bond and determination fuelling us through the chaos. In the end, it was our unity, our unwavering commitment to each other, that saw us through.

As dawn broke over the estate, the rain washing away the remnants of the battle, we stood together, battered but unbroken. The echoes of the past had been faced and silenced, their threat diminished by our strength and unity. In the aftermath of the attack, the estate was a flurry of activity. We assessed the damage, checked on our wounded, and began to regroup. Despite the chaos, the determination in our hearts remained unwavering. I found Leo in the command room, poring over security footage and coordinating with our guards. His face was set with a mixture of exhaustion and resolve.

"Leo," I called out, walking over to him. "We need to increase our security detail. This was just a taste of what's to come."

He looked up, nodding in agreement. "I was thinking the same thing. We need more personnel and better equipment. I'll start reaching out to our contacts immediately."

"Good," I said, my voice firm. "We can't afford any more breaches. The estate is our stronghold, and we need to keep it secure."

Leo set to work, his focus intense. As he made the calls and coordinated the additional security measures, I felt a sense of reassurance. We were taking the necessary steps to protect our home and our family. That evening, we gathered in the war room to review our plans. Judie stood at the head of the table, her presence commanding and reassuring.

"Leo has arranged for additional security personnel," she announced. "They'll arrive within the next few days. In the meantime, we need to remain vigilant and prepared."

Ruby, sitting beside me, added, "We should also strengthen our alliances with the community. Their support will be crucial in times of need." Mia nodded, her expression thoughtful. "And we should continue to gather intelligence on Dom's network. We need to know their movements and intentions." I looked around the table at my family, each one ready to face the challenges ahead. "We'll get through this," I said, my voice filled with conviction. "We've faced worse and come out stronger. Together, we'll protect what we've built." In the days that followed, the additional security personnel arrived, fortifying the estate with their presence. We held training sessions, ensuring everyone was prepared for any eventuality. Mia's expertise in security was invaluable, her meticulous attention to detail ensuring that no aspect was overlooked. The garden, once a place of tranquillity, now served as a centre of strategy and planning. We met regularly, discussing our progress and adapting our plans as needed. The sense of unity and purpose was palpable, our bond as a family growing stronger with each passing day.

As evening came, I walked through the garden with Ruby, I reflected on the journey we had been on. "It's been a long road," I mused, my voice soft. "But we're stronger for it." Ruby squeezed my hand, her eyes filled with warmth and determination. "And we'll keep going, no matter what. Together." As the sun set over the estate, casting a warm glow over the garden, I felt a deep sense of resolve.

THE BLOOD PACT

The echoes of the past still lingered, but they no longer held the power to break us. We were united, resilient, and ready to face whatever challenges lay ahead. The estate was a hive of activity, with new security measures being put in place and plans being refined. Yet amidst the hustle and bustle, a quiet moment had been lingering in my mind—a moment I knew I had to seize.

One evening, as the sun dipped below the horizon, casting a warm, golden hue over the garden, I found Ruby by the rose bushes. She was tending to the flowers, her serene presence a balm to the day's tensions.

"Ruby," I called out softly, walking towards her. She turned, her green eyes sparkling in the fading light.

"Ryan," she greeted me, a smile playing on her lips. "Taking a break from all the chaos?"

I nodded, feeling the weight of my decision pressing down on me. "There's something I need to talk to you about. Something important." Her expression grew serious, concern flickering in her eyes. "What is it?" I took her hands in mine, the warmth of her touch grounding me. "Ruby, we've been through so much together. We've faced challenges and overcome them, side by side. You've been my strength, my confidant, and my anchor." Her eyes softened, and she squeezed my hands gently. "And you've been mine, Ryan."

Taking a deep breath, I reached into my pocket and pulled out a small velvet box. "Ruby, I can't imagine my life without you. Through all the chaos and uncertainty, you're the one thing that has always kept me going. I love you more than words can express." I dropped to one knee, opening the box to reveal a simple, elegant ring.

"Ruby Smith, will you marry me?"

Tears welled up in her eyes, and for a moment, time seemed to stand still. Then, she nodded, her smile radiant.

"Yes, Ryan. Yes, I'll marry you."

I slipped the ring onto her finger, feeling a surge of joy and relief. We embraced, the world around us fading away as we shared this intimate, profound moment. Later that evening, as we gathered in the war room to continue our planning, I couldn't help but feel a renewed sense of purpose and determination. Judie, Leo, and Mia noticed the change in our demeanour and exchanged knowing glances.

"What's going on?" Leo asked, a hint of curiosity in his voice.

I stood, taking Ruby's hand, and addressed my family. "Ruby and I have some news. We're engaged." A chorus of congratulations and cheers erupted around the table. Judie, her eyes shining with pride, hugged us both tightly. "I'm so happy for you both," she said, her voice filled with emotion. Leo clapped me on the back, grinning. "About time, Ryan." Mia, always the pragmatist, nodded in approval. "Congratulations. This is a bright spot in all the madness." As we celebrated this new chapter in our lives, the sense of unity and love that bound us together grew even stronger. The threats we faced were real, but so was our commitment to each other and our shared dreams.

In the days that followed, our engagement brought a renewed sense of joy and purpose to our lives. Despite the ongoing challenges, the promise of a future together strengthened our resolve. The estate, fortified and secure, became a bustling centre of activity as we prepared for whatever lay ahead. One morning, as we gathered in the command room, Leo briefed us on the latest intelligence. "We've intercepted some communications," he said, his voice serious. "Dom's network is regrouping. They're planning something big, and we need to be ready." Judie, ever the strategist, nodded. "We need to stay ahead of them. Ryan, I want you and Ruby to continue building our alliances. The more support we have, the better prepared we'll be."

THE BLOOD PACT

Ruby and I shared a determined glance. "We'll get to work right away," I replied. Over the next few weeks, Ruby and I focused on strengthening our ties with the community and local businesses. We attended meetings, organized events, and worked tirelessly to build a network of support. Our efforts paid off as more and more allies joined our cause, bolstering our defences and resources. One evening, as we walked through the garden, Ruby turned to me, her eyes reflecting the soft glow of the lanterns. "We've come so far, Ryan. But there's still so much to do." I nodded, feeling the weight of our responsibilities. "I know. But we have each other, and we have our family. We'll face whatever comes together."

The tension in the air was palpable as we continued to prepare for the inevitable confrontation with Dom's network. Mia's vigilance and expertise in security kept us one step ahead, her meticulous planning ensuring that our defences were impenetrable. One night, as the rain poured down outside, we gathered in the war room, reviewing our strategies. Mia's voice crackled over the comms, her tone urgent. "I've got movement on the perimeter. Multiple vehicles approaching."

Judie, her calm demeanour never wavering, issued commands with precision. "Positions, everyone. This is it." As the sounds of engines grew louder, I felt a surge of determination. We had faced threats before, and we had emerged stronger each time. This would be no different. The first shots rang out, the clash between past and present erupting in a storm of violence and resolve. We fought with everything we had, our bond and determination fuelling us through the chaos. The estate, our sanctuary and stronghold, stood as a symbol of our unity and resilience. When the dust settled, we stood victorious. The remnants of Dom's network had been defeated, their threat diminished by our strength and unity. The estate had withstood the assault, a testament to our preparedness and resolve.

As dawn broke, casting a golden light over the garden, we gathered to reflect on the battle. Judie, her eyes filled with pride, spoke first. "We've faced a great challenge and emerged victorious. But we must remain vigilant. This is just the beginning." Ruby, standing beside me, nodded. "We have each other, and we have our community. We'll keep building, keep growing, and keep fighting for what we believe in." Leo, ever the pragmatist, added, "And we'll continue to gather intelligence and strengthen our defences. We're ready for whatever comes next." Mia, her sharp eyes scanning the horizon, concluded, "We've proven that we can face anything together. This is our home, our family, and we'll protect it at all costs."

THE BLOOD PACT

Unforeseen Alliances

The estate had become a fortress of resilience and unity, our sanctuary amidst the chaos. But as we settled into a semblance of routine, it became clear that our journey was far from over. The past had a way of lingering, and new challenges were always on the horizon. One evening, as we gathered in the garden for our regular strategy meeting, Leo shared some unexpected news. "I've been approached by someone who claims they can help us," he said, his tone cautious. "An old associate of Dom's. They want to meet." Judie's eyes narrowed, her instincts as a strategist kicking in. "And why would they want to help us?" Leo shrugged. "They didn't say much, but they implied that they're not happy with the current state of affairs. They see an opportunity in aligning with us."

Ruby, ever the empath, looked thoughtful. "It could be a trap. But it could also be a chance to gain valuable information and support." Mia, added, "We need to be cautious. But if there's a way to turn one of Dom's own against his network, it might be worth the risk." I listened to their perspectives, weighing the potential benefits against the dangers. "We'll meet with them," I decided. "But on our terms. We'll choose the location and set the ground rules." The next day, we arranged to meet the mysterious associate at a neutral location—a quiet café on the outskirts of town. Mia and Leo scouted the area in advance, ensuring it was secure.

As Ruby and I arrived at the café, my senses were on high alert. We took a seat by the window, the late afternoon sun casting a warm glow over the room. A few minutes later, a tall, slender man with dark hair and a sharp gaze walked in. He scanned the room before making his way to our table.

"Ryan," he greeted, his voice calm and measured. "I'm Antonio."

I studied him carefully, noting the intelligence in his eyes and the tension in his stance. "Antonio. You said you wanted to help us. Why?" He took a seat, leaning forward slightly. "Dom's death has left a power vacuum. The remnants of his network are scrambling for control, and it's turning into a mess. I have my own interests to protect, and aligning with you could bring some stability to the chaos." Ruby, her green eyes filled with curiosity, asked, "What do you want in return?" Antonio smiled, a hint of something enigmatic in his expression. "I have resources and information that could be valuable to you. In exchange, I want protection and a place in your new order." I considered his offer, aware of the risks but also the potential benefits. "We'll need to vet you and verify your information. If you're genuine, there might be a place for you."

Antonio nodded, understanding the gravity of the situation. "Fair enough. I'll provide you with some initial intel as a show of good faith." Back at the estate, we reviewed the information Antonio had given us. It was detailed and precise, shedding light on the inner workings of Dom's network and their plans. It was clear that Antonio had access to valuable insights. Judie, ever the strategist, was the first to speak. "This information is credible. If Antonio is willing to work with us, we could turn a significant asset from Dom's network into our ally." Leo added, "We need to be cautious, but this could give us the edge we need."

THE BLOOD PACT

Ruby looked at me, her expression a mix of hope and caution. "What do you think, Ryan?" I took a deep breath, feeling the weight of my decision. "We'll proceed, but carefully. We'll continue to verify Antonio's information and integrate him into our operations slowly. Trust is earned, not given." Mia nodded in agreement. "I'll keep a close watch on him. If he tries anything, we'll know." As the weeks passed, Antonio proved his worth. His information allowed us to pre-empt several moves by Dom's network, strengthening our position and solidifying our alliances. He became an asset, working closely with Leo and Mia to enhance our intelligence operations. Despite the initial scepticism, Antonio's integration into our team brought unexpected benefits. His expertise and insights helped us navigate the complexities of our situation, turning potential threats into opportunities.

As the days turned into weeks, Antonio's presence became a familiar and valuable part of our operations. His insights and strategic advice allowed us to pre-empt several moves by Dom's remaining loyalists, solidifying our position and fortifying our defences. One afternoon, as the sun cast a warm glow over the estate, I found Antonio in the garden, his expression contemplative. I approached him, curious about what was on his mind.

"Antonio," I greeted him, "you've been a great help to us. I wanted to thank you for your efforts."

He turned, a small smile playing on his lips. "Ryan, I appreciate that. Aligning with you and your team has been... enlightening. But I must ask, what drives you to fight so hard for this place and these people?" I took a moment to gather my thoughts, feeling the weight of his question. "This estate, this garden—it's more than just a place. It's a symbol of what we can achieve together. It's a sanctuary for our community and a testament to our resilience. We're not just fighting for ourselves; we're fighting for everyone who believes in what we've built." Antonio nodded, his gaze thoughtful. "I see. It's admirable.

I've seen too many people driven by power and greed. It's refreshing to see a cause worth fighting for." Our partnership with Antonio opened new doors and brought unforeseen opportunities. With his help, we expanded our network and strengthened our alliances. His knowledge of Dom's inner circle proved invaluable, allowing us to stay one step ahead of any potential threats. One evening, as we gathered in the war room to review our progress, Judie addressed us with her usual commanding presence. "Thanks to Antonio's insights, we've managed to neutralize several threats and strengthen our position. But we must remain vigilant. Dom's network, though weakened, is still out there."

Leo leaned forward, his expression serious. "I've been tracking their movements. They're regrouping, trying to find a new leader. We need to be prepared for any attempts to reclaim power." Mia added, "Our defences are strong, but we should continue to gather intelligence and stay proactive. Information is our best weapon." Ruby, sitting beside me, looked thoughtful. "We should also focus on our community outreach. The more support we have, the stronger our position will be." I nodded, feeling a renewed sense of purpose. "We'll continue building our alliances and fortifying our defences. Together, we'll protect what we've built." As the days went by, our efforts began to bear fruit. The estate flourished, becoming a beacon of hope and resilience for our community. We held events, organized meetings, and continued to build a network of support that extended beyond our immediate circle.

One afternoon, as Ruby and I walked through the garden, we talked about our future. "I want us to build a life here," I said, my voice filled with hope. "A life where we can thrive, despite the challenges we face."

THE BLOOD PACT

Ruby smiled, her eyes reflecting the same hope. "We'll build it together, Ryan. This place, this community—it's our home. And we'll protect it, no matter what." The alliances we formed, both expected and unexpected, strengthened our resolve and our capabilities. Antonio's integration into our team brought new perspectives and opportunities, proving that sometimes, the most valuable allies can come from the most unforeseen places. As we looked to the future, we knew that our strength lay not only in our unity but also in our ability to adapt and forge new paths. Together, we were unstoppable, ready to face whatever challenges lay ahead. As the weeks passed, the estate buzzed with a sense of newfound purpose. The alliance with Antonio had bolstered our strategic position, and his insights continued to prove invaluable. Our preparations were thorough, but the unpredictability of our circumstances kept us on our toes.

One evening, while Ruby and I were reviewing plans in the war room, Leo entered with an air of urgency. "Ryan, Antonio has just brought in some critical intel. You need to see this." We followed Leo to the command centre where Antonio was waiting, his expression grave. He laid out a series of documents and maps on the table. "I've uncovered a plot against us," he began. "There are factions within Dom's network planning a coordinated attack to reclaim their lost power." Judie, who had joined us, leaned in, her sharp eyes scanning the information. "How credible is this intel?" she asked. Antonio nodded. "It's solid. My sources confirm that they're planning to move soon. We need to act quickly to pre-empt their efforts." Mia added, "We should strike first. Take them off guard and disrupt their plans before they have a chance to mobilize."

I looked around at my team, the weight of leadership heavy on my shoulders. "We'll need to be strategic about this," I said. "Antonio, can you provide us with the exact locations and key players involved?"

He handed me a folder. "Everything you need is in here. We can coordinate our efforts to hit multiple targets simultaneously." The next few days were a whirlwind of preparation. We planned and coordinated meticulously, leveraging Antonio's intel to formulate a comprehensive strategy. The estate buzzed with activity, each member of our team focused on their respective tasks. As night fell on the eve of our planned operation, we gathered in the garden for one final briefing. The atmosphere was tense but resolute. Judie addressed us with her usual commanding presence.

"This is it," she said. "We've prepared for this moment, and now it's time to act. Remember, our strength lies in our unity and our determination. We fight not just for ourselves, but for our community and the future we're building together."

Ruby stood beside me, her hand in mine. "We'll get through this, Ryan. Together." I nodded, feeling a surge of resolve. "Let's do this." The operation commenced under the cover of darkness. Mia and her security team moved with precision, executing our plan with military efficiency. Leo coordinated the efforts from the command centre, ensuring seamless communication and support. Antonio and I led a team to one of the key locations, our movements swift and deliberate. The element of surprise was on our side, and we quickly neutralized the threats, dismantling their operations before they could fully mobilize. As the night wore on, reports came in from the other teams. Each target was successfully neutralized, the coordinated efforts effectively disrupting the factions' plans. The sense of victory was tempered by the knowledge that our fight was far from over.

By dawn, the estate was once again secure. We gathered in the garden, the first light of day casting a hopeful glow over the flowers and plants we had nurtured. Judie, her expression a mix of relief and pride, addressed us.

THE BLOOD PACT

"We've achieved a significant victory," she said. "But we must remain vigilant. This operation has shown us what we're capable of when we stand united. Let's continue to build on this momentum and protect what we've created."

Ruby's green eyes sparkled with determination as she looked at me. "We did it, Ryan. But we need to stay strong. There's still more to do." I nodded, feeling the weight of our journey and the promise of our future.

"Together, we'll face whatever comes next."—-

With an air of anticipation and excitement. The garden was filled with the fragrant scent of blooming flowers, and the preparations for the wedding were in full swing. The morning of the wedding, Ruby and I had a quiet moment together in the garden. The sun was just beginning to rise, casting a soft, golden glow over the vibrant blooms. We walked hand in hand, taking in the beauty of the space that had become so meaningful to us.

"Ryan, I can't believe this day is finally here," Ruby said, her voice filled with emotion. "It feels like a dream."

I smiled, squeezing her hand gently. "It's a dream we've built together, Ruby. And today is just the beginning of our next chapter." As the hours passed, the garden transformed into a magical setting. Twinkling lights were strung along the trees, and the tables were adorned with elegant floral arrangements. Our friends and family began to arrive, each one adding to the joy and love that filled the air.

Before the ceremony, I took a moment to gather my thoughts. Standing at the altar, I could see the smiling faces of our loved ones. The support and love from our community made this day even more special. Finally, the music began to play, and all eyes turned towards the entrance of the garden. Ruby appeared, walking down the aisle with her father by her side. Her dress was a vision of simplicity and elegance, and her eyes sparkled with happiness. As she reached the altar and took my hand, I felt an overwhelming sense of gratitude and love. The vows we exchanged were heartfelt and sincere, each word a reflection of our journey and our commitment to one another. After the ceremony, we celebrated with our friends and family. The garden was filled with laughter, music, and the clinking of glasses. It was a day of pure joy and unity, a testament to the strength of our love and the bonds we had forged with those around us.

As the sun set and the evening ended, Ruby and I found ourselves once again beneath the old oak tree. The garden, now illuminated by the soft glow of fairy lights, felt like a magical sanctuary.

"We did it, Ryan," Ruby whispered, her head resting on my shoulder. "We've come so far, and I can't wait to see what the future holds for us."

I wrapped my arm around her, feeling a deep sense of contentment. "Whatever the future brings, I know we'll face it together. With love and support, we can achieve anything." With an even deeper sense of fulfilment and connection. Ruby and I had just shared one of the most significant moments of our lives, but our journey was far from over. As the days turned into weeks, we began to settle into our new routine as a married couple. The estate, once a place of strategy and tension, had transformed into a home filled with love and laughter. The garden, where we had exchanged our vows, continued to be our sanctuary—a place where we could reflect on our past and dream about our future.

One afternoon, as we strolled through the garden, Ruby turned to me with a thoughtful expression. "Ryan, I've been thinking... I want to invite my parents to visit us here. It's time you met them." I nodded, feeling a mix of excitement and nervousness. "I'd love to meet them, Ruby. What should I know about them? How can I make a good first impression?" Ruby smiled, sensing my apprehension. "Just be yourself, Ryan. They'll love you for who you are. But if it

THE BLOOD PACT

helps, here are a few tips: dress appropriately, be punctual, be polite and respectful, engage in conversation, and most importantly, be genuine." With Ruby's advice in mind, I felt more confident about the upcoming meeting. We spent the next few days preparing for their arrival, making sure everything was perfect. When the day finally arrived, I stood in the garden, waiting with bated breath. The familiar sound of footsteps on the gravel path made my heart race. Ruby's parents appeared, their faces filled with warmth and curiosity.

"Mom, Dad, this is Ryan," Ruby introduced me with a smile.

I extended my hand, offering a sincere greeting. "It's a pleasure to finally meet you both. Welcome to our home." As we sat down for tea in the garden, I found myself engaging in a heartfelt conversation with Ruby's parents. We talked about our shared experiences, our hopes for the future, and the journey that had brought us together. Their kindness and acceptance put me at ease, and I felt a genuine connection forming. The rest of the visit was filled with laughter and bonding. We shared stories, enjoyed delicious meals, and explored the beauty of the estate together. By the time they left, I felt like I had gained new family members. The days continued to pass in a harmonious blend of work and leisure. Ruby and I focused on our personal and professional goals, supporting each other every step of the way. The garden remained our haven, a place where we could find solace and inspiration.

I couldn't help but reflect on the incredible journey we had undertaken. From the challenges we faced to the love we had found, every moment had shaped us into the people we had become. Together, we were ready to face whatever the future held, knowing that our love and the strength of our shared dreams would guide us through.

Dangerous Games

Josh's rivalry with Ryan takes a darker turn. It had been a few, months since the heated confrontation in the university dining hall, where Josh had attacked Ryan out of jealousy. Josh wanted Ruby for himself, but she had never felt the same way about him. The incident had left a mark on Ryan, both physically and emotionally. He had thought that the matter was resolved, but little did he know that Josh's resentment had only festered and grown stronger. Life at the estate had settled into a peaceful routine, but beneath the surface, danger lurked. Ryan and Ruby were focused on their future, their love stronger than ever. However, the shadow of Josh's animosity loomed over them.

One evening, as Ryan was walking through the garden, he noticed something unusual. A note, crudely written and pinned to one of the trees, caught his attention. It read:

"Ryan, this isn't over. I won't let you have Ruby. Watch your back. - Josh"

A chill ran down Ryan's spine. He knew that Josh was not one to make empty threats. Ryan immediately showed the note to Ruby, who was visibly shaken but also furious.

"Josh has been my friend for a long time," Ruby said, her voice trembling with anger. "I can't believe he would do something like this. I don't think he's dangerous, but this threat is unacceptable."

Ryan placed a reassuring hand on her shoulder. "We need to be careful, Ruby. Josh's jealousy has taken a dangerous turn, and we can't underestimate him." Ruby nodded, her eyes filled with determination. "We'll get through this together, Ryan. We have to stay strong." The next few weeks were tense, as Ryan and Ruby took extra precautions to ensure their safety. They informed their friends and family about the situation, and everyone rallied together to support them. Despite the threats, Ryan and Ruby refused to let fear control their lives. They continued with their daily routines, but always remained vigilant. Ryan kept a close eye on their surroundings, looking for any signs of Josh's presence.

One evening, as Ryan was returning from a late-night walk, he heard footsteps behind him. He turned around to see Josh emerging from the shadows, his expression twisted with anger and jealousy.

"Josh, what do you want?" Ryan asked, trying to keep his voice steady.

"I want what's mine," Josh replied, his voice cold and menacing. "You took Ruby from me, and now you'll pay for it."

Ryan knew that a confrontation was inevitable. He stood his ground, ready to defend himself and protect Ruby. The tension between them reached a boiling point, and the confrontation quickly escalated into a physical struggle. Ryan fought with all his might, determined not to let Josh's hatred tear them apart. With the support of his friends and family, Ryan managed to fend off Josh's attack. The authorities were called, and Josh was apprehended, putting an end to his dangerous games. As the dust settled, Ryan and Ruby stood together, their bond stronger than ever. They had faced the darkness and emerged victorious, their love and determination

THE BLOOD PACT

shining through. With Josh apprehended and safely in police custody, Ruby felt a surge of conflicting emotions. Anger, disappointment, and a lingering sense of disbelief weighed heavily on her heart. Despite their long-time friendship, Josh's actions had crossed a line, and she knew she needed to confront him.

Ruby made her way to the police holding area, her mind racing with thoughts of what she would say. As she entered the room, she saw Josh sitting on a bench, his hands cuffed and his expression sullen.

"Josh," Ruby began, her voice steady but filled with emotion. "I can't believe you've done this. How could you threaten Ryan and me like that?"

Josh looked up, his eyes filled with a mix of guilt and anger. "Ruby, I... I just wanted you to see how much I care about you. I thought if I could get rid of Ryan, you'd realize we belong together." Ruby shook her head, her eyes narrowing with determination. "Josh, this isn't love. It's obsession. I've always seen you as a friend, but your actions have shown me that you don't respect my feelings or my choices." Josh's shoulders slumped, and he let out a heavy sigh. "I was jealous, Ruby. I couldn't stand seeing you with him. I thought I could make you see things my way." Ruby took a step closer, her voice softening but remaining firm. "Josh, you need to understand that love can't be forced. It's built on trust, respect, and mutual feelings. What you did was wrong, and it hurt me deeply. I want you to get the help you need to move on and find happiness in a healthy way."

Tears welled up in Josh's eyes as he looked at Ruby. "I'm sorry, Ruby. I never meant to hurt you. I just didn't know how to handle my feelings." Ruby nodded, her heart aching for the friend she once knew. "I hope you can find a way to heal, Josh. But for now, we need to keep our distance. I need to protect myself and the people I love."

With those words, Ruby turned and walked away, leaving Josh to reflect on his actions. As she exited the police holding area, she felt a sense of closure and resolve. Back at the estate, Ryan was waiting for her with open arms. "How did it go?" he asked, concern etched on his face. Ruby sighed, leaning into his embrace. "It was tough, but I said what I needed to say. I hope Josh can find a way to move on and heal." Ryan held her close, his voice filled with love and reassurance. "We're stronger together, Ruby. We'll face whatever comes our way, and we'll do it with love and determination." In the aftermath of Ruby's confrontation with Josh, the atmosphere at the estate began to stabilize. The tension that had lingered for weeks was finally easing, and a sense of normalcy was returning. Ruby and Ryan were determined to move forward, focusing on their future and the strength of their relationship.

Despite the recent challenges, life at the estate continued to thrive. The garden, which had been a place of solace and reflection, was now filled with the vibrant colours of blooming flowers. Friends and family frequently visited, offering their support and sharing in the joy of the couple's journey. One sunny afternoon, Ruby and Ryan decided to host a small gathering in the garden. It was a celebration of their resilience and the love that had carried them through difficult times. As the guests arrived, the garden buzzed with laughter and cheerful conversations. Leo and Mia, ever the supportive friends, brought over a basket of freshly baked pastries. Judie, the organizer, had prepared a beautiful spread of finger foods and refreshing drinks. The atmosphere was light-hearted, and the sense of community was palpable.

THE BLOOD PACT

As the sun began to set, casting a warm golden glow over the garden, Ryan stood up to make a toast. "Thank you all for being here," he began, raising his glass. "Your support means the world to us. Ruby and I have faced many challenges, but with your help, we've come out stronger on the other side. Here's to love, friendship, and the bright future ahead."

The guests raised their glasses, cheering and clinking in celebration. Ruby smiled, her heart full of gratitude and love. She knew that no matter what obstacles lay ahead, they could face them with the strength of their bond and the support of their cherished community. As the evening ended, the garden was filled with the soft glow of twinkling lights and the sound of gentle music. Ruby and Ryan took a moment to themselves, standing beneath the old oak tree where they had shared so many significant moments.

"Ryan, I feel so grateful for everything we have," Ruby said, her voice filled with emotion. "We've been through so much, but we've come out stronger because of it."

Ryan nodded, wrapping his arm around her shoulders. "I feel the same way, Ruby. Our love has been tested, and we've proven that it's unbreakable. Whatever comes next, we'll face it together."

R. STELLAN

Next to come!

Veins of Vengeance awaits: In the next battle for freedom, betrayal would strike when Ryan and Ruby least expected it, and the thirst for vengeance would draw new threats from every direction. The shadows of Ryan's past would close in once more, casting doubt and danger over every choice they made. As old alliances crumbled and unexpected enemies emerged, the depth of their love and loyalty would be tested like never before.

But together, they would face whatever came, determined to break free from the chains of Ryan's past—even if it meant risking everything for a future they could finally claim as their own...

Don't miss out!

Visit the website below and you can sign up to receive emails whenever R. Stellan publishes a new book. There's no charge and no obligation.

https://books2read.com/r/B-A-VPMVC-XAPIF

BOOKS 2 READ

Connecting independent readers to independent writers.

Also by R. Stellan

The Notturno Affair
The Blood Pact

Watch for more at https://rstellan24.my.canva.site/.

About the Author

My name is Riven Stellan, and I'm from a small coastal town in South Africa. Life wasn't easy growing up—I left school early and faced the harsh realities of poverty. Despite the challenges, I built a career in the automotive industry, earning international certification through determination and hard work.

Writing has always been a passion of mine. In my youth, I expressed my emotions through poems and short stories, using them as an outlet to make sense of the world around me. Over time, the pressures of life dulled that creative spark, but not too long ago, something inside me changed. I felt an overwhelming need to channel my personal feelings and frustrations into stories—stories that could connect with others who might be going through similar struggles.

I love crafting gripping narratives, ones that pull you in and make you live in the moment. When a story touches something deep inside, when it strikes a nerve or feels relatable—that's when it truly matters to me. My writing focuses on emotion, on creating characters and experiences that feel real. I aim to craft moments that help readers step into someone else's shoes, to feel what they feel, and to maybe find strength in those connections.

For me, writing is more than just storytelling—it's a way to inspire, to offer understanding, and to remind us all, that we're not alone in our struggles.

Read more at https://rstellan24.my.canva.site/.

Milton Keynes UK
Ingram Content Group UK Ltd.
UKHW020331031224
451863UK00012B/496